Goodbye Holly Jane

GOODBYE HOLLY JANE

Maureen Peters

Constable · London

First published in Great Britain 2001
by Constable, an imprint of Constable & Robinson Ltd,
3 The Lanchesters, 162 Fulham Palace Road,
London, W6 9ER
www.constablerobinson.com

Copyright © 2001 Maureen Peters

ISBN 1-84119-405-0

Printed and bound in Great Britain

A CIP catalogue record for this book is available from the
British Library

1

The house is still there though Holly Jane went away forty years ago. To me that seems like a contradiction. You expect the memories of people to remain bright for longer than abandoned buildings stand. Yet there's nothing tangible left of her at all, not a ribbon or a shoe or even her name written in a book. And the house still stands, high on the hill above the village with the moor creeping to the wall of the garden and the thorn tree twisting in the wind.

Old houses ought to lose a few slates from their roof, to sink a little lower as the foundations crack and the damp creeps in, and that was what I expected to find when I came back here so long after it all happened. The row of cottages where we used to live have been bulldozed to make way for a supermarket and the old school closed down – I don't know when!

I drove here up the M62, leaving the yellowish brick of Lancashire behind me and coming into granite territory, with rows of stone houses and the still blackened chimneys of mills pointing sooty fingers out of the valleys. Our village was – no, why should I repeat the name again? There's been quite enough publicity and decent people still have to live there. I shall call it Linton.

I parked at the side of the supermarket, in the tarmacked car park, leaving my car where, as far as I could judge, old Mrs Aykroyd used to hang her washing. I don't suppose she was really old, fiftyish perhaps but old then to me, in her flowered pinny and the smudge of lipstick on her mouth in case the vicar chanced by.

I climbed up the long hill that still rises out of the main street, the track still trodden earth invaded by weeds and glistening with scree. At each side the lower reaches are lively with long grasses and starred with flowers but fairly soon the track curves round on to the moors proper, and the grass dwindles down into a thin covering for the stony soil beneath with patches of heather and gorse in their due seasons.

The house is called the Tyler house. No sign announces that but it has always been the Tyler house. Nobody knows why though I made up a reason when I was a child. I told Sandra that a man who mended roofs had once lived nearby and had fallen madly in love with the girl who lived in the house but her parents refused to let them marry and the girl had died of a broken heart and the sweetheart had leapt from the high chimney stack to his death.

'To his death,' I repeated solemnly.

'So it wasn't his house at all,' Sandra said.

'They say he haunts it,' I said, believing my own fantasy. 'He climbs about on the roof, slithering over the slates, moaning.'

'Why moaning?' Sandra wanted to know.

'Because ghosts always moan,' Josie said as if she knew anything about it.

Josie made a sometimes unwanted third in our friendship. She was a year younger than me and two years younger than Sandra and she had a peaky little face like an apprentice goblin and light red hair worn in two stubby little plaits. I don't want to think about Josie yet.

The house had been built about eighty years before when men who'd 'made a bit o'brass', as Dad said when he was lapsing into his local accent, had erected large showy houses high above the smoky valleys and the little farms that clung to the edges of the moor. Nobody was sure who the original owners had been. Some said a manufacturer called Tom Taylor who'd gone bankrupt and others said that it had been used as a school but the fees were too high and they, whoever 'they' had been, couldn't get pupils.

What I did glean when I was a child was that something had happened there once. I found out later what it was but at the beginning, when I was twelve years old, adults still wreathed their words in ambiguity. It's difficult for me to explain how innocent we were back in 1960.

Change was in the air, of course, but its winds were no more than a gentle breath blowing our way and fiercely resisted by everybody. We didn't even have a television set in our house. Reception was very poor anyway and Dad said there was nothing on it worth watching, and that the wireless was good enough for him. There were still buses running into Bradford and linking with the railway, and several people had cars.

Even we had a car because Dad worked in Bradford in an insurance office which kept him busy six days out of the week and sometimes late into the evening too. That firm would fall to bits without Dad, or so Mum said.

The summer of 1960 I was twelve years old. One year to go before I became a teenager, Susan said, and smiled her little cat smile because she was seventeen and getting ready to leave her teens.

Sandra had gone off on holiday with her mother to Brighton. Mrs Pirie, who the village suspected wasn't a Mrs at all, lived in the cottage at the other end of the row from ours. She was a thin, smart lady with very blonde hair – 'bottle blonde' said Mum with a little sniff – and she wore heels that were too high for the uneven pavement that meandered along the main street. Most people disapproved of Mrs Pirie without actually knowing why. She kept her cottage neat and her garden pretty and she went into town on the bus every day and came home quite late at night. 'Too late' said Mum with another sniff.

I liked Mrs Pirie. I liked the way she smoked cigarettes through a long holder and the scent she used that smelt musky and forbidden, and I wished she'd invited me to go on holiday with her and Sandra though my parents wouldn't have let me go anyway.

'Not quite the thing,' Mum was wont to say, with a little nod in my direction as if she was calling attention to one whose ears were too sharp for comfort.

What did seem to be quite the thing, though I'd never have thought it, was that Susan should leave home. Mind you, there'd been the usual endless discussions about it with Mum and Susan on one side and Dad on the other. This had gone on over Easter and sounded exactly like somebody playing the same boring record over and over.

'If she's to take the secretarial course, John, she can't be going back and forth every day!'

That from Mum, with the worried look on her pretty face and her fingers pleating the edge of her skirt.

'Why not? I make the daily trip!'

That was Dad with his mainstay of this entire family face on.

He was ten years older than Mum and that gave him the edge in arguments.

Not this time though. Mum said, 'But you often have to be late at the office, dear. That would mean our Susan hanging about in town or having to catch a late bus. And she'd need time and space in which to practise her shorthand and typing. There isn't much room here.'

'You were the one who wanted to come and live in the country when Cordy was a toddler,' Dad said. 'Do you want to uproot us all now?'

'No, of course not!' Mum had flushed, darting her eyes towards Susan who said calmly:

'Melanie Price who's doing the course with me has the chance of a flat in the very next street to the secretarial school. Her parents will let her take it if she shares with me. We can have it for the whole year if we like. The rent's reasonable and if Dad can't afford it I can take a part-time job.'

She was clever was our Susan! Dad stiffened and said exactly what we knew he'd say.

'I've not reached the stage where I can't help out my daughter with her higher education! We'll talk about it some more. No sense in rushing our fences.'

The upshot of all the talking was that Susan moved out just after Easter, making my sleeping space twice as big. Up to then we'd shared the second bedroom at the back of the house, and though we were supposed to have half the room each Susan's belongings overflowed into my half and my half of the wardrobe was crammed with her stuff.

After she'd gone, the boot of the car laden down with suitcases and holdalls and herself in the back seat behind Dad and Mum, I went upstairs and tried to imagine what it would be like going to sleep without hearing the little creaks and shifts with which Susan composed herself to sleep. We weren't very close. The five years between us was too wide a gap at the ages we were then, but the feeling of her still hung in the air. I spread out my own garments to make them fill up the empty spaces and I put some daffodils in a glass jar in the window where they looked quite jolly for a day or two until they turned brown because I'd forgotten to water them. Anyway it wasn't really like having my entirely own bedroom because Susan came home most weekends and left bits of her things around as if she'd never been away at all.

By the time the summer holidays came we were quite used to not having Susan around. At least I was quite used to it. My parents weren't. Mum was still forgetting and laying the table for four and Dad would look up from his newspaper with the idea, I suppose, of saying something to Susan and register the fact that I was sitting there and give a little cough, a vagueness coming into his eyes, before he bent his head over the newspaper again.

'I can't understand why you don't want to come with us,' Mum complained mildly one late afternoon.

They were going to spend the evening with Susan. She had offered to cook dinner for them. Dinner! In our house we had dinner in the middle of the day and high tea at six o'clock, or a bit later if Dad was held up at the office. Our Susan was getting posh, I thought.

'I'm snowed under with homework,' I said, mildly pathetic.

'Surely you've the whole of the summer holidays in which to do it?' Mum said.

'I want to get it out of the road before Sandra comes home,' I said.

'Well, make sure you do then,' she said, trying to sound firm. 'And don't go wandering off anywhere! If you want to ask Josie round –'

'She went shopping or something with her mother.'

'Well, in that case – here's your dad now! He promised to be early.'

She bustled off to get her coat. Mum always wore a coat even in summer as if it was a by-law or something! Dad was honking the horn impatiently as she gave me a quick kiss and went out, picking up a carrier bag on her way. The carrier bag contained a sweater she'd just knitted for Susan and some chocolates. The sweater hadn't turned out quite right and the chocolates had hard centres which Susan didn't much like but it was the thought that counted.

The car drove off again and I looked round the front room, finding myself alone in it for the first time in ages. It was a pleasant room. People always said that when they came in.

'What a pleasant room!' they said, looking round.

Not that we had many visitors. Mum kept herself to herself and Dad was generally at work.

Mum kept our sitting-room as neat as she possibly could just in case – of what she never said. Two of the walls had flowered paper on them and two were painted pale blue which was regarded as very modern at the time. There was a brown carpet with little triangles of yellow and blue in it and a chiming clock on the mantelshelf which was Mum's despair because bits of soot flew up out of the coal fire and covered it with tiny flecks as if the gold-coloured clock had some dreadful medieval disease.

There was a three-piece suite though only Dad ever sat in the armchair by the fireplace; and net curtains stretched tightly over the insides of the two narrow windows as well as blue curtains looped at the sides. The sideboard had Mum's silver fruit bowl in the middle of it with small photographs of us all in varicoloured frames propped up all round this centrepiece in which a few apples sometimes languished for a week or more. There was a whole shelf devoted to photograph albums in the recess at the side of the fireplace and a small table with the wireless, as we still called it, in the adjoining recess. On the blue walls were a handsome photograph of Mum and Dad on their wedding day, she in a droopy-looking suit with a frilled collar and a hat shaped like a saucer stuck on the side of her head and Dad in a dark suit with a carnation, a photograph of Susan as a baby, all dimples and big eyes, and one of me at the same age looking scrawny and sulky.

The kitchen behind the sitting-room had an extra bit that Mum called the breakfast room although Susan never ate any breakfast, Dad gulped down toast and tea, and Mum tried to coax me into finishing up the leftovers she always prepared. I could have eaten the leftovers for every family in our row without putting on an ounce in those days.

It was quiet when they'd gone. The walls pressed in on me and the place was chilly because the fire hadn't been stoked up, it having been a warm day and they having been invited over to Susan's place.

I went upstairs and kneeled on the window seat and looked out over our strip of garden to where the moors rose up with the track curving through them, inviting someone to explore. I tried to pretend that I was Emily Brontë, dreaming through the window and making up deathless poetry, but the mirror on the wardrobe door showed me a somewhat unromantic figure in jeans and the shirt with the daisies embroidered on it that was my normal Saturday wear. And I couldn't think of a single line of poetry that someone else hadn't written first.

Mum had left some ham sandwiches in greaseproof paper and a bowl of salad and opened a tin of mandarin oranges. That was to console me for missing out on the posh dinner that Susan was going to give them, though it was my own choice to stay at home. I put out the food and ate it, putting my elbows on the table and pulling the rim of fat off the ham in a way that would have earned me a telling off but as nobody was there to see me being bad-mannered it didn't carry the same satisfaction. I even cleared away and washed up the few dishes I'd used.

When I came back into the sitting-room the telephone rang. Dad had had the telephone installed as a surprise for Mum's birthday.

'Now you can ring up all your girlfriends and chatter away to your heart's content,' he'd said.

But Mum didn't really have many friends. Acquaintances, I allowed, but not close friends. The problem was that she wasn't from Yorkshire at all. She'd been brought up by an aunt after her parents died when she was a child and though the aunt had been kind they'd lived down on the south coast until the aunt died too and Mum, who was just eighteen, had met Dad who was selling insurance policies in that area and not only sold Mum one but married her too.

'They're a bit clannish round here,' Dad was fond of saying, 'but you'll soon settle in.'

'We've been settled in more than eleven years,' I said to him once.

'It takes time,' Dad said vaguely, and Mum said it was a lovely present and a real link with the outside world.

I picked up the telephone.

'Cordy, is that you?' It was Mum's voice.

'No, it's the Queen of Sheba,' I said wittily.

'Don't be silly, dear,' Mum said in her patient voice. 'Look, we might be a bit late back. Susan booked us seats at the theatre as a surprise. Wasn't that lovely of her? But it means we won't be home until nearly twelve. You can stay up until ten if there's anything good on the wireless or perhaps you'd like to go over to Josie's? You could stay over, couldn't you? Are they on the telephone?'

'I don't think so,' I said. 'I've homework to do anyway.'

'Yes, of course. I forgot.' She sounded flurried. 'Yes, John, I'm just coming! Cordy, if you don't sleep at Josie's bolt the back door and just close the front door. It's self-locking and Dad's got his key.'

'I'll be fine, Mum. Honest!' I suddenly wanted her to have a good time and not be worrying.

'I'll see you later then, lovie, if you're still awake. I'm coming!'

She rang off abruptly before I could say goodnight.

This was the first time I'd had the house all to myself in the evening, but the novelty quickly wore off. There were no secret staircases or tiny dead-end rooms where a lunatic wife might have been hidden. Everything was everyday, boring normal.

Outside it was still light though the sunshine had a mellow tinge. I put on my blazer, then changed my mind and pulled on a sweater instead.

I didn't really want to go and spend the night at Josie's house. She wasn't a real friend. She just tagged round after Sandra and me, her peaky little face poking forward, her eyes watching us anxiously so that she'd know the right time to smile or giggle or look serious.

She lived at the other side of the village near the general store, so I left the back door unlocked – you could still risk doing that back then – and went along our street to where there was a bit of a square with the post office and the greengrocer's as well as the general store and the bus stop.

I hung about for a couple of minutes at Josie's gate until Mrs Simmons came to the door of the general store to tell me it was no use waiting because Josie had gone out for the day with her mum.

'I don't know when they'll be home,' she said. 'Was it important?'

Poor Mrs Simmons was grey-haired and plain and the only important thing that had ever happened to her was being widowed, but that had been so long ago that nearly everybody

12

had forgotten it by now unless she reminded them which she did now as I shook my head.

'I may be only a poor widow,' she said, 'but I can recognise a girl who likes chocolate. Hang on a minute!'

She darted into her shop and came out again with a bar of flaky chocolate. I wasn't supposed to take sweets from strangers but Mrs Simmons wasn't exactly a stranger even if she wasn't exactly a friend either, so I thanked her with real sincerity and had torn off the wrapping and devoured half of it before I was half-way home again.

I decided that I'd take a walk before I went inside. In those days, apart from a very few horrible cases that were front page news for weeks, it was quite safe for children to wander about within reason. We were told there were some very sick people in the world but this was Linton, where everybody knew everybody else and it didn't really feel like being part of the world anyway.

I climbed that same winding track today forty years on, my legs encased in jeans, my sweater tied round my neck. When I turned my back on the spoilt village below I saw that nothing had changed. The heather was still pale, the gorse more green than gold, but the wind smelled the same as it gusted down the hill. Clean and fresh and deceptively innocent as if it never turned into a gale that whipped flowerpots off windowsills or took the branches of a holly bush and tortured them into a tangled ball.

Back then on that particular evening the wind was gentle. It lured me onward, past the last long grasses with their veils of meadowsweet on to the short crisp turf with its outcroppings of stone.

I sat down on one of the rocks that stuck out of the soil and finished off my flaky bar.

Being alone up here felt different from being alone in our neat cottage. Up here I felt light as air with the sensation that if I jumped high enough I would go on rising higher and higher until I was a speck in the sky with the earth spread below me, but when I tried a small experimental jump I sat down abruptly, giggling.

The afternoon was reaching towards evening, with longer shadows creeping over the grass, and in the village below a light flashed on here and there. I supposed that I ought to go home and turn on the electric fire to warm the sitting-room while I sorted out what holiday work I was supposed to finish before school started again, but September was light years away and I couldn't start on the maths anyway until Sandra came home. I was always among the first half-dozen in English and History but numbers floored me, never coming out the same twice when I added them up or multiplied them.

I stood up and went across the sloping ground towards the track. I think I really meant to walk down into the village again but I found myself trudging upwards instead, the first faint stars appearing as the sky grew darker with that darkness that falls so suddenly in the north.

I reached the top of the long hill and the moors lay before me, in fold upon fold, with pools glimmering where streams had cut into the earth over the long slow centuries.

Nobody lived in the Tyler house then. There had been a family living there when we first came to the village but they had gone away years before and nobody talked of them.

'There was a terrible tragedy,' Sandra had whispered to me.

'What tragedy?' I wanted to know.

'Someone suicided.'

'Like the man who tiled the roof?'

'That's just your story. This was real!' she said impatiently.

'So what happened?' I persisted.

But Sandra didn't know. She was only sure that it had been terrible.

That hadn't stopped us going to play in the house. In fact it added a certain frisson of excitement to think that there might be a real ghost there as well as the ones we made up.

There were walls round the house, not low enough to peep over but with gaps in them that were easy to squeeze through and made a nonsense of the padlocked iron gates. There were two large overgrown lawns in front of the building and the remains of a tangled garden behind it with bilberry bushes invading everywhere, and a rain-soaked swing hung on rusty chains from two trees – apple trees, I think, though they never bore fruit. There must have been a child there once. A little girl in a frilled pinafore, I had decided, with a blue ribbon in her hair.

It wasn't a pretty house but ivy had crept over its dark stone and wound its tendrils up the twin pillars of the front porch. There were wooden shutters fastened outside the windows and they had protected the glass behind though there were broken staves in the shutters through which bars of daylight fell across the wooden floors within.

We always went in through the back door which had swollen with damp and didn't close properly. Inside, the rooms opened one out of the other, with unexpected passages that led nowhere in particular and a rather grand staircase with carved banisters and a kind of railed gallery above from where one could look down into the hall below. Some of the rooms had faded carpet in them and high mantelpieces of smooth black marble.

There were pieces of furniture too that had been left behind. Huge pieces they were, a dresser towering up to the roof, a huge billiard table with the green cloth on it ripped and dirty, a four-poster bed and a long table scored with knife marks. It was as if the furniture had always stood there and the house had been built round it.

We weren't really supposed to play in the Tyler house, so of course we did – or rather had done. The thrill of having a secret society consisting of Sandra and me with Josie as acolyte had been fun when we were younger but since we'd moved into the Upper School it had begun to seem a bit too childish.

How odd to look back down the tunnel of the years and see oneself as a small figure standing in the brightness at the end! I have photographs of myself at twelve – a school photograph taken just before the Easter break and making me look stiff and self-conscious in my uniform, and blurred shots of me with my arm partly raised to shield my face from the photographers. I looked so vulnerable then that I can't connect my present self with that child, but returning to this place where it all began I can feel the ache of an old wound and remember how it was to stand between childhood and adolescence and fear to take the next step as much as I dreaded to go backwards.

By the time I had reached the high iron gates the wind had a sighing sound. The gates were wide open, pushed back on to the grass verges at each side of the weedy drive. I'd never seen the gates open before and, for an instant, I felt a little shock of anger

15

as if persons unknown had trespassed in my own private place.

There were tyre marks along the drive. The last flare of sunlight glinted on them and then as I straightened up and looked towards the house the sun went down in a last defiant blaze, lighting the round window above the porch.

I had always liked that window. There were bits of stained glass in the segments of pane that were leaded together to form a circle. In the old days when we played pirates the round window had been a porthole or, after we'd learned something about the Wars of the Roses, it became the window through which Elizabeth of York gazed while she waited to hear the news about the Battle of Bosworth.

In that last dazzle of light I saw, shielding my eyes with my hand, the profile of a girl with long black hair hanging down her back and floating about her face so that the glimpse I had was blurred and indistinct, no sooner seen than gone.

I blinked and shook my head and when I looked up again the window was a round dark blank.

'My mum says that you've got an overactive imagination!' Sandra had told me. 'She says it's best to see what's there.'

Sandra's mum was right, of course, but life would be duller, I thought, if you couldn't trace the features of an old man trapped in the bark of a tree or if clouds were mere clouds with no fantastic animals breaking out of them.

There hadn't been anyone in the window at all. I knew that perfectly well but I wanted to check for myself.

How could I have braved the gathering dark in order to explore what my mind had conjured up? Nowadays, keys firmly in my hand as I walk with conscious briskness the short distance from the garage to my front door, there is a weeping within me for the lost days of innocence when an empty house was as familiar to me as my own and children walked safely through the world. That the world wasn't the sanctuary I believed it to be saddens me more but the innocence was real.

So I went on up the drive without pausing to think about it and since the front door was always locked I went as usual round to the back where there was a cobbled yard and a couple of sheds and a conservatory that jutted out from the back of the house and, unprotected by shutters, showed cracked and missing panes of glass with a jumble of old earthenware pots heavy with dried earth flung about inside.

The back door stood half open as it always did, its wood bulging outward. I stepped into the big shadowy kitchen with its tiled and filthy floor, its old-fashioned range which had once gleamed blackly but now was grey with ash, and the long table with the knife marks scored across it and the dark stain at one end which we'd played was blood left by a sacrificed maiden.

The kitchen was on a slightly lower level from the rest of the building with three stone steps leading up into a small back hall from where a long passage ran to the front hall. The room ought to have been quite dark but there was a candle stuck in a saucer and lighted in the centre of the table.

Somebody had moved in then. There were packing cases scattered about, a couple opened with tissue paper spilling out of them. I had turned on my heel when I heard the light footfall on the step and the voice.

When you first meet a stranger you know that once introductions are over you will never see that person in quite the same way again. But as I was to discover that rule didn't apply to Fay Maitland. I never looked at her with eyes grown accustomed to her. She was always newly minted.

'Hello, little girl,' she said. 'Do you like cake?'

She had a light, slightly husky voice that lifted a little at the end of each sentence so that she seemed to be perpetually questioning. I learnt that later too.

'Yes,' I said simply.

She came down on to the kitchen floor, holding the oil lamp she carried high so that its rays cast honey over her face with its mop of curly fair hair. It looked warm gold in the light but in daylight it would reveal streaks of other shades, a tinge of auburn, a hint of toffee, a sprinkle of grey. I couldn't tell – I would never be able to tell – whether or not she was pretty. What I saw on that first occasion was that her skin was pale and her eyes were a light, opal green which, like an opal, had in them dashes of other colours.

'It's a bought cake,' she said, 'because the electricity isn't turned on yet. Someone is coming to connect it I daresay. I have some cream too. Clotted. Like they eat in Devon. I bought that in the same place as the cake so both are quite fresh. We stopped

17

off for some fish and chips and saved the cake and the cream to eat when we arrived. There are plates and spoons somewhere.'

'In the packing case?' I suggested, mesmerised by the swirl of the long multicoloured caftan she wore as she set the lamp on the table and blew out the candle flame.

'Yes, of course! In the packing case.' She sounded pleased. 'But which packing case? That one perhaps? Shall we look?'

She moved to one of the open cases and bent over it, her long white hands moving among the tissue paper like sea creatures under water.

'Plates!' she said with an air of triumph. 'Four plates I think. And here are soup spoons! We shall use soup spoons though we can't offer you any soup.'

'I'm not keen on soup,' I said politely.

'Then you have never tasted Fred's soup,' she said. 'He uses fresh tomatoes and wild mushrooms with a hint of chervil and a dash of sour cream and sherry. It is like drinking Paradise. Here is Fred!'

I don't know what I expected to see by this time. A knight in armour or a hunchbacked dwarf with a swirling cloak, I suspect. But the heavier tread that signalled his arrival was followed by a stocky, tired-looking man with grey hair receding slightly at the temples and horn-rimmed glasses on a jutting nose.

'We have a visitor,' she said.

'So I see.' He put the cake he was carrying on the table. 'Does our guest have a name or is she travelling incognito?'

'My name's Cordy,' I said blankly. 'Short for Cordelia. Cordelia Sullivan actually but my mum and dad call me Cordy.'

'We shall call you Cordelia,' the lady said. 'That is a beautiful name! Isn't that a beautiful name?'

'It's a lovely name,' he agreed.

'And should never be shortened! We won't ever shorten it ever, will we?'

'We shall pronounce it in its full glory,' he said solemnly.

I wasn't sure whether or not he was making fun but when I shot a glance at him he looked perfectly serious.

'We must introduce ourselves,' the lady said gravely, with a little wave of her hand. A ring glittered on it in the lamplight.

'We are the Maitlands. My name is Fay which cannot be short-ened of course.'

'Your parents chose wisely,' he said. 'Lovely sounds ought not to be cut short.'

'Your parents were less sensitive,' she said.

'They saddled me with Fred,' he nodded.

'Not even Frederick which might have conferred some distinc-tion.' She sounded quite distressed about it.

'At least you can't shorten it,' I said helpfully.

'That's very true, Cordelia. I never thought of that! You can't shorten it,' she repeated.

'Is Cordelia staying for a piece of cake?' he asked.

'Of course she is and an enormous dollop of cream! Two dollops if you like. You look as if you're at the growing stage. How old are you?'

'Twelve, Mrs Mait –'

'Mrs Maitland! Fay, Cordelia dear. Please, Fay!'

'And I'm Fred.' He had bent over one of the packing cases and straightened up again with a knife in his hand. 'We don't stand on ceremony with our friends, do we, Fay?'

'We never have before,' she replied. 'The truth is that we haven't any friends here yet on account of – of what, Fred?'

'On account of we only just arrived,' Fred said, starting to cut the cake.

'We brought some bits and pieces but the rest of our stuff arrives – is it tomorrow, Fred?'

'It'd better be, I paid him a hefty deposit,' he said. 'Not that our furniture will fill this house.'

'You're really coming to live here then?' I sat down as Fay patted the bench beside her with her hand.

'Did you think we were trespassing then?' He pushed the plate with its large slice of pale yellow cake on it across to me.

'We've rented it,' Fay said. 'Fred wanted somewhere quiet where he could write, didn't you, Fred?'

'Fred will be lucky to get three minutes' peace with you around, my love,' he said, his eyes crinkling behind his glasses as he smiled at her.

'Take no notice of him. He's only teasing,' Fay said. 'Did you bring the cream?'

'It's in the jar on the shelf. I'll get it.'

19

'I thought I saw a girl – in the round window,' I ventured.

'Oh, that must've been Holly Jane,' Fay said. 'Our daughter. Fred, she did say that she was tired and didn't want anything but this cake looks so delicious –'

'I'll go up and ask her,' Fred said. 'You carry on!'

He disappeared up the three steps.

'You have a daughter?' I looked at Fay.

'Holly Jane is thirteen. She's going through a difficult phase. Won't eat properly in case she gains any weight; doesn't want to make friends because she's shy,' Fay said. 'She used to be such a friendly little soul but recently – it's only a phase I know but I'm longing for her to grow out of it! Daughters can be a great anxiety though one wouldn't be without them! I suppose your mother says the same thing about you?'

'Not to me she doesn't,' I said.

'Then I'm sure she thinks it – is she coming down, Fred?' She broke off as his solid figure filled the doorway again.

'She's already rolled up in her sleeping bag. You'll have to meet her another time, Cordelia.'

'Shall I save her cake?' Fay looked at it doubtfully.

'It'll be stale by morning. This isn't your real home-made cake, darling. Perhaps Cordelia would like another piece?'

'No, honestly. This is lovely,' I said.

Fay had put two spoonfuls of the yellowish cream on top of the sponge and on top of the chocolate I was starting to feel slightly nauseated.

'You eat it, Fred – oh no!'

She broke off abruptly as a feeble wailing sounded from above.

'I must've disturbed him when I went up,' Fred said with a grimace. 'It will be better when we get the carpets laid. I'll go up.'

'Him?' Spoon poised, I looked at Fay.

'Our little boy.' She patted her mouth with a scrap of silk. 'He's only eight months old. To tell you the truth his coming was a great surprise. We thought that Holly Jane was destined to be solitary which was rather sad for her but then Edward was born.'

'Is that his name?' I said disappointed.

'For Fred's sake,' she said gently. 'He never complains but

I know he must feel a bit out of it being just plain Fred when Holly Jane and I have more romantic names. Edward is a very sound, steady name, don't you think?'

'Like Fred,' I said.

'Exactly like Fred!' She sounded approving. 'The longer one knows Fred the more one appreciates his sterling qualities. The world has never really acknowledged his worth but then he says he can do without the world as long as he has my approval.'

'He's a writer?' I recalled what had been said.

'He translates learned books into English but he also writes short stories though so far they have failed to find a market. I am hoping that good fortune will smile on us here.'

'It already has,' Fred said, coming back into the kitchen. 'Cordelia is our first visitor.'

'You can frame a compliment with the best of them,' Fay said, laughing. 'Did you get Edward off without too much trouble?'

'Like a lamb! He was slightly damp so I changed him. He went straight back to sleep.'

'And Holly Jane?'

'Sleeping like a princess! The long drive wearied her. I could do with a cup of tea!'

'We might build a fire with sticks,' Fay suggested.

'Darling, that would take for ever! Never mind, I'll survive until –'

'There'll be some in the thermos flask!' Fay cried, beginning to rise. 'We didn't drink it all I'm sure.'

'My wife,' Fred said solemnly, 'is the brains of this outfit! Did you bring the thermos indoors?'

'It will be in the van, between the two front seats,' she said. 'Shall I get –?'

'It won't take me a moment to pop into the garage. Perhaps Cordelia will want to wash down the cake too?'

'I think I ought to be getting home,' I said, suddenly realising that the sky beyond the unshuttered window was quite dark.

'We've kept you too long,' Fred said. 'Will your parents be annoyed?'

'No. They won't mind at all,' I said brightly.

'They won't mind if you come to tea tomorrow then?' Fay said.

'Darling, why not make it the day after tomorrow?' Fred

interposed. 'We have the electricity people coming tomorrow as well as the rest of the furniture. We shall have no time to devote to Cordelia! Tea, the day after tomorrow? We shall be getting things straight by then.'

'Meaning Fred will be getting things straight!' Fay said. 'I shall be supervising. This has been a good day, hasn't it, Fred?'

'And will be even better when I have had some tea,' he said.

'The day after tomorrow then!' Fay sank down on the bench again. The lamp glowed on her curly hair.

'Thank you for having me,' I said, remembering my manners.

'This way then! Where did I put the torch?' Fred said.

'In the van!' Fay said, giggling. 'You're getting forgetful!'

'Age creeping on,' he said wryly.

'Not you, Fred! Not you.' Her voice ended on a dying fall.

'Not either of us, my love. Come along, Cordelia! I'll walk with you to the gate.'

I left her seated at the table, her long curving finger tracing an old knife scar on the wood. Outside in the yard the cobbles glinted faintly under a thin young moon.

'I do know my way,' I said.

'Nevertheless . . .' He let the word trail into the darkness. 'I shall stand at the gate and watch you go down the hill. There are streetlights in the village so you will know your way from there.'

As if I didn't already know my way everywhere in the area with my eyes closed!

When we reached the open gates he shook hands with me solemnly as if we were both grown-ups and then I turned and went on to the track that fell in a gentle slope towards the hill.

I looked back once and he was still standing there. Watching me.

2

'I let you sleep in,' Mum said when I came downstairs the next morning. 'You never stirred when we got back. Did you make a good start on your homework?'

'It's going to take a bit of time,' I said vaguely. 'Mum, I –'

'You should've come with us,' Mum said. 'It's a nice little flat, very convenient for the secretarial college. The two girls have done it up a treat. Melanie's a nice girl. Comes from Rochdale. Sensible type. Your dad was quite relieved. You know how he –'

'Mum, about last night –' I said.

'Worries about you two. But she stayed and chatted for a bit while our Susan was getting the dinner. She'd made prawn cocktail – Susan I mean. And the show was very good. An Agatha Christie story. Very –'

'I was going to tell you –'

'Will you just look at the time! I've a million and one things to do before – why don't you run over and play with Josie? Or Sandra.'

'Sandra went on holiday. I told you!'

'Yes. Sorry, love! I get quite muddled about all your friends.'

She emerged from the larder and shot me a flurried smile.

'I think I've made some new ones,' I said. 'I wanted to tell –'

'Have you, love? That's nice! Make the most of childhood is what I always say. Now do hurry up and get out from under my feet!'

I got out from under. It wasn't my fault if she was too busy to listen. Mum and Dad hardly ever went out and when they did Mum always scoured the house as if she'd been away for a year.

'Do you want anything from the shop?' I asked automatically.

'I don't think so, love. Now where did I put –?'

I left her looking for something or other she'd only just realised she needed.

Outside the sun's rays bladed down through little clouds and sent them dashing all over the sky.

There was a little knot of people at Josie's front gate. Not doing anything, just staring at the house and shuffling their feet.

I squinted at them doubtfully and heard a hissing noise behind me.

'Sst! Cordy, a moment, please!'

Mrs Simmons was at the door of her shop.

'Yes, Mrs Simmons?'

In olden times she'd've worn a big mobcap and been known as the Widow Simmons. These times she wore a flowered overall and her hair was curled in regular little ringlets over her head. It had a bluish tinge.

'Don't stand gawking, dear. It's ill bred,' she said, her eyes piercing past me towards the crowd. 'It really is none of our business!'

'What isn't our business?' I enquired, following as she turned and went inside.

For a wonder the shop was empty, the shelves standing at attention as if they waited to be inspected by a general who never came.

'You haven't heard?' She lifted the flap of the counter and invited me behind it, a mark of special favour. 'Would you like some lemonade?'

'No, thank you,' I said. Mrs Simmons made her own lemonade and it was always full of pips.

'You haven't heard about Josie?' she said.

'She went shopping with her mum.'

'She's run off,' Mrs Simmons said, lowering her voice.

'Josie's mum?' Mrs White was small and neat and prettier than her daughter.

'No, dear, of course not! Josie's run off,' Mrs Simmons said.

I stared at her.

'Run off where?' I said at last.

'Nobody knows.' Mrs Simmons clicked her tongue against her teeth, making them wobble slightly. 'She and Mrs White went over to Halifax to do some shopping. Why Halifax I cannot imagine but maybe they wanted a bit of a change or something.'

24

'Doesn't Mr White work in Halifax?' I remembered. 'Maybe they were going to have a meal with him after they finished shopping.'

'Mr White's meals are generally liquid,' Mrs Simmons said acidly. 'If I were in Mrs White's position –'

'So what happened?' I asked hastily, knowing that her next remark would be that though she was a poor widow now she could always be thankful that the late sainted Mr Simmons never touched anything stronger than tea and her pip-heavy lemonade.

'They were in Harvey's. Buying some jumpers – or was it a cardigan? Anyway Josie said she was going up to the next floor to look at the jewellery there and she didn't come back.'

'Where did she go?'

'Nobody knows, dear.' Mrs Simmons took a genteel sip from a cup of coffee near the till. 'Mrs White finished her purchase and went up to the next level. She took the lift but Josie may have walked up the stairs. The place was quite crowded so Mrs White wasn't too worried when she didn't see her at once, but after ten minutes she did get a mite fussed and began asking the sales staff if any of them had seen Josie. They put out a message for her on the tannoy. Finally they called the police.'

'And then? What happened then?' I was still trying to digest the fact that Josie had actually run off.

'Apparently they managed to get hold of Josie's father. She knew where his office is so they hoped she'd turn up there, but he'd been out of the building most of the afternoon and his secretary said Josie hadn't been there.'

'Maybe she was kidnapped,' I ventured.

I couldn't think of a single person who'd want to kidnap Josie but I found it impossible to imagine her running away either.

'In broad daylight? In the middle of a crowded store? But one hears such dreadful stories these days.'

'I don't,' I said. 'Mum doesn't let me read the Sunday papers.'

'You may take my word for it,' Mrs Simmons said. 'Anyway after the police were called the Whites were persuaded to come home and wait until – in case Josie turned up.'

She sounded as if she wanted to go on talking but a couple of women had just entered the shop and, sensing a fresh audience, she lifted the counter flap and whisked me back to the customers' side of the shop.

I wandered outside and saw the crowd at Josie's gate had slightly increased. There was a policeman there now and a man with a flash camera.

'Cordy!' The front door of the house opened abruptly and Mrs White came out on to the step, raising her voice shrilly.

'Cordy, please come in for a minute!' Her hand reached out and clutched me as a camera clicked and the policeman called impatiently:

'Move along there! There's nowt to see!'

The little crowd fell back slightly at the policeman's instruction and I went through the gate and up the path.

'Please come in!' She pulled me into the hall and shut the door.

A man in a plain grey suit was standing in the sitting-room and a police sergeant was sitting by the window making notes.

'Mrs White, you'd do far better to leave it to us,' the grey-suited man said.

'You don't understand. Inspector! Cordy is one of Josie's friends! She may know something!' Mrs White said in a hopeful, flurried kind of way.

'We are planning house-to-house enquiries later today,' the sergeant said.

'Cordy, is it?' The other man was looking at me.

'Cordelia Sullivan,' I said loftily.

'And you're a friend of Josie's?' I hesitated.

'She's younger than I am,' I said awkwardly. 'She sort of – yes, we're friends.'

He had glanced at the police sergeant who snapped shut his notebook and rose, saying in a soothing kind of voice, 'Mrs White, shall I give you a hand to make a pot of tea?'

'I . . .' She looked imploringly at me, then went obediently into the kitchen.

'My name's Archer, by the by,' the grey-suited man said. 'Detective Inspector Archer. You were going to say that Josie sort of . . .?'

'Tagged after us. I didn't want to hurt her mum's feelings,' I said.

'Us?'

'Sandra Pirie and me. Sandra's on holiday with her mum.'

'And Sandra and you are best friends?'

'I suppose.' It sounded childish. I added hastily, 'We let Josie come round with us though.'

'When did you last play together?' he asked.

'Last weekend. On the moor. Well, it was more talking really.'

'About what?'

'School, homework, the holidays, nothing in particular.'

'Boyfriends?'

'We're too young,' I said virtuously.

'I bet you get crushes on them though?'

'On the boys at school? No, of course we don't!' My respect for him was diminishing. I said, 'We don't much like real boys. We like film stars and rock and roll stars and – you know!'

'Of course. Silly of me!'

'And even Josie isn't daft enough to run away to see one of them,' I said. 'We don't even know where they live.'

'I'm a fan of Audrey Hepburn myself,' he remarked.

'My dad likes her too. He says she looks like a real lady.'

'That's true.' He nodded. 'So you haven't seen Josie since last weekend?'

'Not to play with but I've seen her once or twice, in the village and that. Just to wave.'

'Has Josie ever talked about running away?'

'No more than the rest of us,' I said. 'I mean everyone thinks about it after they've had a telling off or if they've got to go to the dentist, but nobody ever does it.'

'And you and Sandra and Josie tell one another everything?'

'Not really every single thing,' I said. 'I mean we never told Josie she was a bit of a nuisance – not that we didn't like her but she's awfully young. I'm sure she wasn't planning to run away though. She was going out with her mum to do some shopping and she was going to buy a book. She likes reading.'

I broke off as the sergeant came in, carrying a tray with cups and saucers on it. Behind him Mrs White was carrying a round biscuit tin, her fingers beating a nervous little tattoo on its sides.

27

'I don't think Cordelia has been able to tell us very much,' Detective Inspector Archer said.

'She wouldn't run away,' Mrs White said, her voice thin and rasping. 'She wouldn't do that. Someone took her. I know someone took her.'

She stopped abruptly, staring at her tapping fingers as if they belonged to someone else and she wanted the drumming to stop.

'You sit down, Mrs White,' the sergeant said kindly. 'I'll hand round the tea.'

'Perhaps Cordy would like some pop?' Mrs White said, forcing a silly, twisted little smile as if somebody had told her she must behave like a hostess.

'I'd better get off home,' I said. 'Mum might be worried.'

'Better go out the back way,' the sergeant advised. 'There's more at the gate now.'

'I can't think what they expect to see,' Mrs White said dully.

'I'm sure Josie'll be back very soon, Mrs White,' I said uselessly.

'Thanks for your help,' Detective Inspector Archer said. 'If anything else comes to mind let the sergeant here know. He'll be around for the rest of the afternoon.'

I nodded and went out into the passage and turned towards the back door that led into the strip of garden. Josie's school blouses and navy blue knickers were blowing on the line that stretched between two posts. Mrs White must have hung them there before they caught the bus to Halifax.

They looked limp and empty as they swayed in the warm breeze.

There was a shed by the back gate. We weren't supposed to go there because Mr White housed sharp garden tools in it and Mrs White was scared that one of us might fall and get a cut and die of lockjaw. Not that we ever wanted to play in the shed or in Josie's garden come to that! Her dad was liable to turn up at odd hours and breathe whisky fumes over us.

'My dad has a cold,' Josie always said. 'A drop of whisky with lemon and honey makes it go away.'

Mr White, I thought, had a perpetual cold but we never heard him blow his nose or cough.

He was in the shed, seated on an upended barrel. Once, when

28

Josie wasn't looking, Sandra had lifted the lid and we'd looked down at the empty bottles stacked neatly inside.

He had nothing in his hands now though his breath stank just the same as he shifted his burly torso forward and peered at me through bleary eyes.

'My Josie's not home yet,' he said.

He had reddish hair like Josie and his skin looked damp.

'She probably will be soon,' I said.

'She went out the wrong door,' he said. 'Went out the wrong door and found herself in the street. Got confused. Went out the wrong door. That's what she did.'

'Yes, well . . .' I reached to unbar the gate.

'Don't you ever,' he said suddenly, threateningly, 'go through the wrong door! Don't you ever!'

'I won't,' I said, and got myself through the gate.

'Dinner's nearly ready,' Mum said when I arrived home. 'Have you been playing with Josie?'

She hadn't heard. Her face was still untroubled, wisps of hair escaping from beneath the brightly coloured scarf she had tied over her head.

'Josie ran off,' I said.

'Maybe her mum had a meal ready. Would you like some chips?'

She started slicing potatoes quickly and expertly.

'Yesterday,' I said. 'She ran away yesterday.'

The knife slipped and a thin line of scarlet appeared on her thumb. She stared at it for a moment, then lifted her head and looked at me.

'What on earth are you talking about?' she said sharply. 'You said something about her going shopping.'

'With her mum. Yes. They went to Harvey's to buy a skirt or something. Josie went up to look at the jewellery – said she was, but she never got there. The police are at Mrs White's now. A man's taking photographs outside for the papers, I think.'

'My heavens!' Mum was turning on the cold tap, holding her thumb under the running water. 'Get me an Elastoplast, there's a good girl. They'd've rung the police yesterday I suppose. You didn't –?'

'I had homework to do,' I said virtuously, fishing a plaster out of the tin.

'And we were in Bradford. So – did Josie ever talk about running away?'

I shook my head.

'How dreadful!' Mum was pouring oil into the chip pan. 'Her dad works in Halifax, doesn't he? Perhaps she got muddled and tried to find her way to his office.'

'She knows where he works,' I said. 'Anyway she'd've asked a policeman the way.'

'That poor woman!' She dropped a square of bread into the oil and watched it browning. 'Ought I to go over?'

'There are people standing at the front gate and a policeman trying to move them on.'

'Morbid curiosity seekers! I won't intrude. Maybe it was a silly prank and now she's scared to come home. What d'ye want with your chips?'

'A fried egg, please.'

'You ought to eat more vegetables,' she said, sliding the chips into the oil and bringing out the frying pan. 'Don't go hanging about at the Whites' and getting in the way. I'm sure Josie'll be home soon.'

She said it as if she was trying to convince herself as well as me.

The chips were crisp and the egg just set. Dad said that even if an earthquake occurred Mum would still dish up something tasty for dinner!

'Do you want any help?' I lingered to ask.

'I think I'll make a start on the kitchen cupboards. They need a bit of a clean-out. No, you take advantage of the sunshine, there's a good girl. And don't go poking your nose into the village!'

'Right!' I slid from my chair and reached for my jacket.

'Don't be late for tea,' she said absently, her mind already in the kitchen cupboards. 'And don't talk to strangers.'

'Mum, when I was on the moor yesterday –' I began.

'And wipe your shoes when you come in again.'

'Yes,' I said.

Before I'd closed the door I heard the rattle of crockery as she lifted out stuff from the cupboards.

Our end of the street was quiet. Usually there were small children hanging around but today the little patches of front garden were deserted, doors and windows closed. I guessed they'd all gone to watch the Whites' house.

I went up the track past the long grass with the nodding flowers. It was warm so I slung my jacket over my shoulders in the way Susan sometimes did.

I wished I had a dog but Dad got hay fever from cats and dogs. It was an allergy and he was sorry about it, but there was nothing to be done. Once I had invented a dog – rough-haired with brown eyes and a furiously wagging tail. I invented him so strongly that if I closed my eyes I could feel the rough texture of his hair under the palm of my hand. But when I opened my eyes there was only empty air under my hand and that made me miss the dog I didn't have even more, so I uninvented him and though once or twice after that I tried to picture him again I never could do so.

I had reached the level ground from where I could look down into the village. The houses and cottages, the cobbled square, the store and the post office and the bus shelter looked like a toy village and the people moving about were like ants. There was a positive anthill at the gate of the Whites' house. I could see the light flashing off the windscreens of several cars parked in the square.

Josie had been excited the last time I'd played with her. I went on walking more slowly. Sandra had been with us, showing off about the posh hotel where she and her mother were going to stay. I didn't mind that because I'd've showed off too if we'd been going to stay in an hotel. I'd let her witter on and made all the right noises and tried not to mind that I'd be stuck with Josie for a fortnight, and Josie had listened too with her eyes glowing in her peaky white face.

'You look as pleased as if you were going on holiday yourself,' Sandra had noticed. 'Are you?'

'Not on holiday, no,' Josie had answered quietly but her eyes were still glowing and her skinny little frame thrilled slightly like the strings of a violin someone has just finished playing.

'Then what?' Sandra had demanded.

'Nothing.'

Josie had closed her lips into a thin white line and ducked her head. She did that sometimes as if she had some marvellous

31

secret she was unwilling to share but, as she never had one anyway, we never bothered to ask.

'Be good!' Sandra had called back to us as she ran ahead down the hill.

'And if you can't be good be careful!' we chorused after her.

Had Josie been careful, I wondered? I equated being careful with not getting run over and never going out with unwashed underwear on in case you did get knocked down by a bus and the nurses in the hospital saw your dingy vest.

I'd come to the gates of the Tyler house. They were still open and I could see fresh tyre marks on the soil. I wondered if they'd gone to pick up the rest of their furniture. The van had been in the garage when I'd been there the night before so I hadn't seen it. It would have to be a very large van to get a lot of furniture in, I thought.

I looked doubtfully up the long weed-covered drive. It was silly but I'd never had a second thought about squeezing through the gaps in the wall when the gates were closed. Now they stood invitingly open but the house was occupied. It would be more like trespassing.

Anyway, I consoled myself, I was soon going there as an invited guest for tea. I'd have to tell Mum about the Maitlands then. Tea in our house was a holy ritual! She'd probably insist on coming with me to check them out. I could picture her only too clearly with her good shoes and coat on, introducing herself in that slightly affected voice she used on the telephone, her eyes taking in the grimy floor and the swollen wood of the door and Fay in her caftan of many colours with her crop of curly fair hair and Fred with his spectacles and slightly frayed sweater.

She'd be very polite and smiling and she'd let herself be talked into staying for a cup of tea and a slice of cake herself, but she wouldn't approve of them, not one little bit!

I hesitated, then squared my shoulders and marched up the drive and round to the back of the house. Perhaps Josie had really run away and was hiding here.

There was a van parked outside the kitchen door and the door itself had been removed. I could see straight into the kitchen where wires were tangled across the floor and three men in overalls were sitting at the long table drinking beer and eating sandwiches.

32

'Need any help?' one of them asked, lifting his head to look at me.

'I was looking for Mr and Mrs Maitland,' I said.

'They went off to Scarborough for the day,' he told me. 'We're connecting up and getting the switches fixed.'

'No central heating though,' said the one seated next to him. 'Can't run to that seemingly.'

'Bill likes his radiators, don't you, Bill?' The first man grinned and winked at me.

'Well, thank you anyway,' I said.

'Don't go fiddling with any cables!' one of them called after me.

He must've thought me a baby, I decided indignantly. As if we didn't all get it drummed into our heads that electricity was dangerous.

There was no point in hanging around. Without the men there I could have spent a couple of hours pretending something. I didn't suppose Fay and Fred would really mind if they came back early and found me.

I would have pretended to be a detective – an inspector. A lady inspector who solved crimes. Something dreadful had once happened in the Tyler house but nobody talked about it to children. Nobody had lived there for years and years.

Why had Josie looked so excited when Sandra had been talking about Blackpool? Where had she gone?

I had reached the gate again and I stood, frowning up at the wall. It had been built of the same stones as the house and was clearly intended to mark the boundary between common land and private estate, but had failed to last as the house had lasted, or perhaps the builders had not taken so much care because the stones stuck out from the wall in irregular lumps and the mortar between many of them was dried and cracked, and had forced the stones apart. Even in the places where it wasn't possible to wriggle through there were gaps. We'd used them as spyholes when we were waiting for the Roundheads to attack, but the lads had tired of the game and run off to play football and Sandra had got sick of being a Roundhead all by herself.

The next summer we'd had a secret society with passwords but only girls were allowed to join. The society didn't last for very long either because once four of us had formed it and made all the rules we weren't certain exactly what secret societies did. Two of the members, Iris and Jean, left after a couple of months and joined someone else's secret society at the other side of the village and that left Sandra and me to struggle on.

That was when Josie had started trailing after us everywhere. We never knew exactly what was so attractive about us. I suppose it was because we didn't shoo her away or tug at her stubby little plaits to make her cry, and she made quite a useful member of the society carrying messages between Sandra and me, and leaving coded signals in smaller gaps in the wall.

By the time the holidays came round again we'd lost interest in the secret society but Josie was now in the habit of tagging along with us and we still left occasional notes in the spaces between the jutting stones.

I went through the open gates and began to skirt the wall, looking for a betraying flicker of white paper.

And there it was! As a detective I was first class, I decided, easing out the wedge of paper and unfolding it carefully.

'Goodbye for now,' Josie had written in her neat, round hand. 'I am going away for a day or two to become very famous. Don't tell. Love, Josie'.

So she had run off somewhere after all! I was pleased she hadn't been kidnapped though I'd never really believed that anyone could be taken away by force in the middle of Halifax. She'd be home again by tomorrow if she wasn't home already.

Josie famous? At what? She was in the group below me but her reading was so good that she came up to our group for that. But nobody got famous reading unless it was on the BBC. I didn't think the BBC offered jobs to girls of eleven without letting their parents know. And she wasn't pretty enough to be discovered like Lana Turner at a soda fountain. We'd read that in a magazine and thought that America must be a wonderful place with fountains of soda water coming out of the ground.

I folded up the note again and put it in my pocket. I'd wait another hour or two before I showed the message to the policeman. Sneaking on someone was the worst thing to do even when it involved a silly kid like Josie. On the other hand it wasn't safe for her to be wandering around in a big town whether she was getting famous or not.

With my conscience more or less at ease again I struck off

across the moor. There wasn't much point in detecting things all by myself and it was harder than usual to think up another pretend.

I could be Jane Eyre, wandering and starving on the moor after she'd run away from Thornfield Hall, I considered, but I was still rather full of chips and anyway I'd thought her a bit feeble to take off like that and not go with Orson Welles to a tropical island and be a mistress.

The moors were lovely. Visitors often came in the summer to tramp over them with cameras and haversacks but they couldn't know them as I knew them, in every season. They didn't know where to find the first wood violet by the stream, nor were they aware that the long-horned cow which lowed at them from the brow of a hill threateningly was so placid that children could ride on her broad back.

I looked back towards the Tyler house, or rather to its roof rising beyond the walls. Where I stood the grass dipped into a hollow. If I went on a little way I would be able to see more of the building.

'You'd think someone would buy it or rent it or something,' Sandra had remarked.

'It has a reputation,' I'd replied darkly.

'What's that?' Josie had piped.

'Things or people that have stories told about them. The stories make the reputation.'

'But what did happen there?' Sandra spoke more gravely than usual. 'Not pretend happen but really happened. I asked Mum but she didn't know.'

Mrs Pirie wouldn't know, I thought. She and Sandra had come to the village at about the time I was starting Junior School. The neighbours soon found out she was divorced – perhaps not even married! That was whispered but Mum said that it was malicious gossip and I must be nice to Sandra and polite to Mrs Pirie.

'Someone killed themselves in the house,' I said. 'I don't know any more than that really.'

'When?' Josie enquired. 'A hundred years ago?'

'When I was little. I don't remember anything about it.'

The remembered conversation faded in my mind as I went up

the nearest rise and looked over into the hollow that enclosed the village.

There were more cars coming along into the square from the main street. Black cars with the sun striking their windscreeens. I could see the group of black ant figures scatter and divide as if someone had thrust a stick into the middle of them.

Perhaps Josie had come back! I forgot about the Tyler house and set off across the sloping turf on to the track again, arms swinging as I marched down towards the village.

It would be useless asking Mum what was going on. She'd be busy mopping the floor or ironing tea towels or something else equally time-consuming and silly! In any case she didn't mix much with the neighbours.

'They're a bit clannish here,' she'd told me once. 'It takes twenty years to belong in a place like this.'

So I hurried past my house and the row of cottages to which it was attached and went on into the square.

The Whites were just coming out of their house and I knew then that Josie hadn't come home. Mrs White was always a quietly dressed lady with her hair neatly combed and very little colour in her face, but now she looked white as wax and her eyes were closed as if the light hurt them.

A policewoman was guiding her into a black car, arm round her shoulders. Behind them Mr White shambled, clearly very drunk. The police put him into the car behind. Maybe they were afraid that he was going to be sick or something.

The tall inspector got into the front of the second car and the policeman at the gate made more shooing noises. People were drifting away to form smaller groups, heads together, talking.

Mrs Simmons was standing at the door of her shop. It must have been a day with few customers, I thought, weaving my path towards her.

'They found a body,' she said.

Usually she had a gossiping, slightly breathless kind of voice but now it was flat and toneless and her eyes had a startled glare like the eyes of a rabbit caught in the glare of Dad's headlamps once when we'd been to the cinema. He'd swerved to avoid it but when I looked through the rear window it was still sitting in the middle of the road.

'Whose?' I asked.

'A child's. That's all I heard.'

'They must think it's Josie,' I said.

'Go home, Cordy!' She looked at me properly for the first time, her eyes focusing. 'Go on home, child.'

There must be some mistake, I decided. Josie had run away to be famous so how could she be a body? It had to be a mistake.

I felt chilly suddenly though the sun was still shining. I could hear the low conversations going on all about me, split into broken phrases.

'– blindfolded. Constable Spelling told me.'

'– playing chicken?'

'– has to be someone else. She went – in Halifax, didn't she?'

'– always thought that –'

I turned and went home, carefully avoiding every third cobble.

'If I miss every third cobble then Josie is alive. She'll come back and explain everything.'

I reached my own gate with every third cobble untrodden. I went up the short path and pushed open the front door. To the left of our little square hall Mum was in the sitting-room, the telephone receiver held to her ear.

I couldn't see her until she turned and when she did turn she looked – I had no word then to describe how she looked.

'Wipe your shoes, Cordy,' she said. 'Your dad's on the telephone. He has some very bad news. His secretary just told – Cordy just came in. Yes, I'll break it gently. Try to get home early, dear.'

She put the receiver down very gently and looked at me.

'Josie's mum and dad are going off with the police,' I said.

'Formal identification. I think we could both do with a cup of tea. Let's go into the kitchen.'

She'd finished the cleaning and every surface sparkled.

'Tea,' Mum said, standing stock still in the middle of the room and looking vaguely round.

'I'll make us a pot of tea,' I said.

That seemed to wake her up. She gave herself a little shake and said, 'The idea! You'd probably scald us both! You get the cups. This has been – I keep hoping there's been some mistake.'

'What did Dad's secretary say?' I asked.

'She went out to buy some filing paper. The usual order hadn't arrived and at this time of the year a lot of people going on holiday take out extra insurance so there's quite a rush on at the office. Anyway she came back in an awful state, poor girl! Said she'd just seen a little girl knocked down and killed.'

'Accidentally?'

'What? Yes, of course. People don't run children over deliberately! It was a lorry and she just ran right out in front of it without stopping, Miss Johnson said. He didn't have a chance to stop, poor fellow!'

'Josie was run over by accident,' I repeated.

I'd thought that she'd been murdered. The police, the crowd at the gate, the whispering had heralded a drama that never was.

'Do stop standing there saying that!' Mum said impatiently. 'Accidents do happen you know.'

'But she disappeared yesterday afternoon,' I said.

'They think she ran off out of naughtiness,' Mum said. 'Miss Johnson did manage to tell me a little but then she started crying and your dad took the phone. He's pretty shaken himself. I mean – it isn't every day – get the sugar, love.'

I got the sugar and she put two big spoonfuls in each cup.

'How did she get from Halifax to Bradford?' I asked.

'I've no idea. By bus maybe? Maybe she got on the wrong bus and instead of coming home landed in Bradford. I don't know.'

'But why would she run out of the big store and get on a bus anyway?' I said.

'Cordy, I don't know! Who knows what goes through a child's mind? Perhaps she and her mum had an argument in the shop or something. I'm sure we'll find out the truth of it before very long. Do you want a biscuit?'

I shook my head. For once I wasn't hungry.

'I blame the parents,' Mum said suddenly, fiercely, sitting down. 'Mrs White never has a word to say for herself and as for that husband of hers, he –'

'Drinks like a fish,' I supplied.

'That's enough, Cordy! No sense in repeating idle gossip. Josie's gone and we must come to terms with that.'

Come to terms with a death. It was exactly the kind of stupid remark that grown-ups offered as if it were wisdom.

I said in a small voice, 'I never knew anyone who was dead before.'

'It just shows you –' Mum said, stirring more sugar into her tea. 'We should never take our loved ones for granted. Maybe Josie went into the cinema or something when she got to Bradford – to teach her mother a lesson for scolding her or something – and then it got later and later and the last bus went and she got scared. The police will find out what actually happened.'

'I heard someone in the crowd say she had a blindfold,' I said.

'A blindfold?' Mum stared at me. 'Miss Johnson said something about a scarf round her neck. She didn't know who the child was but she stood there until a policeman ran up and he said it looked like Josephine White who'd gone missing yesterday. Miss Johnson just stood there. Shock I expect.'

'Will the police be asking us all questions?' I enquired.

'I don't think so, dear.' She got up to pour herself more tea. 'I keep on thinking that your dad and I were having a nice time with Susan last night and while we were enjoying ourselves poor little Josie was likely wandering around Bradford, not knowing what to do next.'

'I never heard her mum scold her,' I said.

'Well, we shall hear about it I daresay.' She sat down at the table again and looked at me. 'Cordy, this is an awful thing to happen right at the beginning of the summer holidays. You know terrible accidents do sometimes happen. They're very rare so I don't want you to worry about them. Were you very friendly with Josie?'

She was getting ready to be comforting and motherly. Susan would have burst into tears and sobbed that Josie had been her dearest friend. I wasn't like Susan. 'Born spiky,' Mum sometimes said when I evaded a hug or said something flippant when she'd cooked something special for me.

'She trailed round after Sandra and me,' I said. 'She was all right, I suppose.'

'Her poor mother!' There were tears in my mother's eyes. 'Oh, I just can't imagine how I'd feel if – it doesn't bear thinking about. I shall feel obliged to go over tomorrow and take some flowers. Or a hotpot? I don't suppose that Mrs White will have had time to cook anything.'

'I've been asked out to tea tomorrow,' I said.

'Sandra's away,' Mum said.

'Sandra isn't the only friend I've got!' I said crossly. 'I've lots more. It isn't only Susan who has friends, you know.'

'I never said it was, Cordy.'

She gave me a hurt, reproachful look.

'In fact,' I said, wondering why I was getting so angry inside, 'in fact I spoke to the inspector earlier on. I told him that I hadn't seen Josie since last weekend. That was before they found her.'

'You mustn't go bothering the police,' Mum said frowningly. 'They have work to do, Cordy. They don't want little girls pushing themselves forward. Who's this friend who's asked you to tea? Oh, that'll be Susan ringing. John said he'd ring the college and you know how considerate she is.'

The shrilling of the telephone stopped as she picked up the receiver and I heard her voice raised eagerly.

'Susan? Oh, how lovely of you to call. Did Dad let you –?'

'Her name is Holly Jane Maitland,' I said aloud to the empty room.

3

When you are twelve you think of death as something which stands apart waiting until you are old. I realise now, of course, that the old see it as waiting for the very old.

At twelve I had never come within a whisper of death. Both sets of grandparents had died before I was born so I hadn't even a dim and distant memory of them. I didn't know quite how to react in these circumstances. There was a chilly feeling inside me, because if Josie could be here one day and gone the next then the world wasn't as safe as I'd painted it.

I went up to my bedroom where Susan's presence still lingered and began tidying out the drawers of the dressing-table. In that I was like my mother, I realised, sitting back on my heels and hurriedly pushing everything back in its original jumble. I loved Mum but I didn't want to be like her, hemmed in by kitchen walls, forever dusting and cooking and keeping the world at bay.

Dad came home early, his face drawn into a sombre mask. He and Mum sat together in the kitchen over yet another pot of tea while I spread out some homework project – geography, I think – on the table in the sitting-room and puzzled over trade routes as their voices murmured on.

While Mum was making tea Dad got up and came into the sitting-room. He usually read an evening paper at this time but today he had evidently neglected to buy one and without it he was like a baby without a dummy. He came over to look at the map I was drawing, took a few turns about the room, fiddled with a little bunch of silk flowers on the sideboard, then said abruptly, 'Your mum says that you've taken all this very well!'

I gave a little shrug and he patted my shoulder in an awkward way as if he was afraid that I might burst into tears. There was nothing men hated more than a crying woman, Mum had told me.

'It was a dreadful accident,' Dad said. 'Just shows you can't be too careful on the road. You always look both ways, don't you?'

'Yes, I do,' I said.

'That's a sensible girl!'

He patted my shoulder again and wandered into the hall, opened the front door and meandered down the path.

'He's gone to pick up an evening paper,' Mum said, coming through from the kitchen. 'Men are lost without their evening papers.'

We had a silent tea which wasn't that unusual because Dad liked eating in peace without chattering going on all round him.

'Any news?' Mum said at last, beginning to clear away.

'Not really.' He shook his head. 'They were saying in the general store that she's to be buried in Leeds. Apparently the Whites have a family plot there.'

'Were they – you know – insured with your firm?' Mum asked.

'Mary, you know I can't discuss clients.' He put his knife and fork neatly together. 'As a matter of fact they weren't. Mr White isn't a person I'd regard as a good risk anyway. Cordy, why don't you help your mother?'

I helped Mum though, looking back now, I can see that I was in her way. She had her own routine and I was at the stage when fingers easily become thumbs and dishes slip through thumbs.

'Why don't you take your homework upstairs and finish it there?' she said. That meant she and Dad wanted to discuss what had happened with the wireless turned up loud. I wished that parents didn't try to protect their children so carefully. I wanted to know where Josie had been all night and why she'd run straight into the path of the lorry but I'd never hear it from them.

I collected my books from the sitting-room and was rewarded with an approving nod from Dad as he turned a page of the newspaper.

'That's the ticket! Work hard and you'll do well,' he said. 'Don't spend all your holiday with your nose in your books though. We all need a spot of relaxation.'

'I'm going out to tea tomorrow with –'

'That's the right idea! Go along then.'

The newspaper rustled as he folded it carefully.

Nobody, I reflected as I trudged up the stairs, was really interested in what I did. Nobody was much interested in what any child did provided they wiped their shoes before they came into the house and got reasonably high marks in school. Nobody had been interested in Josie until she got herself knocked down by a lorry.

From below came the sound of the wireless turned up high. That meant Mum and Dad would be talking about what had happened. I closed my bedroom door and took the folded note Josie had left in the wall out of my pocket.

If I gave this to the police it might be a useful clue. On the other hand it might look as if I was pushing myself forward, trying to make myself look important. And when I told them where I'd found it they might go on up to the Tyler house and start looking for more clues. I had only met Fred and Fay once but I already knew they would hate having strangers poking about their property. Fred needed quiet for his writing and Holly Jane was very shy. Anyway Josie might've stuck the note in the wall weeks back in the course of some game or other and forgotten about it.

I opened the door and went into the bathroom, tore up the note into little bits and flushed it down the lavatory. The tiny white pieces with the neat round letters on them whirled round and round and went down with a great swoosh.

'Cordy, don't forget to wash your hands!' Mum called up the stairs.

Mum always said that even if I had only gone in to brush my teeth.

'All right, Mum!' I called back, and ran the tap over my fingers as if I was flushing the last of Josie away.

In the morning I slept late which was a kind of escaping, I suppose. Years later I find the same tendency in myself when there are problems to be solved or emotions to explore.

'You look a bit peaky today,' Mum said, whisking my breakfast from under the grill. 'I know I said to get your homework done but you're not working too hard, are you?'

'No, honestly, Mum.'

'I thought I might slip over to see Susan later on today,' she said. 'She has the afternoon off and –'

43

'I'm going out to tea,' I reminded her.

'With your school friend, yes.' She brushed a wisp of hair out of her eyes. 'I'll drive home with your dad.'

Susan at seventeen was practically grown up, so it was only natural for Mum to want to talk over what had happened with her.

'Are Josie's mum and dad back yet?' I asked.

'I've no idea.' She gave a reproving little frown. 'Cordy, when something very sad happens in a family they don't want people moithering them. They need some privacy to come to terms with their loss. You're to stay away from the Whites and you're not to go gossiping in the village either! Now I want you to promise me.'

'I promise,' I said.

'And don't talk with your mouth full! Right, now where did I put that list?'

I slept late and Mum made lists and cleaned out cupboards. We neither of us liked real sorrows very much.

Dad must have gone off early to make up for coming home early the day before because the morning paper was still folded on the table. Usually he took it to work with him and bought an evening paper before he came home later in the day. Mum only ever glanced at the headlines and read her stars though she said the forecasts were quite ridiculous.

'I think I'll give the bedrooms a bit of a turn-out,' she said now with a brisk air. 'Don't get into any mischief.'

I'd promised not to go to the Whites' house or gossip in the village but I hadn't promised not to read the paper. I waited until I heard her moving about upstairs and then I quickly unfolded it.

There was nothing about Josie on the front page. There was an item on the third page headed, 'Tragedy In Bradford'. Underneath the headline was a photograph of the Whites' front door with the blurred figure of Mrs White just emerging and an indeterminate figure on the step which might or might not have been me.

I heaved a little sigh of relief and started reading the column.

West Yorkshire police are investigating the circumstances

which led to the accidental death of Josephine White, 11, yesterday afternoon. Josephine had been reported missing by her parents the previous day after vanishing from Harvey's store in Halifax where she had gone with her mother on a shopping trip. Nothing further was reported of her until three o'clock yesterday afternoon when she ran out into the main road under the wheels of a lorry. She was killed instantly. The driver of the lorry was treated for shock and later made a short statement to police. Several witnesses gave statements which absolved the driver from any blame.

Formal identification of their daughter was made by Mr and Mrs Charles White who have remained in Bradford to assist the police with their enquiries. Two witnesses have already come forward to report that they saw a child answering Josephine's description board a Bradford bus in Halifax town centre the day before the tragic accident.

Anyone having any information to impart should contact –

I folded the paper hastily as Mum came down the stairs. She had a bundle of garments in her arms.

'I wish you'd put your clothes in the proper place, Cordy,' she said, 'when they require washing. I hate having to grope for socks under the bed! You do know where the clothes basket is by now!'

'Sorry, Mum.'

'And don't tip the chair like that. It weakens the legs! Why don't you finish your homework or something?'

'I thought I'd weed my patch,' I said.

Susan and I both had our separate plots at the end of the back garden. Susan had grown spring onions and lettuces and radishes in hers.

'You can't buy stuff as fresh as this from the greengrocer,' Dad had always boasted.

I'd planted flowers, meaning to fill vases with them, but I planted them too close to the surface or something because the birds had a feast and only a few mingy strands of exotic ivy and misty bluebells came up, along with the dandelions and daisies and several tough thistles.

'Well, I don't suppose you can get up to anything there,' Mum said.

Mothers were peculiar, I decided, going through the back door. When I was somewhere else mine assumed I was playing happily but when I was under her eye she assumed I was planning all kinds of wickedness.

My plot was smothered in weeds. Some of them were as pretty as flowers. Susan had dug over her plot before she left and told me I could have it. I decided that I might make a rockery there, but not just yet!

Instead I started pulling up weeds, carefully not thinking about Josie or what I'd read in the newspaper. When a thin prickle of thistle stung my hand and brought tears to my eyes I was more glad of it than not.

I went in when Mum called me and washed my hands, pressing out the tiny blob of blood and wondering whether or not I'd get tetanus and die.

'Always wear gardening gloves,' Dad had instructed. 'There are germs in the soil which can get into your bloodstream and cause tetanus; that's lockjaw which is very dangerous.'

'Do worms get tetanus when you chop them in half?' I'd wanted to know, and Dad had smiled and said he didn't think so.

'What time are you due at – what's her name?' Mum asked, setting stew before me.

'About three o'clock,' I invented. 'We might have a play on the moor first.'

'Well, as long as you don't go near any roads. I'm catching the two thirty bus else I'd walk over with you. Where does –?'

'Will Susan be coming back with you?'

Effectively diverted she looked regretful.

'I wish she would but we can't keep dragging her home again now that she's so nicely settled in the flat. You miss her, don't you?'

I considered the question for a minute. Did I miss Susan? I wasn't sure but I said, 'Yes, but she had to leave home sometime.'

'If the college had been nearer . . .' Mum sighed, her eyes dreaming Susan so vividly that I almost saw my sister seated at the table, small white teeth biting into a chunk of bread, her blue eyes laughing at us.

'Have you heard anything else about – you know?' I asked.

'Where would I have heard anything?' she said. 'I don't have people running to feed me the latest gossip! It's very sad but it isn't our business, Cordy. I shall send a card and some flowers to the funeral – now ought I to send them to the house or will there be an announcement? Susan will know. I'd better give her a quick ring just to make sure she hasn't got other plans.'

Mum had on a flowered shirtwaister dress and her navy blue summer coat hung, freshly brushed, on the hallstand. She'd rolled her hair into a pleat the way Susan had shown her and she had her good pearl ear-rings on. Typical, I thought! Anyone else would've rung first to find out if the visit was convenient, but Mum probably knew already that Susan would be pleased to see her again so soon, so that they could enjoy a mother-daughter chat about the terrible accident.

She was already on the telephone, voice pitched high.

'Are you sure it's no bother, love? You hadn't made any other plans? I'd not want you to –'

Susan would be reassuring her that she'd love to see her. I pictured my sister's smile and the genuine warmth with which she greeted people as if she was really delighted to see them. I hadn't learnt that gift.

Mum was off at last, fussing that she had enough change in her purse and that the dishes were soaking properly in hot water.

'Make sure that you're home by eight,' she said, kissing me. 'Leave the back door key under the mat. Don't outstay your welcome.'

'Holly Jane is looking forward to me going there,' I said.

'Yes, of course, love. Of course! Now where did I put my sunglasses?'

Her mind was already on the bus wending its way to Bradford. She had never once stopped to wonder just who this new friend was or exactly where she lived. It wasn't Mum's fault. She liked to think of me as a popular girl with too many friends to count. Of course Susan had been popular. I was Susan's sister so it followed that I must be popular too.

When she'd gone I went upstairs and took a bath. In our house baths were for evening three times a week with hot chocolate to follow and hair towelled and combed with a styling brush that never did a thing for my heavy mouse brown bob. It felt wonderfully wicked to lie in the hot water scented with a plentiful handful of Mum's bath salts that were perfumed with lilac and feel one's body buoyed up slightly by the water.

What did it feel like to die? Mum had said once that it was exactly like going to sleep. I thought it had to be more than that. Otherwise nobody would ever go to sleep for fear of dying. Susan had said once that she thought you stepped out of your body. I tried to imagine Josie, seeing the lorry bearing down on her and leaping out of her body. Had she stood there watching all the people crowd round her and the policeman come running, and try to touch someone and tell them she was there still?

I held my nose and slid under the surface of the water, keeping my eyes open. If I stayed here long enough I might swim out of myself. They would say that I had drowned in my bath and Mum would be sorry that she hadn't appreciated me when she had the chance and Dad would arrange the cards of condolence all round the family snapshots and think of happier times – I shot into a sitting position coughing and spluttering out a mouthful of lilac-scented foam.

I put on my gingham dress with the white collar. It was a tiny checked material in red and white which looked rather jolly. I brushed my hair and put on sandals with white knee socks because I was going as a guest and I even remembered to put the key under the mat.

When I set off up the track I was full of anticipation and virtue. It was a lovely afternoon.

Today, given the same situation, I would feel regret and pain that Josie wasn't able to see the blue sky or the waving grasses or the darkening gold of the gorse, but the young are selfish. They are only glad to be alive, striding on and up over the tumbling scree. As I was on that sunny afternoon.

By the time I reached the open gates of the Tyler house I had decided not to tell the Maitlands about Josie unless they mentioned it first. They hadn't known her, I reasoned, and it would be mean to worry them when they had only just come to live in the district. They might get the idea that it wasn't safe to allow Holly Jane to play out on the moors with me even though Josie had disappeared in Halifax and been knocked over in Bradford.

I hesitated as I approached the house. Visitors usually came to the front door when they'd been invited to tea, but I already guessed the Maitlands didn't always do things the way other people did.

My dilemma was resolved for me by the front door opening wide and Fay coming out on to the steps with her hand stretched towards me in welcoming style.

In daylight she looked insubstantial as if one could, by squinting, see the light through her. She was wearing a loose ankle-length dress of some flimsy almost transparent stuff, patterned all over with brown and green leaves with here and there a little curling scarlet leaf. Her hair curled over her head and round her face and her eyes were wide and green.

'Oh, I hoped you'd be early!' she said, her long pale fingers grasping my own as she drew me after her into the high-ceilinged hall with its wide staircase that curved up to a gallery above. 'You must come and see how beautiful we have made the sitting-room!'

She urged me into the big room at the back out of which the conservatory led. Sandra and I had often played there, draping school scarves round our shoulders and practising court curtseys.

The floor had been swept and polished and several thin, bright rugs laid across it. There was a long sofa, and where patches on the walls betrayed mirrors or paintings had once hung there were shawls pinned, dozens of them in every shade, some threaded with gold or silver, others embroidered. There were also beanbags scattered here and there on the shining expanse of floor and a big gramophone with a trumpet-shaped speaker sticking out of it.

'It's lovely,' I said reverently.

Fred came through from the conservatory. He'd replaced the cracked and broken panes of glass and swept the floor, and the broken flowerpots were piled in a wheelbarrow. He looked absolutely, somehow reassuringly, solid.

'Your parents didn't mind your coming then?' he said to me.

'No. With Sandra away and – well, Mum's pleased that I've found a new friend,' I said.

'As to that I'm afraid we've got a bit of a disappointment for you,' Fred said.

'We simply couldn't cope with getting the place shipshape and getting rid of all the dust with poor Edward coughing his little lungs up and since he knows Holly Jane already and is so fond of her –' Fay said.

'We drove over to Scarborough and left the pair of them with Fay's sister for a few days,' Fred said. 'She wasn't awfully keen on going to her aunt's once she knew that you were coming but she'll be back next week, so you can meet her then.'

'And Edward! Oh, Cordelia, you'll love Edward,' Fay said. 'He is quite the most remarkable baby ever born, isn't he, Fred?'

'He certainly has the biggest appetite,' Fred said with a wink at me.

'My sister will love having him,' Fay said. 'She never had any of her own so in a way it's a treat for her. She's a widow so she hasn't got a Fred either.'

'She doesn't seem to feel the lack,' Fred said.

'Everybody ought to have a Fred,' Fay said.

There was a loving look on her face and her hand touched the sleeve of his frayed sweater in a light, tentative caress. For an instant I felt shut out from something precious, just as I did when Susan and Mum had one of their little chats.

'And everyone ought to have a Cordelia too!' She swung round and caught my hand and laughed on a high, tinkling note.

'Holly Jane will be the first to agree with that when she meets you,' Fred said. 'I believe that she will lose her shyness once she has seen you and talked to you.'

'We are working very hard,' Fay confided, 'to make the house comfortable for the children. Ooops! Holly Jane would never forgive me if she heard that. She's a teenager now and that makes a great difference! Come and look at these. We got them this morning from the nurseries.'

She swooped upon one of the beanbags and scooped up a pile of large packets with brightly coloured flowers on them.

'I'm by way of being a bit of a gardener,' Fred said modestly.

'Fred! You are not!' Fay let the packets fall round her feet. 'Don't heed him, Cordelia! He can't tell a rose from a buttercup!'

'But I'm good at the digging,' he said.

'That I'll grant you!' Fay knelt in the circle of packets, picking up a couple and shaking them. 'We shall begin with autumn blooms and then move on to spring bulbs. Fill the house and the conservatory with colour.'

'And Fred will do the digging,' he said.

'Very thoroughly!'

She rose in a graceful movement and took my hand again, her opal green eyes moving over my gingham dress and spanking clean shoes and socks.

'You're so prettily dressed today that our house doesn't do you justice,' she said.

'She pays a compliment to her hostess,' Fred said.

'One which is appreciated. Fred, it's so warm! Why don't we have tea in the garden? You'd help us carry the things out, wouldn't you, Cordelia?'

'Yes of course. I love picnics,' I said.

'In heaven, according to my wife, there are endless picnics,' Fred told me.

'Also balls and sleigh rides and fat babies,' Fay said solemnly. 'Now that we have electricity we can make pancakes and pies and puddings and all kinds of marvellous things to eat.'

'What Fay means is that I can make them,' Fred said with a grin.

'My dad can't even boil an egg,' I said, a trifle unfairly because I couldn't picture Mum letting him try.

'Well, I whipped up a trifle in your honour,' Fred said. 'Cakes and pies must wait until another day. There are salmon sandwiches and marzipan biscuits and stuffed choux pastry – cream cheese and chives.'

'One of Fred's specialities.'

They were looking at me expectantly.

'It all sounds delicious,' I said sincerely.

'We're still unpacking but the table in the kitchen is laid,' Fred said. 'We can carry the stuff out to the end of the garden. There's a swing there.'

'Yes, I know,' I said.

'Of course you play here, don't you? You and your friends. You probably know the place inside out,' he said, leading the way to the kitchen.

'Used to play here,' I said. 'We only came here because the house was empty.'

51

'It's still pretty empty,' Fred said. 'Our furniture hardly fills a corner of it.'

'You will earn a lot of money from your next translation,' Fay said. 'In any case it's fun to do things little by little. You see we have the cooker in and the refrigerator already.'

They stood gleaming self-consciously next to the old range.

'And the new door is on,' Fred said.

And the food, I saw, was ready too, as Fay opened the refrigerator and brought out bowls and a large plate of sandwiches under greaseproof paper.

'Don't we have a proper picnic basket somewhere?' Fred said, looking round.

'Over here!' Fay darted into the pantry. 'Fred, I must be psychic! There was no reason for me to unpack it.'

'We'll load it.' He took the big square wicker basket from her and began to put the various dishes carefully into the separate compartments.

'Shall we make the tea or would you like something else?' he asked.

'Tea, please.'

I was still young enough to enjoy drinking tea.

'I'll make the tea!' Fay darted to the kettle.

We went out into the garden and took the narrow overgrown path that led down the side of the garage to the acre or so behind the house.

It had once been a late Victorian garden, with shells edging the flowerbeds and a separate kitchen garden with a low hedge round it. There was a lawn which hadn't been mowed for years so that it was now a meadow, where one stood knee deep in buttercups and meadowsweet.

The two apple trees that never bore fruit were at the end of the lawn, branches beginning to tangle together above the swing with its rusty chain.

'Edward will adore the swing when he's a little older,' Fay said, carrying one half of the basket with Fred.

I had been entrusted with a wooden bowl piled with fruit and little packets of cheese. I put it on the grass – in would be a better word for it sank down and the tall needles of grass closed around it.

'The soil seems very fertile here,' Fred said with a professional air. 'The former owners must've had compost brought over the moor. Nice for a bit of a dig.'

'Fred is in his element with a spade in his hand,' Fay said, trying to flatten down an area of grass and set out the dishes.

'Or a knife,' said Fred.

'A knife too. He is quite useless with a needle, but that's my strong point. I love sewing. Do you, Cordelia?'

'I never do any,' I said truthfully. 'I can knit a little.'

'Cordelia is the intellectual type to my way of thinking.' Fred passed round the sandwiches.

They weren't the dainty ones I associated with afternoon tea but thick cut rounds of brown bread packed with salmon and cucumber and slices of tomato.

'We leave the crusts on because it's such fun to throw them away,' Fay said, peeling off a crust and flinging it over her shoulder.

'Great fun!' Fred tore off a crust from the sandwich he was holding and flung it in the opposite direction.

'Your turn.' Fay nodded at me.

Mum would have a blue fit, I thought, tearing a crust loose and throwing it to land by Fay's.

'The birds will come and gobble up the crusts and spare the worms for another day,' Fay said.

I saw the logic of that.

'Do you have a garden outside your home?' Fred enquired.

'Quite a long one at the back,' I said. 'It isn't like this one though. I'm not very good at gardening either.'

'Cordelia is too modest,' Fay said, passing round the fluffy-looking pastries.

I'd never eaten éclairs stuffed with cheese before. I wasn't sure that I liked them though I politely finished mine. Fred ate his too in a couple of big bites. Fay polished off the rest.

She had an appetite bigger than me, I thought in awe. And yet she sat there with her skirts foaming round her and took quick, mouselike nibbles at a tremendous speed. She ate as if she hadn't eaten for a week but she did it in a way that made the speedy disappearance of the goodies on offer a matter of wonderment.

'Susan wouldn't agree,' I said, giggling as I spooned up trifle.

'Who is Susan?' Fay asked.

'My sister.'

'You have a sister? Oh, Fred, how rude of us not to have invited her too!'

'She doesn't live at home now,' I explained. 'She lives in a flat in Bradford with a girlfriend. They both go to the secretarial college.'

'How old is she?' Fay asked.

'Seventeen.'

'Oh, grown up.' She sounded disappointed.

'We all grow up,' Fred said gently.

'It seems such a pity. Why was she named Susan?'

She asked questions in a simple, straighforward manner that made her seem not far from childhood herself.

'Mum was brought up by an aunt who was called Susan.'

'Then why Cordelia?'

'Oh, she and Dad went to see a Shakespeare play –'

'*Lear*. Of course.' Fred nodded.

'And Cordelia was the most honest of the daughters. And the name itself is so musical.'

'Do you like Shakespeare?' Fred asked.

'We've done *The Merchant of Venice* and *Twelfth Night*. Read them in school, I mean. I read *A Midsummer Night's Dream* by myself.'

'Ill met by moonlight,' Fay said softly.

'Except that it's not moonlight and we are not ill met,' Fred said.

'The sun is sinking lower.'

Fay had risen, holding out her skirts, her head tilted slightly back so that as she moved into the sunshine her hair seemed enveloped in flame.

'We are in luck,' Fred said in a low voice. 'She is going to dance!'

We sat there with the remains of the picnic nestling into the long grass and watched her.

I had never seen dancing like it before. She raised her arms and her long loose sleeves fell down to her elbows like the wings of butterflies, and with no music except the breeze she began to circle gently in slowly widening circles, her sandalled feet brushing the grass so lightly that she gave the impression of hovering slightly above it, cushioned by air.

She bowed to the four corners of the wind and then began to circle again, toes pointing, her hands coming together in a series of quickening claps that kept pace with the flying circles her feet made over the grass.

And then the dance was done as suddenly as the globe of the sun dipped down behind the high wall.

I looked at Fred, wondering whether applause was in order, but he was looking at Fay, a stillness about him.

Then a bird swooped down on one of the abandoned crusts and Fay laughed and became earthbound again, as far as a creature like her could be bound to the earth.

'Let's drink the tea before we go indoors,' she said.

Fred unscrewed the big thermos flask and we drank the tea which tasted rather odd as it was full of sugar but bereft of milk, and Fred made up silly riddles and even sillier answers when Fay and I couldn't guess them, and we fell about laughing.

'It's getting chilly, sweetheart.' He stopped telling riddles and looked at her anxiously.

'Then we must go in,' Fay said. 'Your parents would be very cross if you caught a cold because of our neglect! Help me pick everything up, Fred.'

I thought that my parents would be even crosser if they could have seen me flinging crusts with gay abandon all over the place or caught a glimpse of Fay's whirling dance.

We put everything except the thrown bread into the picnic basket and screwed on the lid of the vacuum flask and Fred carried the picnic basket by himself since it was no longer necessary to be careful with it, and Fay took my hand and ran with me across the garden and up the narrow path to the kitchen door again.

I remembered what I'd been warned about overstaying my welcome and held out my hand.

'It was a wonderful picnic,' I said. 'Really wonderful.'

'You're not going already?'

'Her parents will be expecting her,' Fred said. 'You didn't get into any trouble the other night?'

'No. It's quite safe for children round here,' I said.

'Safe,' Fay said, wrapping her arms about herself. 'That's a nice word.'

'It goes with Fred,' I said.

'Like toast and soup and blanket,' she agreed. 'You'll come again?'

'Give us a few days to get everything more organised,' Fred put in. 'We are going to have a telephone installed and make a couple of shopping trips to buy new curtains and some paint.'

'We want to decorate a bedroom for Holly Jane for when she gets home,' Fay said. 'Come to lunch on Monday. Will that suit you?'

'I'm sure it will.'

'I'd like to start planting some flowers in pots in the conservatory,' Fay said. 'You could help me with that unless you'd rather not?'

'I'd love to!'

I hardly recognised myself as the girl who couldn't be bothered to dig holes deep enough for the bulbs.

'And Holly Jane will lend a hand as soon as she gets back,' Fred said.

'If we can coax her nose out of a book,' Fay said playfully. 'I'll see you out at the front door. Like high society!'

She went ahead of me down the long passage into the front hall and opened the door. Outside the sky was streaked with gold and scarlet, orange and pink.

'Such loveliness,' Fay said softly. 'Sometimes I feel as if I could drink down the sky! Goodbye, Cordelia. Come again on Monday!'

Four whole days away, I thought, going down the steps. It stretched ahead in an eternity.

When I glanced back at the gates she was still there, the last spear of sunlight striking fire from the ring on her waving hand.

Mum and Dad were already home. The afternoon had flown by as fast as a good night's sleep.

The back door was ajar when I went round and I could hear Mum's voice, cajoling.

'It's a big opportunity for her, John.'

'Hardly the kind of opportunity I'd've chosen for a daughter of mine,' Dad said.

'Surely it's an honour? To be picked to represent the college in a promotion pamphlet! And she's a pretty girl. You can't deny –'

I pushed open the sitting-room door and they turned and looked at me. They were sitting like bookends one at each side of the fireplace. The electric fire had been switched on and the pretend flames quivered on the metal behind the two red bars.

'Did you wipe your feet?' Mum asked automatically.

'Yes. What's Susan going to do?'

'Nothing's been settled yet,' Dad said with a weighty air.

'The college is going to bring out a pamphlet advertising the various courses on offer and our Susan has been asked to be on the cover,' Mum said.

'In a bathing costume?'

'No, of course not! Don't be so silly, Cordy. In a white blouse and a dark skirt, seated at a typewriter. It'll be very tasteful.'

'You're merely repeating what Susan said. You cannot know for certain.'

'Susan is always truthful,' Mum argued.

'Of course she is, but she's still young and as a concerned parent –'

'Honestly, John! You talk as if she was going to be photographed for the *News of the World*!' Mum said, exasperated.

'It might help your business,' I said. 'Susan Sullivan, elder daughter of Mr John Sullivan, Bradford insurance agent?'

'They want to advertise the college, not the insurance game,' Dad said. He sounded marginally less cross.

'Did you want anything?' Mum gave me the look that said she was pleased to see me, but she wanted me out of the road.

'No. No, I had tea,' I said.

'You must have Holly – whatever over to tea in return,' Mum said. 'John, Susan will be terribly disappointed if you don't let her do this.'

'New people?' Dad looked at me.

'Fairly,' I said.

'Glad you're making new friends.' He frowned slightly. 'I never did like the amount of time you spend with the Pirie girl.'

'With Sandra? Why not?'

'Too full of herself. Like her mother if you ask me.'

'Sandra's on holiday with her mum.'

'And sundry admirers I daresay!' He chuckled at what to me was an almost incomprehensible remark.

'About Susan?' Mum said in a tentative tone.

'We'll see. I'd not want to stand in her way – and if it's done in a very tasteful way. You'll give me no peace until I agree, I can see that!'

'I'll give her a ring!' Mum was on her feet, hand reaching for the telephone.

'Did you hear anything else about Josie?' I ventured.

'Your mum sent a card to the house. The Whites aren't home yet. Cordy, you mustn't let what happened prey on your mind,' he said. 'That poor child should've stayed with her mother and not gone wandering off by herself. Playing a silly trick, I shouldn't wonder! It's the lorry driver I feel bad about. Must've been a terrible shock.'

'I don't think she got run over on purpose,' I said.

'No, of course not, but it just proves you must always look both ways. You do, don't you?'

'Yes, but I usually play up on the moor.'

'She'll come to no harm up on the moor,' Mum said, covering the mouthpiece briefly with her hand. 'Hello! Susan? I've been talking to your dad and he sees no reason why –'

I turned and went quietly out of the room.

4

These days time whizzes by. In those days time was elastic. It could be stretched as tightly as an arrow string or as loose as a game of cat's cradle abandoned in a limp tangle of thread halfway through. That weekend was a mixture of the two, with moments when I remembered Josie and felt the weight of all the years she would never know descend on my shoulders, and the long slow evening hours when I sat in the bedroom where Susan's personality still lingered and tried to concentrate on the holiday homework we had to do. Downstairs Mum and Dad did what they usually did after tea. Dad read his paper and listened to the news on the wireless and Mum moved about and carried out various small tasks and from time to time I heard a few words exchanged between them as if they rationed out conversation.

On Sunday we went to church where there was a brief extra service in memory of Josie. Dad wasn't a regular churchgoer since he thought religion was best left to women but on that Sunday he put on his best suit and came with us. Mum fussed around before we set off.

'I don't think actual mourning is required, do you? It isn't as if we were relatives or anything like that. On the other hand one does like to show respect.'

'Put on your navy blue coat and the small hat,' Dad suggested. 'That's respectful without overdoing it. Anyway the Whites aren't home yet.'

'Staying in town for the inquest I daresay.'

He nodded.

'Well, an inquest won't bring her back,' Mum said. 'Cordy, put on your blazer, there's a good girl. It looks smarter under the circumstances.'

Privately I didn't see how looking smart had anything to do with Josie being dead, but back then people set store by quaint traditions, and I put on the despised school blazer and the beret with the badge at the side and wished that I could feel real sadness. The trouble was that I hadn't liked Josie very much when she was alive and her being dead didn't make her more attractive. It was the way she had died that made her interesting. I knew there was a lot about it in the newspapers but Dad didn't leave his paper lying around for me to glance at, and when I looked for it it was a soggy torn mess in the bin with potato peelings emptied all over it.

Church was full. Most people went to church in our village – or to be more accurate the mothers and children went and the fathers went for a quick pint at the pub. Mr White always did that and went straight to sleep when he finally got home, not bothering with his dinner drying up in the oven.

The Whites weren't there. There were more fathers present than usual and several children I knew from school. I was the only one in school blazer and beret and I felt too humiliated even to acknowledge them.

It was a service like any other save for a few words of condolence from the vicar who told us that Josie had fallen as a flower and would rise as a star. He probably got that out of a book. The funeral would be in Leeds the following afternoon and those who wished to pay their last respects were welcome to attend, after which, having given official permission as it were, he beamed round and announced the last hymn.

'We ought to go,' Mum said as we walked home. 'What d'ye think, dear?'

'Seems the decent thing to do,' he said. 'What about Cordy?'

I didn't want to go to the funeral. It wasn't that I'd really liked Josie but I hadn't disliked her either, and going to the funeral would be like finally admitting she was actually dead and shut up in a coffin.

'Cordy's going to a friend's,' Mum said. 'Can you get time off work?'

'I've a couple of days owing to me. We could meet Susan and go together.'

'I was hoping she might come home this weekend,' Mum said. 'Weekends are for families I always think.'

And it wasn't family unless Susan was home. I knew that as plainly as if she'd said it out straight.

'You were the one who insisted she live away from home,' Dad said. 'I'd my doubts from the start.'

'Oh, but girls need some independence,' Mum said. 'To teach them to deal with the real world! And she seems to be doing awfully well at her course.'

'Girls can be anything these days,' I said. 'They can drive tanks and lots of things.'

'Only in Russia,' Dad said, with the dry little chuckle which signalled he'd made a joke.

'Cordy's just being silly,' Mum said.

'It's a phase,' Dad said mildly.

All children went through phases. They said that to each other at intervals every time I tried to express myself. There were, as far as I could make out, never any good phases. Presumably they stopped when people grew up.

After dinner I mooched into the garden and squatted to pull up a few weeds.

Fell like a flower and rose like a star. It was pretty but it wasn't true. Josie had been a bit of a nuisance all told and she hadn't fallen gracefully like a dying rose. She'd run in front of a lorry and been squashed. With a scarf tied at the back of her neck and pulled down past her chin, as if she'd been wearing a blindfold. That much I'd gleaned from the soggy bits of newspaper. And she hadn't risen like a star. That was Sunday school nonsense like saying of a dead person they were better off as if anyone could be certain of that.

There were little yellow weeds in the patch of garden. Sad little weeds with spiky leaves. I looked at them for a bit and then I stood up and put my foot down on them hard and twisted them into the soil, and let myself be angry because that was easier than crying.

'Now make sure you don't outstay your welcome,' Mum said the next day.

'I won't,' I said in the submissive tone that ought to have alerted her suspicions but didn't on this occasion because her mind was already moving ahead to the funeral.

'Nice for you to get friendly with Melanie,' she said, putting on her hat and frowning at herself in the mirror.

Melanie Deacon lived at the far end of the village and had her own group. Mum however had got it into her head that it was

Melanie I was going to see. I saw no point in setting her straight. The Maitlands belonged to me. They were my own special friends and I saw no reason why I should share them with Mum who would insist on paying them a courtesy visit and embarrass me by talking about things I was sure they wouldn't have any interest in.

'Are you coming?' Dad asked with the slight edge to his voice that meant he was getting impatient.

'Ready, dear.' She aimed a kiss in my direction and was gone, her hat at a jaunty angle. Too jaunty for a funeral for I saw Dad say something to her as they got into the car and she straightened it.

It was hard to believe but the waiting was over. This was the day I would see the Maitlands again. I wondered if they would have changed. Would they, in the brief space since I had seen them, have become ordinary? I was sure they wouldn't have done but one never knew with grown-ups.

I hoped that Melanie and her parents wouldn't be at the funeral in Leeds. That would give the whole game away. Fortunately they weren't people who went along and did what everybody else was doing, so I reckoned I was safe.

I waited until there was no likelihood of Mum and Dad coming back for something they'd forgotten and then I changed my dark skirt and blouse for a pair of jeans and a flowered shirt that Mum had picked up in a sale and never liked on me much.

The street was quiet when I let myself out of the house. I guessed that a lot of people had gone to the funeral. They would tell themselves that they were going out of respect but some of them would be going to see if Mr White managed to turn up sober and some would be going because there might be reporters there with cameras and a general air of excitement.

I turned in the opposite direction first and walked along to the square. The shop was closed and Mrs Simmons had put a neatly printed notice on the door. 'Closed for today'. Out of respect for Josie, I supposed. I made a little face, wondering if Josie knew that so much respect was being offered to her. Then I turned and went back, past my house and its neighbours and up the long track that led to the moors and the Tyler house.

On the high ground where the grass was short and littered

with rocks and the placid cow grazed I always felt light and free. Usually the prospect of spending the day with a couple of adults in a big, half-furnished house would've filled me with gloom, but the Maitlands were different.

I'd played up at the old Tyler house so often that I knew every inch of it, yet it was always subtly different as if the games of pretend we made up there had altered its shape and changed the angles of the walls.

This day I stood at the open gates for a moment savouring the prospect of arrival and then I walked rapidly up the weedy drive. I had it in mind to go round by the back door as usual but Fred must've been waiting for me at the window because he opened the front door as if I was regular grown-up company.

'Exactly on time! How are you, Cordelia?' he said.

'Very well, thank you,' I said.

'And that takes care of the formalities,' he said, putting an arm round my shoulder as he ushered me into the wide hall with the main staircase rearing up and the long passage beyond it.

'It's all polished!' I said, looking round.

The dark wood gleamed with damson and honey lights and a thin scarlet runner like a licking tongue ran along the passage.

'Wood is a friendly thing,' Fred said. 'Warm and living. We are going to have lunch in the small breakfast room. That too has been made ready.'

The small breakfast room was one of those opening off the passage. We had used it once or twice when we acted out the murder of Rizzio in the little supper chamber at Holyrood House. I'd been Mary of Scots and Sandra had been all the murderers and we'd persuaded Josie, who never needed much persuading because she was so glad to be included, to be Rizzio. She hadn't been able to act worth twopence but she'd done her best, though she'd complained the floor was filthy and she'd get into trouble when she got home.

The floor was clean today, swept and polished, and the walls had been given a coat of glossy pale yellow paint and a pair of deeper yellow curtains hung at the window that looked out at the side of the house on to a path choked with brambles.

Fay came in, wearing tight black trousers with a gauzy skirt over them and a black top that tied on one shoulder in a bow. Her hair was as yellow as the curtains today and her skin looked white as milk when the cream has been removed and a faint blue tinge shows through. Her eyelids were pink and slightly swollen, dimming the opal green of her eyes. For a moment she looked almost plain.

'Is something wrong?' I asked.

'Onions,' Fred said. 'Darling, you should've let me peel them for the stew. You know how sensitive your eyes are.'

'I shall peel them under water next time,' Fay said. 'Give me a moment while I repair the damage. Fred, give Cordelia a cocktail.'

'Not a real one,' Fred said, smiling as she whisked out again. 'Lime and orange mixed together. Fay and I sometimes have a small whisky in the evenings but during the day we abstain.'

There were two big glass jugs on the round table in the middle of the room and three tumblers and he began mixing the drinks with a long pointed skewer.

'Fay and I have been looking forward to having our first guest for lunch,' he said. 'Your parents didn't mind your coming?'

'They've gone to Leeds. To a funeral,' I said.

The long skewer made a little clattering noise against the glass.

'Better not mention that to Fay,' he said, resuming his stirring. 'She is sensitive about the mention of death or funerals. Some people are. Not a relative of yours, I hope?'

'No. She was – it's been in the newspapers,' I said.

'We never bother with the newspapers or the wireless. Too much reality can be demoralising. Now taste that and give me your honest opinion.'

'It's super!' I sipped and then drank deeply.

'The secret is a little crushed mint in the bottom. Ah, here she comes now!'

He spoke with such pleasure in his voice as if they'd been a long time separated. I liked that. It never happened at home.

She had powdered her eyelids and put some green stuff on them. It made her eyes look paler.

'Make way for the stew! It's bubbling hot so be careful! We have bought apple cake for afters and coffee. Is this mine? It's delicious, isn't it, Cordelia?'

She had put a streak of colour across each cheekbone too. Her manner was excited like a small child at a party. Like a child she had the gift of living in the moment.

'So what have you been doing since we last met?' Fred enquired as the thick brown stew with its chunks of meat and vegetables was served into large shallow bowls.

'I went to church and –'

'No, what have you been doing that's adventurous!' Fay cried. 'Don't you play pretend games in your head? Surely you do!'

'Yes. Lots of times.'

'You used to play them here, didn't you say? When the house was empty?'

'We didn't damage anything,' I said quickly.

'Of course you didn't! But you played – where?'

'All over the house,' I admitted.

'Different games for different rooms, yes?'

'In this room I was Mary, Queen of Scots,' I said.

'Meeting her lover Bothwell. How romantic!'

'Not exactly.'

'Where would one find a Bothwell in the wilds of Yorkshire?'

Fred was chuckling.

'We didn't do much about Bothwell at school,' I said.

I wondered whether or not to carry on and talk about Rizzio but she was sensitive to death so I spooned up carrots instead.

'We must clear away those brambles when we have a spare hour or two,' Fred remarked.

'And then have a bonfire?' Fay spoke eagerly, spoon poised on its way to her mouth.

'Of course! A big bonfire. One can get rid of a great deal on a really big bonfire.'

'And Cordelia must come and help! You must, mustn't she, Fred?'

'Cordelia must feel free to help when and if she likes,' Fred said.

'Will Holly Jane and Edward be home by then?' I asked.

'I reckon my long-suffering sister-in-law will be relieved to offload the pair of them by then,' Fred said.

'We have made a start on the bedrooms,' Fay told me, rising to collect plates. 'Edward is to have a frieze of elephants round his walls. He adored the elephants when we went to the zoo, didn't he, Fred?'

'Find me a child who doesn't adore elephants,' Fred said.

'Blue elephants,' Fay said in a dreamy tone. 'Blue as – as what, Fred?'

'As elephants,' Fred said.

'And at the bottom of the garden near the old swing we are going to make a sandpit,' she rushed on. 'Edward will adore a sandpit. We took him to the beach before we came north and it was the most marvellous fun, wasn't it, Fred? You should've seen his little face when he tried to pick up the sand and all the grains slithered through his fingers! It was really funny, honestly! And Fred had run out of film and couldn't take a photograph of it. Oh, let's go out into the garden now and eat our cake there. We can make coffee later on if anyone wants any.'

She was on her feet again, gauzy skirt whipping round black-clad legs as she went out.

'It looks as if good old Fred is going to be wielding shovel and paintbrush very soon!' Fred said with a wink at me.

There was a sudden loud squeal from the kitchen. He was out of the room before my ears had properly registered it. I went after him into the big kitchen with its incongruous mix of old and new.

Fay stood at the table, knife and cake in front of her, staring at her finger where a thin line of scarlet was barely visible.

'The knife cut me,' she said. 'It made blood, Fred.'

'Only a trace, darling. Only a trace.' He was holding her arm tightly. 'Knives are my job, sweetheart. Not your job. Look, we'll put your finger under the tap and then find a bit of Elastoplast and Cordelia will put out the plates and I'll slice the pretty cake. More pie than cake, don't you think so, Cordelia? A pastry base and sponge with caramelised apple slices. Come to the tap, darling. There! not a drop left now. The plates are on the side, Cordelia. Would you . . .?'

The plates were blue and white with a lacy china border. I set three of them on the table while Fred ran cold water.

'It's only a tiny cut,' Fay said. 'Look, the skin's closing over already. I won't need any plaster. Shall we go into the garden now?'

'When I've cut the cake,' Fred said, moving to the table and picking up the knife.

'We shall eat every bit but leave crumbs for the birds,' Fay said, her hand on the latch of the back door. 'Come on, Cordelia. Race you!'

She set off as she spoke and I raced after her through the overgrown garden. She ran faster than I could but my own pace was slowed by the thoughts in my mind. Fay was sensitive to lots of things. And yet she was so happy, so carefree. The way children were supposed to be but parents and teachers made jolly sure they weren't. I couldn't imagine my own mother making such a fuss about a tiny cut but then I couldn't imagine her dancing in a garden or anywhere else for that matter.

'I won! I won but I had a head start on you!' Fay called, leaning against one of the old fruit trees. 'And here comes Fred, balancing three plates like a waiter in a very busy restaurant!'

We sat down and ate the cake and scattered crumbs for the birds.

'Where shall we dig the sandpit?' Fay demanded.

'You mean where shall Fred dig the sandpit, don't you?' he teased. 'Here? Not too near the swing. There's a natural hollow here where we could dig and fill it with sand. We'd need a groundsheet to cover it in wet weather or we'll end up with a mudpit. Can you see Edward with mud all over his face?'

'Edward looks adorable whatever his face is covered with,' Fay said.

'I'll paint the swing too,' Fred said. 'What colour?'

'Red!' Fay said. 'Swings should be red.'

'And elephants blue,' I put in.

'And elephants blue. Pre – cisely!' Fred said.

'And your room is to be yellow,' Fay said.

'My room?' I looked at her.

'That was going to be a surprise.' There was mild reproach in his voice.

'Darling, I'm sorry but I just couldn't resist saying something,' she said. 'We've talked about it, Cordelia, and we've decided that you must have a bedroom of your own here when you stay for the weekend. Pale yellow curtains and a green carpet. Like dozing inside a daffodil.'

'I've got a bedroom at home,' I said stupidly. 'At least – it's

Susan's too but she has a flat in Bradford now and so it's mine.'

'That's for everyday. Your yellow room will be for occasional weekends,' Fred said.

'Occasional indeed!' Fay said indignantly. 'You sound most unwelcoming, Fred! Many happy weekends, Cordelia. Many! Your parents will lend you to us now and then, won't they?'

I nodded, thinking privately that my parents would probably be quite happy to give me away for keeps most of the time.

'We must show Cordelia the room that we've picked out for her,' Fay said.

'It was intended as a surprise,' Fred reminded her.

'Expected surprises are the best ones,' she said, taking my hand. 'Let's run again and this time you shall win!'

We ran back to the house and Fred plodded after us, carrying the plates. Fay stopped when we'd almost reached the back door, pretending to double up with a stitch, and I ran on.

'You see I always keep my word. You won!' she said, coming up laughing. 'The back stairs were built for the servants here, I daresay, but you and I, being ladies, will mount the grand staircase. Hurry up, Fred!'

We went through to the front of the house and up the curving staircase. I'd been up it countless times before but seldom as myself. Now I didn't have to pretend! I could be myself, Cordelia Sullivan, invited guest.

On the upper storey two wide landings were divided by the little gallery with the rose window.

'There are attics above but they're full of rubble,' Fred said, coming after me. 'I'm not sure the floors are too safe either.'

'They're a bit rickety,' I told him.

'Of course. You will have played up there already. Children love caves and attics,' Fred said. 'Now Fay will show you the Cordelia room.'

It was one of the main bedrooms where the walls had once been papered with a design of roses but were now discoloured and peeling. There was a divan bed and a white chest of drawers there already – new to my eyes – and several pots of yellow paint stacked near the door.

'You see we have begun already,' Fred said indicating them.

'But you won't have much time to write your book,' I said.

'The book will be written.' His face was suddenly grave. 'There's no sense in rushing anything.'

'Have you played in this room?' Fay asked. 'Happy plays?'

'We played being presented at Court here once,' I remembered. 'Sandra was the Queen and I had a tablecloth as a train. Mum was mad when she found out I'd borrowed it.'

'We shall make the room fit for a young lady being presented at Court,' Fred said solemnly.

'Come and see Holly Jane's room,' Fay invited. 'We're further on with it than yours of course but then she's our own daughter. She decided on rose pink in the end and Fred has already put up the wallpaper.'

The room was bigger than mine – I already thought of it as mine – and the wallpaper was pale pink with a border of deeper pink and a couple of fluffy white rugs on the polished floor. There was a divan bed here too and a matching wardrobe and dressing-table. Fay had opened the wardrobe door to display the row of garments with shoes on trees ranged below.

'Lots of pinks and scarlets!' she said. 'Blue jeans. Why do girls love wearing blue jeans these days? We shall have to buy uniform before term starts. She took only a few things to her auntie's. Pale pink or rose for curtains. Which do you think?'

'I don't think it matters which,' I said.

'No, it doesn't matter.' She looked thoughtfully at the garments hanging in the wardrobe and then closed the door.

'What time do your parents expect you back?' Fred asked.

'They said not to outstay my welcome.'

I wondered if his remark had been a hint, but he gave his broad, warm smile and said. 'That you could never do! But they might worry about you if you're gone too long.'

'You could come and meet them sometime,' I suggested.

'We're not much for socialising,' he said. 'We're bound to run into them down in the village sooner or later. Anyway –'

'You'll come again soon?' Fay sounded anxious as if my going there really mattered to her. 'Don't wait for an invitation –'

'But leave it for a couple of days. We want to do more work on your room,' Fred said.

By the time I came again Holly Jane would be back, fresh from her auntie, and she'd find another girl coming in and out, staying over for the weekend. I thought that if I was Holly Jane I wouldn't relish that very much.

'Holly Jane will be so pleased to find a friend,' Fay said. 'And Edward too. Of course he's only a baby yet. Not much of a companion. We shall have picnics out on the moor and scatter food for the birds. If I weren't a person I'd love to be a bird. What animal would you be, Cordelia?'

'A dog I think.'

I remembered the dog I'd imagined, felt his coat under my palm.

'I don't like dogs,' Fay said.

'A cat then?'

'That's much nicer! A gentle tabby cat who never chases the birds. Fred?'

'I'd be a parrot I think,' Fred said thoughtfully. 'Rather jolly to sit on a perch and swear.'

'You only swear when you're hanging curtains,' Fay said severely. 'You will have to refrain from hanging curtains in future. Edward is at the age when he'll soon begin to imitate people.'

'If he imitates me he won't go far wrong,' Fred said with a wink.

'Perhaps he'll grow up to be a photographer,' Fay said. 'Fred is very good at taking photographs, Cordelia.'

'Haven't time these days,' Fred said, rather brusquely I thought.

'No.' Fay sounded thoughtful. 'Too many decisions to make. Come again soon, Cordelia. We truly love having you around.'

They stood at the front door waving as I went down the drive. I thought about the pretty room they were preparing for my weekend visits. Mum certainly wouldn't allow me to stay over with people she didn't know, which meant that sooner or later she'd have to meet them. And Fay and Fred were less sociable even than my parents. They were different from any other grown-ups I'd ever met, and deep down I didn't want to share them.

I could already hear the comments after the first visit between them and my parents was done.

'Rather a vague sort of person, dear. Those floaty clothes and her hair! Looks as if she dyed it at some stage and didn't keep it up.'

'Seems a nice enough chap. Doesn't seem to have a regular job though. Money in the family perhaps?'

At the foot of the hill I saw a familiar figure just emerging from our garden gate.

'Cordy! Hey, Cordy!'

'You're still supposed to be on holiday!' I said.

'We came back a few days early,' Sandra said. 'Mum heard about Josie. I can't believe it, really I can't! Do you know what happened?'

At thirteen Sandra was taller than me and already growing breasts. They stuck out in front of her like twin cones and she had one of those tape-measure belts that declared her waist was twenty-two inches.

'Only that a lorry knocked her down,' I said.

'But she went missing the day before.' Sandra's eyes were bright with curiosity. 'Our Josie skipping off by herself! She wouldn't say boo to a goose! You know she wasn't raped?'

I stared at her.

'It was in the paper this morning,' Sandra said. 'Wherever she'd been no one had raped her. There was a post-mortem.'

Not for the world would I have revealed that I wasn't absolutely sure what rape was. It had to do with sex and it was violent and people never explained it to children. In those days they explained very little to us. We didn't even do human reproduction until we were fourteen and even then we had to have a note from our parents.

'That would be just awful,' I said in a small voice.

'Yes, it would.' Sandra sounded unusually sober. 'I feel bad now about all the times I teased Josie, went a different way to stop her tagging along. She wasn't a bad kid. Where is everybody?'

'They went to Leeds – to the funeral.'

'Poor old Josie! Didn't you want to go? There would have been reporters from the newspapers and the television I daresay.'

'I didn't feel like it,' I said.

'Poor old Josie!' she said again.

'Is that why you came back early? Because of Josie?'

'No, not really. Mum had a bit of a row with her friend and decided to cut her losses and come home.'

Mrs Pirie frequently had bits of rows with various boyfriends. Some of them left her with a cut lip or a bruised eye she disguised with a little sequinned veil.

'Was Brighton nice?' I asked.

'Nice?' Sandra rolled her eyes and leaned closer, lowering her voice. 'Just wait until I tell you what –'

Our car purred along the street and stopped, disgorging Mum and Susan.

'Come along in, dear!' Mum had shed a few tears but her voice was loud and breezy. 'Oh, Sandra. Did you enjoy your holiday?'

'It was super!' Sandra said. 'I was just –'

'Then you'll be wanting to unpack and give your mother a hand, won't you, dear? In view of the circumstances it'd be better if you didn't play out today – showing respect to poor little – Susan has some exciting news for us, Cordy.'

'See you tomorrow,' I said hastily to Sandra, aware that Dad had turned a disapproving eye in our direction. 'Bye now!'

'See you later, alligator!' Sandra turned and sashayed down the street, her hips waggling.

'Getting more like her mother every day,' Dad said gloomily, getting out of the car. 'Don't stand there with your mouth open, Cordy! Go and help your mother.'

Mum and Susan were already brewing up tea in the kitchen. Susan gave me a quick salute, her blue eyes sparkling. In her smart black suit and high heels she looked terribly grown-up.

'Any tea going?' Dad asked, coming in after me.

'In your direction, d'ye mean?' Susan sounded teasing, familiar, in a way that would've got me a telling off for being cheeky.

'Good! I'm parched!' He went into the sitting-room and sat down.

'They didn't have any refreshments after the service,' Mum said to me. 'Understandable under the circumstances but one likes the chance to unwind, lighten the mood a bit.'

She meant telling jokes. People always ended up telling jokes over the ham sandwiches as if to push the facts of death a bit further off. It would have been hard to find anything funny to say after Josie was buried.

'Were there a lot of people there?' I asked.

'Hundreds!' Mum spoke with awe. 'There's been a lot of publicity about it of course, even allowing for that! We went round to Susan's flat afterwards for a spot of lunch.'

'Didn't you go to the funeral?' I asked Susan.

'She had lectures this morning,' Mum spoke for her. 'Anyway it was lucky that we went because she's had rather an exciting offer. Quite a big PR opportunity, isn't it, love?'

'Only some publicity stuff for a cosmetics firm.' Susan had flushed, embarrassed by Mum's eager tone. 'Anyway it's only for a couple of weeks. No big deal!'

'I do wish you wouldn't use slang!' Dad complained from the other room. 'How can you be doing a PR job while you're still a student? Doesn't make sense to me!'

'You forget the college doesn't have a long summer vacation like most other places,' Susan said. 'It's an intensive course, Dad, but we can take paid employment during the time we do get off. It's a real compliment to be asked. Melanie is dead jealous!'

'Talking of Melanies,' Mum said. 'Did you get a decent lunch?'

'Yes and I didn't outstay my welcome,' I said.

'Melanie?' Susan raised newly plucked eyebrows.

'The Deacons,' Mum said. 'Cordy's got quite friendly with the child over the last week or so. Not that we know too much about them but it's better than hanging round with the Pirie girl.'

'About that –' I began.

Now was the time to tell them about the Maitlands, carefully censoring my account.

'Not now, Cordy! I'm trying to make the tea,' Mum said. 'I'm all of a fluster today. This business has really upset me.'

'Have they found the man who –?'

'Little pitchers have big ears, Susan. No, not yet. Let's not go into it.' ▪

'Fellow needs shooting!' Dad proclaimed.

'I don't even want to think about it.' Mum rattled cups into saucers, her mouth in a thin line.

'I had a big lunch,' I said.

'That's nice, dear.' She gave me a distracted glance as she went past me. 'I wish you could stay overnight, Susan. It seems wrong having you start this holiday job straightaway before your dad and I have had a chance to check it out.'

'The college checks out all job offers,' Susan said patiently.

'Even so!'

Mum always said that when she lost an argument.

'Mum, would you mind if I stayed over –?'

'I hope you're not thinking of turning up for work in that skirt,' Dad was saying.

'What's wrong with it?' Susan wanted to know.

'Too short,' he said succinctly.

'Oh, Dad, don't be so stuffy!'

Susan was laughing.

I put my foot on the rung of a kitchen chair and tilted it crossly. When Susan came home I became completely invisible. Not existing. The two words sent a cold shiver down my back. Not existing. Like Josie. Fall like a flower. Rise like a star.

Fay's eyes red-rimmed like Mum's as she got out of the car. Only there hadn't been any onions at all in the stew!

5

Sandra turned up the next morning just after Dad had left for the office and Mum was complaining that the silverware – photograph frames and a rose bowl – needed cleaning. She had on jeans and a sweater that wasn't as tight as usual and Mum gave her a smile that was more approving than usual.

'It looks a bit like rain,' she said, casting a glance towards the window. 'Perhaps you ought not to –'

'Not to play out, Mrs Sullivan.' Sandra was at her most polite. 'Mum's gone shopping and so I thought Cordy would like to see my holiday snaps. We had really good weather.'

'That's nice, dear.' Mum's eyes had wandered back to the rose bowl. 'Well, I see no reason why not. Would you like to come back here for dinner?'

'Mum left something for us both,' Sandra said.

I wondered how since she couldn't have had much chance to buy any food but Mum nodded vaguely, her fingers twitching towards the silver polish, and I grabbed my jacket and followed Sandra through the door.

'How could your mum leave anything if she needed to go shopping?' I asked.

'She left money so we can buy some chips or something. Do get a move on! I've absolutely loads to tell you!'

I trotted after her, thinking that this time I'd have loads to tell Sandra as well, if I chose. There was the Josie business and our Susan getting a PR job for a couple of weeks and the Maitlands. No, for some reason I didn't want to tell Sandra about the Maitlands or about Holly Jane. From what I'd heard about Holly Jane she and Sandra wouldn't get on together very well.

Mrs Pirie's house was at the other end of our row just before the square with its few shops. The front garden always looked bright and pretty with perfect flowers filling the space at the right seasons.

'Plastic, dear!' Mrs Pirie had once said when I had remarked on them. 'Just stick them in, give them a bit of a dusting, take them out when the next lot of flowers is due to bloom. Labour-saving!'

There were big dahlias and Michaelmas daisies and chrysanthemums that would never droop and die decorating the plot at this time. Sandra let us in at the front door and we went upstairs to her bedroom.

I'd always envied that bedroom, not least because Sandra had always had it entirely to herself with no Susan to clutter up the wardrobe. It had a pattern of little rosebuds on the wallpaper but these could hardly be seen because Sandra had covered the walls with posters and pictures of film stars, and the room itself was a pleasing muddle of clothes flung over the backs of chairs, and magazines and jars of half-used cold cream and shiny lipsticks and a row of little model animals on a shelf.

'I went by Josie's house early on,' Sandra said, plonking herself on the bed. 'There was a furniture van there, and the men were carrying out the three-piece suite. The Whites weren't around.'

'I daresay they can't bear to come back here,' I said.

'I wonder if the men will take away all the empty bottles,' Sandra mused.

I was wondering if anyone had taken Josie's clothes off the washing line or if they still hung there limp and unoccupied.

'Tell me about your holiday,' I invited.

'Oh, it was super! Honestly, if you knew how many boys were there you'd be astonished!' Sandra said.

'There are boys everywhere,' I said gloomily.

Most of them were a nuisance, catcalling and making faces in the playground and swaggering outside the chip shop.

'Not those kinds of boys,' Sandra said impatiently. 'I mean real men with muscles and – you know – tight trousers?'

'I know,' I said solemnly. 'Did you . . .?'

It was the question we always asked each other when we hadn't met for a few days. 'Did you . . .?' The question was never completed, probably because we weren't sure what we were asking.

'I had the curse on,' Sandra said. 'Honestly, Cordy, you can't imagine what an utter bind that is!'

'Not yet,' I admitted.

'Well, it just puts paid to having any fun,' Sandra said. 'I tell you, men don't know how lucky they are! Anyway we had some photos taken down there, mainly on the beach. Let me get them.'

She rummaged in a canvas bag hanging on the bedpost and fished out a buff folder.

'This is one of our hotel that Mum took. That was our room. Well, two rooms actually. There were real palm trees in the lobby. Terribly elegant. This is Mum sitting on the wall that runs down to the beach. This is me coming out of the hotel and this is me in my bathing costume before I got the curse – and this is Mum with a gentleman friend and this is me . . .'

Me, me, me. Sandra coming out of the hotel, going into the hotel, seated in a deckchair, not seated in a deckchair, smiling, laughing, eating an ice-cream.

'There are new people living in the Tyler house,' I said.

'Really? Gosh, I never thought anyone would ever live there again,' Sandra said. 'Not after what happened.'

'But what exactly did happen?' I said.

'Someone got murdered. Raped and then murdered,' Sandra said. 'A boy went and hanged himself before the police could arrest him. It was ages ago. You know that already.'

'Josie wasn't raped,' I said. 'She got on a bus and the next morning she ran right under the wheels of a lorry.'

'Shivery!' Sandra grimaced and fished in the canvas bag again. 'I got you a present. Here!'

It was a rather expensive lipstick, unused. Expensive was a quality that didn't match Sandra's pocket money.

'Did you nick it?' I enquired.

Nicking things had been quite a hobby of ours the previous summer though I was always scared of getting caught and was relieved when Sandra lost interest.

'No, I didn't nick it!' she said, hurt. 'One of Mum's gentlemen friends gave me some money to buy myself something while he and Mum were occupied. D'ye like it?'

'It's lovely,' I said truthfully, wondering how many years would have to pass before I could put on lipstick without giving my parents a heart attack.

'Anyway I haven't told you my real news yet,' Sandra said. 'Swear never to tell!'

'I swear.'

'No, say it. If I ever tell may my body be washed up at high tide and my soul be –'

'No, I don't want to swear that,' I said uncomfortably. 'I'll just swear on cross my heart.'

'All right then.' Sandra pouted slightly. 'So say it!'

'Cross my heart not to tell. Tell what?'

'Just before we went down to Brighton, there was an adver-tisement in one of the local papers.' Sandra sounded important. 'Did you see it?'

I shook my head.

'There are lots of adverts –'

'This one said, "Wanted. Young ladies to pose for cover of new teenage magazine. Good career prospects for the right appli-cants."'

'You never answered it!'

'I did! I wrote from Brighton, asking for an interview. I put the address of the hotel on it and used a false name. Tara Fallon.'

'That's a pretty name.' Fay would like that name, I thought.

'Anyway I got an answer by return of post. I swiped it before Mum saw it. Not that she'd mind me trying to make something of myself but quite honestly I wanted to do something off my own bat for a change.'

'What did the letter say?'

'It wasn't really a letter. It just gave a time and date and an address. French's Photographic Studio in Bradford. I tore it up and put it in the dustbin.'

'What date?' I asked.

'This Wednesday,' Sandra said.

'So you'll have to tell your mum now.'

'No I won't!' Sandra bounced up off the bed, almost sending me off balance, and swung round, her hair whipping across her face. 'It's going to be a surprise for her. If I get featured on a magazine cover then they'll have to pay me and I can buy Mum something nice as a surprise.'

'If you do that you'll have to tell her then or she'll wonder where you got the money from.'

'Of course I'll tell her then. She'll be ever so thrilled about it.'

'My mother wouldn't be,' I said.

'Your mother,' Sandra pronounced, 'is very nice but she lives in the dark ages a bit, doesn't she? I bet she doesn't know very much about – you know – it.'

'She had Susan and me.'

'Well, she might know a bit,' Sandra conceded, 'but I bet she doesn't know everything. She probably thinks that fellatio is an Italian ice-cream.'

I laughed, wondering what it was but determined not to ask.

'Is that why you came home early?' I asked instead.

'No. I was planning to think up something but Mum read about Josie in one of the dailies and she was having difficulties with her gentleman friend so we came home and I didn't have to think up any excuse,' Sandra said.

I didn't ask what difficulties or who the gentleman friend was. Sandra never named any of them, possibly because the various gentlemen didn't use their own names when they were with Mrs Pirie.

'But what time is the interview?' I wanted to know.

'Seven thirty.'

'In the evening? How are you going to manage that?'

'I'll tell Mum that I'm going to the pictures,' Sandra said calmly. 'With you.'

'With me? Mum only lets me go and see a film on Fridays.'

'That's in term time, silly! This is still holiday time. She'd let you come with me, wouldn't she?'

'It depends what's on.'

'I looked at the paper,' Sandra said with the air of clinching the matter. 'They're showing a whole week of Doris Day films with a different one on every night. Your mum wouldn't stop you going to a Doris Day picture, would she?'

'I suppose not.'

'And you'd be going with me. We can catch the six thirty bus into town and come back on the nine thirty bus.'

'But you said you were going for an interview.'

'Wake up, Cordy!' Sandra rolled her eyes heavenward and groaned. 'You can watch the film and we'll meet up afterwards at the bus stop. Then on the way back you can tell me what the film was all about. Of course I'll tell Mum the truth eventually but until then you have to keep your cross my heart swear. Promise!'

'Yes, all right then,' I said weakly. 'But you ought to find out a bit about this studio first. He might be a dirty old man.'

'Dirty old men don't advertise for girls to appear on magazine covers in our local newspaper, silly!'

'Maybe some do,' I argued.

'If I didn't know better,' Sandra said, 'I'd say you were jealous.'

'No I'm not!'

But perhaps deep down I was a bit jealous. I'd not started having the curse yet and my chest was still flat.

'The problem is what to wear,' Sandra said, abandoning her attack and pulling open several drawers out of which various garments burst. 'A magazine cover has to attract attention, doesn't it? Hey, what d'ye think of this?'

She pulled out a vivid scarlet bikini top and held it against herself.

'Is that new? Did your mum buy it?'

'It's brand new. I haven't worn it yet.'

'Then you nicked it. Is that all there is of it?'

'No, stupid, there's a bottom bit. Here! I shoved it away when we got home in case Mum noticed. She's awfully broad-minded about most things but she doesn't like me nicking things. What d'ye think?'

'You'll look like Marilyn Monroe,' I said admiringly.

There was indeed a faint resemblance. Sandra had the kind of skin that tanned easily and glowed and her hair was the same colour.

'I'll put it on under my jeans and T-shirt,' Sandra said. 'Now don't go mentioning it to anyone. It's a dead secret.'

'I swear,' I said.

If I told my parents that Sandra had nicked a scarlet bikini I'd never be allowed to play with her again.

'So that's settled then!' Sandra found a brown paper bag and put the two bits of the bikini in it. 'What shall we do now? Oh, blast! It's raining!'

Little gusts of wind were driving the raindrops against the window pane.

'We won't be able to play up on the moor,' I said, and discovered that I was rather glad of that.

Sandra would want to take a look at the old Tyler house and meet its new occupants and I didn't want to share the Maitlands.

'Playing on the moor is kid stuff,' Sandra said loftily.

She hadn't thought that before she went to Brighton.

'Let's try on some make-up,' I suggested.

'All right.' She shrugged amiably.

We went into her mum's bedroom and spent the next couple of hours delving into wardrobe and cupboards in the happy knowledge that Mrs Pirie didn't mind a couple of kids rummaging among her things. My own mum would've had a fit but then my mum wore sensible clothes and hardly any make-up and dabs of lavender water behind her ears which you couldn't smell unless you were whispering to her. Mrs Pirie had low-cut blouses and tight velvet trousers and stiletto shoes and bottles of perfume with exciting labels like Mitsouko and Casbah, and dozens of bottles and boxes of half-used skin creams, rouge, lipstick, eyeshadow and mascara.

We settled that if Sandra looked like Marilyn then I looked like Audrey Hepburn. That was patently untrue but at the time we believed it, or at least decided to believe it, and the queer little feeling of distance between us that I'd experienced when Sandra first arrived went away. We giggled and postured and Holly Jane melted into the shadows. When she returned would be time enough to tell Sandra about her, introduce her as the one who might turn a twosome into a trio again.

By midday we'd exhausted the possibilities of Mrs Pirie's belongings and dutifully scrubbed off the make-up. Not that Sandra's mother would have minded but we wanted to go to the village shop or the little chippie on the corner and some busybody would certainly have told my mother that good little Cordy was all smeared with green eyeshadow and dark red lip gloss.

The chippie was closed but Mrs Simmons was behind her own counter, with a narrow black band round one arm of her flowered overall as if she had been a relative of Josie's or something.

'Good morning, Cordy. So you're back, Sandra. Did you have a nice time?'

Her voice cooled slightly as she addressed Sandra. Mrs Simmons didn't really approve of her, more on account of her mother than anything else.

'Lovely, thank you,' Sandra said in her best behaviour voice.

'You heard about . . .?' She touched the armband meaningly.

'Yes. That's why we came home early,' Sandra said.

'Nice to hear that your mother has a sense of what's fitting.'

I tried to work out why it was more fitting to stop enjoying yourself because someone you knew had died. I didn't believe

81

that Josie would've wanted people to cut short their holidays or wear black armbands just because she'd been run over by a lorry but I wasn't really sure. I'd never been very interested in what Josie thought about things.

'So what can I get you?' Mrs Simmons was enquiring in a more indulgent tone.

'A large box of crisps and two bottles of Corona and some runny cheese and – shall we get some chocolate?' Sandra looked at me.

'Not chocolate and cheese,' Mrs Simmons put in. 'That can give you a bad migraine. Have some fruit salad instead.'

Sandra was clearly keen to make a good impression because she meekly agreed and we carried our purchases back to the house where Sandra found a jar of pickled onions to go with the crisps and cheese.

I've eaten thousands of meals since but for some reason that one, with the pair of us dipping crisps into the soft cheese and crunching the onions and washing it down with the fizzy dandelion and burdock, has stuck in my memory as if my mind took a photograph which won't go away.

'Did you see that armband?' Sandra giggled. 'Honestly! The Whites aren't even here any longer!'

'She thinks it's fitting,' I said and dissolved into giggles with her.

It sounds so heartless now, the pair of us stuffing ourselves and making mock when a girl we'd played with at the old house had run away and then been run over. Perhaps the death didn't seem quite real to us. Perhaps the young in order to survive have to be callous.

'Let's see if there's anything in the paper,' Sandra suggested.

'I didn't see you get that,' I said as she spread it wide.

'Nicked it from the stand on the way out,' Sandra said.

'Because it was fitting,' I finished for her, and we choked with mirth again.

'What shall we do this afternoon?' Sandra demanded, both elbows on the table, bits of crisps in her teeth.

'What's in the paper?' I countered.

'Enquiries are progressing. No details at all. What shall we do?'

'Mum expects me at home,' I said. 'I'm supposed to tidy up my bedroom.'

It wasn't true or not entirely true. Mum was always at me to tidy my room – 'It was never in this state when Susan was at home.' The real truth was that I was a bit fed up with Sandra's company. I couldn't put my finger on the exact reason why, but I found the idea of Holly Jane's return was becoming more attractive all the time.

'OK.' Sandra sounded resigned. 'What time shall we meet up tomorrow?'

'You said for the six thirty bus. That's if Mum lets me go.'

'She will if you tell her it's Doris Day. You won't let me down, will you? And you won't tell?'

'I already swore,' I said with dignity.

'See you tomorrow then.'

'Right!' I said and took a quick look in the hall mirror to make sure that every bit of lipstick had been wiped off before I went out into the street.

The rain had stopped without our noticing it sometime during the morning, and there was a shining on the cobbled bits of pavement as the sun came out.

When I went into my own house the smell of silver polish killed any lingering traces of Mitsouko.

'Is that you, Cordy? Is Sandra with you?'

'No. She had some things to do.'

'Did you wipe your feet?' Without waiting for an answer, which was lucky because I'd forgotten, she went on. 'Did you have a proper dinner?'

'A sort of snack one,' I said.

'Would you like a cup of tea?'

'No, thanks. I think I'll tidy my bedroom.'

And make true the lie.

'Without being asked?' Mum looked at me.

'Well, sometimes I do,' I said defensively.

'I'm not complaining! The dusters are in the usual place so don't go using a towel like you did last time! If you come across anything of Susan's put it in the bottom drawer, will you?'

'Is she coming home this weekend?' I asked.

'She starts the PR job tomorrow, or at least travels down for it. Dad and I are seeing her off. It's quite a big occasion for her so we want to give her a good send-off.'

'Tomorrow evening?'

'Yes, why?'

'Nothing. It's just that – Sandra and I thought of going to the pictures. To see Doris Day,' I added coaxingly.

'Tomorrow? To the matinée?'

'To the first house show,' I said, and mentally crossed my fingers since Mum might offer to take us both into Bradford and bring us home again which would make everything a bit awkward.

'Dad and I are going over earlier on,' she said. 'At least I'm going to help Susan pack and then your father will meet us from the office and drive her to the station. In fact he's all for taking her part of the way to save her having to change trains too often.'

'Susan's seventeen. She can catch trains by herself,' I said. 'I bet you wouldn't be so worried if I was going away to do a PR job.'

'Don't be silly, dear. You're too young to be offered a job and when you are your father and I will be just as anxious about you,' she said.

'I suppose so,' I said reluctantly. 'Anyway can I go?'

'Go where?'

'To see the Doris Day film. Sandra and I can get the six thirty bus and come home on the nine thirty one. If we miss it –'

'I'd not want you catching the ten thirty,' she said frowningly. 'There are often rowdies on it, teddy boys and –'

'Mum, teddy boys are out of fashion now! Even in Bradford you won't find teddy boys!'

'I'm sure I'm pleased to hear it,' she said primly.

'So can I go?'

'Your dad and I might be late back if we take Susan part of the way. I don't like your being in the house by yourself after dark.'

'I can stay over with Sandra or with the Maitlands!'

'Your father doesn't approve of your spending too much time with – who are the Maitlands?'

'They've moved into the Tyler house. Mum, I told you!'

'You haven't been up there bothering them? You know we don't like you talking to strangers.'

'They're not strangers. They just moved in.'

'Where from? I haven't heard anything about them in the village.'

'You don't often go into the village,' I pointed out, sensibly

84

I thought. 'Anyway they're perfectly respectable. They've got a girl called Holly Jane who's about my age and a baby called Edward. Holly Jane has long dark hair and Edward is ever so cute.'

'Oh, they have children.' Mum sounded relieved.

'So can I?'

'No, of course you can't! Playing with – Holly Jane is all very well and it's nice for you to make another friend, but you can't go inviting yourself to stay overnight until we know them better.'

'They'd be delighted to have me. They think I'm a very interesting girl and an ideal friend for Holly Jane.'

'That's nice, dear, but until we're properly introduced – now don't start sulking, Cordy! Since you're going to the pictures with Sandra then you might as well stay over with her in case your father and I are late back. And you make sure that you catch the nine thirty bus back.'

At least I had leave to go and she hadn't offered to come in with us and meet up with Susan early and take us all for tea or something frightfully embarrassing like that!

'I promise,' I said.

'When we get back we must see about calling on the – what name did you say?'

'The Maitlands. Fred and Fay Maitland.'

'We must make the effort,' she said vaguely.

It was inevitable, I knew. I couldn't keep Fay and Fred all to myself for ever. Sooner or later Mum would make a duty call and after that – if I knew Mum – she'd find reasons why I shouldn't go up to the Tyler house. She didn't trust people who were different from other people.

'I'd better get the tea on,' she said, vanishing kitchenward.

She expected me to do what I'd said I was going to do and tidy my room, but my head was suddenly full of the Maitlands and how awful it would be when they met up with my parents. Perhaps I could explain just how dull and stuffy my own family was, give them the hint to behave – well, differently?

I went quietly through the door again and ran along the shining cobbles on to the moorland track.

I loved the moor after it had rained when the long grass bent beneath the heaviness of raindrops and the air had a fresh clean scent. This day, however, I didn't linger but ran straight through the front gate and round to the back.

Fred was there, potting some plants in earthenware containers. He had on gardening overalls and a narrow black band round his arm, and as I skidded to a halt he stood up and looked at me as if I'd just arrived for the first time and he hadn't a clue who I was.

'Have I come at a bad time?' I said. Mum used the phrase when she occasionally called on anyone without prior notice.

'Cordy! No, of course not! It's only that – bad news, you see,' he said. 'We have received very bad news.'

'Oh?' I stared at him.

'Yes, very bad news.' He set down a pot carefully and looked at it.

'Bad news?' I said.

'Terrible news. No point in beating about the bush. Holly Jane. Our girl – she died.'

'Died?' I stared at him, hearing the word echoing in my head.

'In Scarborough. At my sister-in-law's. We drove over this morning to see them – Holly Jane and Edward – yes, to see them. It was just a whim on Fay's part. She had a sudden longing to check up – odd, that.'

'But what happened?' I said blankly.

'A traffic accident,' Fred said. 'A couple of hours before we got there. My sister-in-law had taken Edward for an early morning walk and Holly Jane went out to look for them, to walk back with them I daresay. Anyway she spotted them and started across the road and – a motor bike came round the corner and – the young man only had cuts and bruises, but she – she was killed outright.'

'I'm sorry,' I said helplessly. 'Really I'm most dreadfully sorry.'

'We drove back in a kind of daze.' He rubbed his hands down the front of his overalls. 'Fay's sister is arranging everything. She's the practical one on that side of the family. We wanted to get some of Holly Jane's things, to leave with her.'

'I'm awfully sorry,' I repeated.

'Life can be very cruel,' Fred said. 'Very cruel.'

'Yes,' I said dully.

I felt dull – confused. It was a bit like hearing about Josie all over again and I couldn't get my head round it.

'We shall be returning to my sister-in-law's this evening,' Fred said. He pushed his glasses up on his nose and left a smudge of soil there. 'I'm just occupying myself,' he said, and looked round at the plants as if he couldn't work out what they were doing there.

There were quick light footsteps within the house and Fay came into the conservatory and through the french windows to where Fred and I stood.

She was wearing a black skirt and a high-necked black tunic over it and a black lacy scarf over her hair, the two ends falling like plaits at each side of her face. She was so pale that her skin would've shamed milk and her eyelids were swollen and heavily powdered.

'Cordy, I'm so glad you're here!' she said in her breathless way. 'You are the one person I could bear to see today – apart from Fred, of course.'

'I'm so terribly sorry,' I said.

'Yes. Of course you are. Of course. You were looking forward to meeting Holly Jane, to making a new friend,' she said jerkily. 'Everything is spoilt now. Everything seems so hopeless.'

'Darling, we still have Edward,' Fred said.

'Where is Edward?' I asked.

'He's still with my sister,' Fay said, knuckling her forehead. 'We shall bring him home – when are we going to bring him home, Fred?'

'Soon. Very soon,' Fred said.

'Yes. Very soon. This house needs children. It needs – Holly Jane didn't suffer, they told us. It was very quick.'

'I wish there was something I could do,' I said.

I felt helpless in the face of such grief.

'Your coming is the best comfort of all!' She put out her hand and touched my arm very lightly. 'On the way back, in the car, I said to Fred, "The only thing that makes me able to bear this is that we've met Cordelia and made her our friend." I said that, didn't I, Fred?'

'Yes, my love, you did,' he assured her.

'And you are our friend, aren't you, even if you can't be Holly Jane's friend now?'

'Yes, of course,' I said.

'When we get back from the funeral we must finish preparing your room. Daffodil yellow and moss green. The colours of spring. Yet it will soon be autumn and then winter. Earth locked up and bars of ice.'

'And then spring,' Fred said.

'And then spring,' she echoed softly. 'You're right, Fred. And Holly Jane wouldn't like us to go on being miserable. We ought to let the sunlight into our lives again.'

'And there's plenty of work to be done,' Fred said, squaring his shoulders as if he were about to start digging.

'I think we ought to have a couple of rugs in a nice spicy nutmeg brown in your room,' Fay said. 'To provide a contrast to the daffodil and green.'

'That would be charming, sweetheart,' Fred said.

'And plants on the windowsill and music. You like music, don't you, Cordelia? We brought back the old gramophone from Scarborough and some records. Wait! I'll put on one now. Don't go!'

She vanished indoors. Fred looked at me.

'She's taking this very hard,' Fred said.

Music floated out through the open windows.

'*Hansel and Gretel!*' Fay came tripping back. 'Holly Jane loved this, you know. The children are so happy. They don't know the kind old lady plans to eat them.'

She looked as if she had finished her grieving, though her eyelids were still puffy. But it was an illusion. As the music swelled out and a chorus of children started singing in high bell-like voices her eyes filled with tears again.

'Too soon for music, darling,' Fred said. 'Come and help me with the plants instead.'

'Yes, too soon.' Fay nodded, twiddling the ends of her black lacy scarf between her fingers. 'I shall leave it on though. Holly Jane may be listening and this song was her particular favourite. Oh, I do hope that we can live here for a very long time! We move on so often. I get very weary, always moving on. Shall we get the seed catalogues and look at them, Cordelia? You must have your say about what goes in the garden.'

'I really have to go,' I said. 'I'm supposed to be tidying my room. I'm – please accept my condolences.'

It was a phrase I'd heard Mum use once or twice when someone had died.

'Thank you, my dear.' Fred put his hand on my shoulder.

'They go quite innocently into the cottage, you know,' Fay said. 'When they get inside the roses grow thorns and they can't get out. Holly Jane used to sing along to this bit.'

She began to hum, swaying gently in time to the music, the ends of her scarf floating gently as herself.

'Even grief becomes her,' Fred said in a low voice. 'Darling, you must rest a little.'

'I think I shall make some gingerbread and put it in a tin for when Cordelia comes again!'

Fay stopped swaying and nodded at me.

'When we get back from Scarborough,' Fred said.

'Yes,' I said and because they weren't the kind of people who needed any formality I nodded back at them both and went quietly away round to the front of the house again. Behind me, as I went towards the gate, I could hear the last faint strains of the singing children.

Josie had died and Holly Jane had died. Suddenly I was in a world where death struck at children. It was all wrong somehow. Old people died and when there were wars people got killed, but children weren't supposed to die.

Dad's car was outside when I reached the house. It was early for him to get home and I remember that a little shiver of foreboding ran through me because this was a day for bad news, but when I went in he was having a cup of tea in the sitting-room, seated in his usual armchair, and Mum was letting down the hem of a pink skirt that Susan hadn't bothered to take with her.

'I turn my head and you're off like a streak of lightning again!' she complained as I walked in. 'Why didn't you make some effort to – what's wrong?'

She broke off, staring at me, and Dad looked up.

'She's dead,' I said.

The word was heavy in my mouth.

'Dead? Who's dead? What are you talking about?'

'Holly Jane. Holly Jane's dead.'

'Who?' said Dad.

'The daughter of some new people who moved into the old Tyler house,' Mum supplied. 'Cordy, what's happened? Where've you been?'

'Out. Fred – Mr–Mr Maitland told me. She'd gone to Scar-

89

borough to stay with her auntie and she was run over by someone on a motor bike and killed. Killed stone dead.'

'Good God!' Mum had paled and her eyes went wide. 'John, d'ye hear that? Oh, those poor people! What a terrible thing to happen. Anyone would think there was a curse on that house!'

'I don't see any connection between the Grant business and this,' Dad said.

'Well, not directly perhaps, but it was a child died then and Larry Grant hang –'

'Not now, dear.' Dad nodded in my direction.

'No, of course not. And this child – Holly Jane? She died in Scarborough?'

'She went to stay with her auntie. They're going over there tonight.'

'We ought to do something.' Mum looked round in a flustered kind of way. 'The trouble is I hadn't got round to introducing myself and –'

'You know my views on letting Cordy run around with strangers,' Dad said.

'Yes, dear, but with Sandra Pirie away and – should I go up there? No, they won't want a complete stranger intruding at such a time. I could send up some flowers.'

'I think you ought to stop fussing,' Dad said. 'They won't want people they don't know intruding.'

'But Cordy knew them – knew the child anyway. You got on with her very nicely, didn't you, Cordy? And you mentioned a baby?'

'Edward, but he's only little.'

'Even so it must be a comfort though they won't realise it yet. Cordy, go into the garden and cut a few flowers. Just a little posy. I'll write a card and you can take it up to them. I'd come with you but I ought to get this finished – and I'm not dressed –'

'Better get the skirt finished,' Dad advised. 'Unless you want our elder daughter to walk round with the tops of her legs displayed for the world to see. Cordy, you heard your mother! Go and cut a few flowers. You can take a couple of my roses if you like.'

I went into the garden and broke off two of Dad's roses and snapped off some purple stems of lavender.

90

'Pink roses?' Mum finished writing a card and took the flowers from me. 'Wouldn't white –?'

'Holly Jane loved pink,' I said.

'In that case. Yes, that looks very suitable. I hate big, ornate wreaths. Let me tie the stalks.' She had bitten off a thread from the skirt she was altering. It was pink too. 'There! That looks very sweet. I still think I should – well, perhaps not. Cordy, be sure to give our condolences and say we look forward to meeting them soon. And come straight home. They won't want you hanging round and making a nuisance of yourself.'

It was no use trying to tell her or Dad that they liked me hanging around. I took the posy and went out again, feeling a certain importance as I walked up the track.

Holly Jane dead seemed more my friend now than when she'd been alive. Alive she might've been jealous or bossy or dull, but death gave me dignity.

When I reached the front gates I walked sedately up the cracked and weedy drive. This was a formal visit which meant using the front door, I decided, and went on up to the steps.

The door was open and the sound of a crying child filled the hall. For a moment I fancied it was still part of the *Hansel and Gretel* music, and then I saw the pram at the foot of the stairs. The hood was up and Fay was wheeling it up and down, a few feet in each direction. She looked up as I stepped inside.

'Flowers? For Holly Jane? Oh, what a lovely thought!'

'Mum sent them. Did your sister bring Edward home?'

'Yes, she – I'm not supposed to say but since it's you – yes, Edward came home,' she said.

The crying rose to a long sustained wail. Fay shook her head at me, half smiling as she bent to the pram.

'Edward, that's enough. Cordelia will think you're a naughty baby instead of my chugalug pumpkin,' she said.

The wailing stopped abruptly as she bent lower and then turned to face me again. In her arms a large teddy bear stared at me out of brown glass eyes.

I am in the same spot now, in the wide front hall with dust thick on the boards that were shining and polished that day. I look down at the floor and decide with a trace of wry humour that there ought to be a plaque there engraved with something to mark the instant when I was turned into a block of ice, chilled, rigid, silent with shock.

91

Fay jiggled the bear a little, held it over her shoulder and patted the furry back.

'That's all you wanted, wasn't it?' she said in a cooing voice. 'A little cuddle and all's right with your world again. He's growing out of his daytime naps now, and soon he'll be crawling everywhere, investigating everything, won't you, pet? Now lie down like a good boy and go sleepabyes for a bit longer.'

She bent again to lay the bear in the pram. I stood watching her, the posy clutched tightly in my fingers.

'Hopefully the motion of the van will soothe him as soon as we set off,' she said, straightening up again. 'Shall I take the flowers? I'll give them a little sprinkle with water to keep them fresh on the way to Scarborough. You say your mother sent them?'

'For Holly Jane, yes.'

Her long cool fingers touched mine briefly as she took the posy and held it up to her face.

'They smell delicious. Holly Jane is – was so sensitive to perfumes. Do thank your mother from me. People aren't always so kind. Holly Jane had to learn that, poor child!'

'Was – Holly Jane like – Edward?' I heard myself ask.

'Oh no, dear.' Fay gave her lovely wide smile. 'She was much bigger with long dark hair. And of course she was a girl. Edward is a boy. Bound to be a difference! Fred, look what Cordelia's mother has sent for Holly Jane! Wasn't it kind?'

Fred had appeared at the end of the long passage leading to the rear of the house. He was still in his gardening overalls with a little rake in his hand. He had stopped dead, his face shadowed because the sunlight didn't stretch so far, but it glinted on his glasses as he came slowly towards us.

'Very kind,' he said.

'I'll wheel Edward through to the kitchen and put some water on these,' Fay said.

She wheeled the pram around and set off down the passage, the posy still in her hand.

Fred sat down on the stairs and scraped the little rake across the wood with a faint screaming sound.

'Edward's a lovely baby,' I said carefully.

'A man likes to have a son,' Fred said. 'His being back will give Fay something to occupy her mind.'

'Yes,' I said.

'And your coming here with flowers. That was very sweet of you. Fay always responds to small kindnesses.'

'Yes,' I said again.

'Do thank your mother for us,' Fred said. 'We'll be away now until – probably Thursday or Friday.'

'The funeral,' I said.

'Somewhere on the moor I think. Fay always gets very upset on these occasions.'

'There were – other children?'

'Two before we got Holly Jane. Eloise and Linnet. Fay takes great joy in the naming of them.'

'Were there,' I asked, 'ever any children like me?'

'Twins.' He laid down the little fork. 'A boy and a girl. Babies.'

'What happened?'

'Fire,' he said briefly. 'Fay blamed herself. Not her fault of course, but despair can play tricks on the mind. I took the decision about Holly Jane myself. I said to Fay, 'Holly Jane and Cordelia won't hit it off.' She saw the sense of it but naturally she was very distressed.'

'There weren't any onions in the stew.'

'We took the decision that day. Sooner or later there would've been questions anyway. We move on all the time.'

He sounded weary, defeated.

'I'd better go.' I took a deep breath and added, 'Edward's a nice baby.'

'Tell your mother we're grateful for the flowers. I hope she understands we don't socialise very often. We don't have any friends.'

'It's difficult when you have young children,' I said.

'You're a remarkably kind child, Cordelia,' he said.

I went out then through the open door. When I looked back he was still sitting on the stairs, scraping the little fork to and fro.

6

Looking back it's all clear to me now. Well, perhaps, because at the time it seemed clear to me too. I went slowly down the track, pity like a sickness inside me. Had I been older my reaction and perception would have been different, but I was a child. To me the creation of a fantasy to bandage the wound of reality seemed logical. And a small part of me felt important because I was privy to a secret that I knew I must guard.

'How are they?' Mum asked when I went in.

She'd finished the alterations to Susan's skirt and was peeling potatoes at the sink.

'They said to thank you for the flowers,' I said. 'They're not really up to having visitors yet. Anyway they're going back to Scarborough for the funeral.'

'Ought I . . .?' She paused in her task and looked at me uncertainly.

'It's to be strictly private.'

'Such a dreadful thing to happen.'

She was, I think, privately relieved that she was spared from giving personal condolences to two strangers whose child she had never known.

'Yes,' I said.

'I've been talking to your dad about the cinema visit,' Mum said. 'He isn't very keen on your hanging about with Sandra but under the circumstances he agrees with me that you need something to cheer yourself up, take your mind off things. So you can go, provided you get the nine thirty bus home. No talking to boys, mind.'

'I don't know any boys I'd want to talk to,' I said truthfully.

'Yes, but Sandra might – your dad and I will see Susan off and drive straight back so we'll probably be here before you. He's out in the back tidying the shed so you can thank him when he comes in for tea. You've got time to get your bedroom neat.'

Once the notion of cleaning something or tidying somewhere had entered my mother's head nothing dislodged it. I went upstairs without arguing because I didn't want to answer any more questions about the Maitlands and half-heartedly dusted the furniture and made hospital corners on my bed which struck me as being as pointless as always wearing clean underwear when you went anywhere in case you got run over and killed. Had anyone taken Josie's things off the washing line or found the store of empty bottles in the shed?

'Well, young lady!' Dad was in an expansive mood when we sat down for tea. 'So you're off to the cinema tomorrow?'

'To see Doris Day,' I nodded.

'Nice wholesome actress,' he pronounced. 'A shame about your friend – Holly?'

'Holly Jane,' I said.

'These new-fangled names! Still, each to his own choice. So you'll be needing some money – bus, cinema seat, some sweets to eat, eh?'

He was bringing out the leather purse in which he kept his silver. He counted out a generous amount, winked at me and dug into his boiled ham.

There was enough there for two return trips to Bradford. I thanked him with real enthusiasm.

'It just keeps nagging at me that Susan isn't here any longer to go with you,' Mum said.

Mum had her fantasy too, I thought. She made out to herself that Susan and I were devoted sisters who loved going everywhere together, whereas the truth was that the five years between us had yawned wider as we grew up until the most that could be said was that we tolerated each other with a fair degree of amiability. Susan certainly wouldn't have wanted to go to any cinema with me.

'You were the one insisted she leave home,' Dad said.

'Only because it was more convenient for her, gave her a taste of independence, dear,' Mum said placatingly.

I bent my head and got on with my tea, thinking gloomily that it would be even harder for me to get away and live in a flat like a real grown-up person when the time came. Mum would be bound to talk about the last chick in the nest. On the other hand by then she might be used to me having weekends at the Tyler house.

Children are callous souls. I look back at myself now and

marvel at how easily I could eat my tea and look forward to the future, when a person I had played with had been killed. Killed, though her death had been an accident. And my shock at finding out about Edward and Holly Jane was muted too. I believe it even crossed my mind that it was better she had only been pretend because I could slip more easily into the place she had held in the enchanted world.

That night, though, I dreamed. Not the nightmare that flees when one wakes but a dream vivid as reality. I was walking through the old Tyler house and in every room Josie sat, holding the posy of roses and lavender that Mum had sent up for Holly Jane. Josie simply sat in every dusty room, with the eager look on her pointed face she'd always worn when she'd tagged after us. She said nothing, but somewhere in the background the tune from *Hansel and Gretel* which Fay had played sounded, young voices high as bells. And I woke up shivering and was glad it was day.

There was no sign of Sandra. There often wasn't on holiday mornings. Unlike our house where breakfast was served on the dot Mrs Pirie often slept until noon and left Sandra to get her own. I took the short shopping list Mum gave me and went along to the square.

Perhaps Mrs Simmons would have more news about Josie, I thought.

The shop was fairly crowded and the customers were still talking about Josie White's funeral. I stood politely near the door and listened to the scraps of gossip being tossed about over the groceries.

'Stone cold sober –'

'For a change! The one day when nobody would've blame –'

'Grilled for hours by the police. I mean it's often the nearest and dearest who –'

'And leaving so quickly. Guilty conscience d'ye think?'

They drifted out, shocked and sorry and enjoying their emotions. Mrs Simmons looked over at me.

'What was it you wanted, Cordy?' she enquired.

'Mum gave me a list.' I handed it over the counter.

'At least she still does most of her shopping here,' Mrs Simmons said, scanning with an experienced eye. 'Not like some.'

'Some?'

'There's talk of new tenants up at the Tyler house. Bert Ransom was up there connecting the electrics the other day. Big house for two people. Not that they've been into the village yet. Grand nobs I daresay. Not that I envy them living up there. Not after the Grant business.'

'I don't remember it,' I said.

'You were just a baby. I remember your mum coming into the shop just after you moved here. Susan was with her too. She'd've been about six then. She was ever so bonnie, with those lovely eyes and the curly hair. Seems a long time ago now but it was just a few months after Mr Simmons – God rest his soul – passed away.'

'Larry Grant hanged himself,' I prompted.

'Always a bit peculiar was poor Larry! Hand me that tin of peaches, dear. Yes, not mad – at least nobody thought then that he was mad – but kind of vacant-looking, gormless as you might say. The Grants were middle-aged when he was born. Anyway he used to wander about the village, do odd jobs for a bit of pocket money or some chocolate.'

'He didn't go to school?'

'He was nineteen – maybe twenty. I think he'd spent time at a special school. He used to like playing hopscotch with the children. Loopy Larry they called him – not unkindly but nowadays we might think it wasn't very nice. Sometimes they teased him and ran off and he'd shake his fist, but we all thought he was harmless.'

'Mum said the little girl –'

'Cathy Benson. She was only nine. Such a pretty little girl too. She used to come in here for sweets. Larry started following her about, watching her. One or two people noticed but nothing was said. Nobody thought.'

Normally Mrs Simmons would've shut up like a clam by this time but the gossip had loosened her tongue, and she leaned both elbows on the counter and gave me a long, meaningful look.

'Still waters run deep, my dear,' she said. 'If only we'd known but we never thought of it, you see. Never even considered it. In my opinion if poor Mr Simmons had lived he'd have begun to suspect, I'm sure of it. The late Mr Simmons had a great knowledge of human nature, but it wasn't to be. Cathy went out to play one Saturday. Some of the other children went with her but it came on to rain and they scattered. Cathy must've gone up to the Tyler house or perhaps Larry Grant lured her there. Anyway she didn't go home for tea and when it started to go dark they organised a search. They found the poor child buried near the garden wall at the back of the Tyler house and Larry Grant hanging from the tree nearby. The Grants had gone out for the day to do some shopping and didn't get back until late. It was plain what had happened. That was a dreadful time. I really don't like talking about it but since your mother talked about it –'

But not as fully as Mrs Simmons had talked, I thought, threading the bits and pieces I'd heard over the years into the narrative.

'What happened to the Grants?' I asked.

'They moved away after the inquest. Murder and suicide.' Mrs Simmons folded her hands beneath her chin and gave me a sombre look. 'There was a family rented the house about six years ago but they only stayed a few weeks. Well, let's hope the new people stay longer. Now was there anything else, dear? Does your mother need any washing powder?'

'I think she's got plenty left.'

'Well, I'll pop in a packet just in case – she can pay me next week. If Mr Simmons had lived we would have started deliveries I'm sure, but as I don't drive – Take a bar of chocolate from the shelf as you go out. And, Cordy . . .'

'Yes, Mrs Simmons?' I took the filled basket.

'Better not mention to your mother about our little chat. It's not a subject to be dwelt upon.'

'I won't say anything, Mrs Simmons. Thank you for the chocolate.'

I felt heavy with secrets as I turned and went out of the shop.

'Did your mum say that you could come to the flicks?' Sandra called from across the road.

'Yes!' I called back.

'Good-oh! I'm going to have my hair done. See you later!'

She held her thumb up and went off with her hips swaying. I had tried to walk with swaying hips but since at that time

I didn't have any hips worth mentioning, the result, seen in Mrs Pirie's bedroom mirror, had been disappointing.

I lugged the basket home and was met by my mother, in what Susan would have called 'a bit of a lather'.

'Where on earth did you get to? You didn't go off with Sandra, did you? I expected you home ages ago!'

'There were lots of people in the shop,' I said.

'Gossips I daresay!' She sniffed, distaste screwing up her mouth. 'I know you think I'm fussy about the friends you make but I cannot stand ghouls!'

'What's that?'

'People who take pleasure in other people's misfortunes. It made me so cross to see them at Josie's funeral, elbowing one another, trying to get a good look at her poor parents.'

There were tears in her eyes and for an instant I was terrified she was actually going to cry. Mothers weren't supposed to cry. They were there to cook meals and nag you to get your homework finished and tidy up your room.

'No good dwelling on it!' she said to my relief. 'Life has to go on. I'm catching the early bus so that I can spend a bit of time with Susan before your dad meets us from work. Shall we just have a snack now? I'll leave you something you can have for your supper but I daresay that your dad and I will be home before you get back. Don't go stuffing yourself with too many sweets now, will you?'

The dangerous moment had passed. She was Mum again, fussing that my shoes were clean because you never knew who you might meet.

'I don't suppose the Queen will be going to see Doris Day,' I said.

'Don't be silly, Cordy! Eat up now. I've got to get ready.'

Catching a bus was a major operation in our house. Mum hardly ever used one since she seldom went anywhere without Dad. Sometimes when I saw her glance at him with that little teasing look which she always seemed to save for Saturday nights I used to wonder what it was like to be in love with someone after being married to them for years and years.

'Right then! I think I'm ready. Now don't go getting into any mischief.' She gave me an anxious look. 'Straight home after the pictures, mind. I'll give Susan your love and wish her luck from you, shall I?'

I thought Susan was big enough to see herself off on a train but Mum would only have said that I was jealous if I'd opened my mouth, so I said like a bright obedient girl, 'Tell her lots of luck! See you later.'

She couldn't leave like an ordinary person of course. She had to turn back and find a nice bag to put that wretched pink skirt in. Susan wouldn't thank her for letting down the hem, I thought. Then she had to remind me to close the windows and leave the key under the mat and then finally she was off.

I wanted to slip up to the Tyler house but I wasn't sure if Fred and Fay would want even me there when they were having their pretend funeral for Holly Jane. So instead I sat down and feeling very saintly finished off my holiday project.

I put on my jeans and a clean shirt and a neat blue jacket that Mum had bought for me and made sure that the key was under the mat and all the windows closed before I left the house. There was always the chance that Dad would come to the bus stop after the film and bring Sandra and me home in the car with Mum and himself. He wouldn't like it if I wasn't neat. I'd've liked to put on some lipstick but if I did they'd be bound to turn up.

'All by yourself, Cordy?' Mrs Simmons, who saw as much as God, came to the door of her shop as I reached the bus stop.

'I'm going to the pictures with Sandra, to see Doris Day,' I said, and wondered if she might think it wasn't respectful to Josie or something, but she said approvingly:

'That'll be nice for you! She's a lovely actress is Doris Day.'

'She's got a lovely voice,' I said.

'And she always takes a good part. Isn't Sandra at home?'

'She went to have her hair done. Mrs Simmons, did you ever hear of a photographer called Mr French?'

'French in Bradford? Aye, old Mr French died years back but I heard his son came back from Australia and took over the old place. Why?'

'There was an advertisement in the paper,' I said vaguely.

'Everybody has a camera these days,' Mrs Simmons said. 'Professionals find it hard to make a living. Well, enjoy yourself, dear.'

She went back inside and I looked round for Sandra. Perhaps she'd thought better of getting herself on the cover of a teenage magazine or her mum had found out and put her foot down for once. Then I saw her coming along the street towards me.

She had on jeans and shirt like me but her hair had been curled under into a long pageboy style and as she reached me I could see the blue shadow on her eyelids and the pink gloss on her lips.

'So what do you think?' She struck a pose in front of me, wobbling slightly on the platform heels of her sandals.

'You look ever so glamorous,' I envied.

'I've got the bikini on underneath,' she lowered her voice to say. 'You didn't tell anyone?'

'About the – no, of course not. Where's your mum?'

'She has a dinner date tonight with a gentleman friend. So it doesn't matter if we get a later bus home.'

'It does to my mum,' I said. 'I promised faithfully to catch the nine thirty.'

'Never mind.' She shrugged.

The bus chugged up, made its customary circuit of the square and drew up beside us. We got on, giggling as Sandra almost fell into her seat.

'These heels!' She crossed her legs and studied her platform sole with a self-conscious frown. 'One suffers for fashion.'

'I don't.' I looked down at my neat slip-ons with the sensibly low heels.

'You will!' Sandra said darkly.

The conductor came round for the ticket money. Sandra, paying him, gave him an upward flirtatious look through her smudgy black lashes.

'I don't want to wear things that hurt,' I said sulkily.

'You will!' Sandra went again.

I looked out of the window at the little grey houses with the moors lying behind them. Now and then the bus slowed down to allow a couple of sheep to cross the road. You don't see that nowadays since the motorways have multiplied and the villages cower as the huge lorries roar through them.

The sun lay low over the landscape and the grass verges were still sparkling from the recent rain. At my side Sandra said, 'It's so boring up here! Now Brighton was something else again! Ever so smart!'

'It must've been fun.' I tried to match her mood of world-weariness. 'I don't suppose there is much to do round here.'

'London's the place to be,' Sandra said. 'Night-clubs and Chinese restaurants and hundreds of boutiques. Fab!'

'You've never been to London!'

'Honestly, Cordy, you can be dim sometimes,' she said impatiently. 'You don't have to go to London to know what it's like!'

'Oh,' I said.

We chugged into Bradford and got off.

'We'll have to get a move on,' Sandra said. 'The main feature starts in ten minutes.'

'Are you coming with me then?' I felt a sudden rise of relief though I didn't know I'd been worrying.

'I'll meet you back at the bus stop in time for the nine thirty bus, silly. Pay attention to the film because Mum might ask me what it was about.'

'Where is the studio? Maybe we ought to go together –'

'It's in Saddle Street. You go and see the film and I'll see you later. And you're still under oath to keep quiet until I say it's all right.'

'But you'll have to tell your mother sometime,' I argued.

'When the contract's signed and I've been paid some money. I'm going to give half of everything I earn to my mum,' Sandra confided. 'Then she won't have to rely on her gentlemen friends for nice jewellery and perfume. It's a surprise so don't you dare say anything, Cordy Sullivan!'

'I won't say one word, cross my heart!'

'See you later, alligator!'

'In a while, crocodile!'

We touched palms and then she turned and sashayed off, still wobbling slightly on her stacked platform heels.

I am walking up the wide dusty staircase now, leaving faint palm prints where my hand clasps the banister. There is still furniture in the upstairs rooms and in one room – my weekend room – the walls glow faintly yellow like a withered daffodil holding the last of spring within its trumpet petals. That conversation is so clear in my memory but I can't recall any part of the film I sat alone to watch. I think Rock Hudson was in it too, or perhaps it was James Garner. I don't know. It is as if everything that happened blotted out that brief Technicolor time when I sat in solitary state in the darkened auditorium and sucked the boiled sweets I'd bought in the foyer.

When I came out the sun had gone and the buildings were crowding closer, looming over the crowded streets. There were people queuing for the last showing of the film and people strolling along the pavements and looking at the brightly lit windows of the closed shops, and a group of mods at the corner of the road, striking ciggies from the soles of their shoes and slicking back their duck's-arse hairstyles.

It was twenty past nine. I stood in the short queue at the bus stop and waited for Sandra. She knew the time of the bus so surely she wouldn't be so mean as to make me miss it.

It seemed that she would be. More people joined the queue. I saw the bus arriving and the prospective passengers all hurried to get on. I got on myself, clutching my return ticket, and gazed anxiously out of the window, but no figure in jeans and platform heels came wobbling towards the vehicle. Obviously Sandra had misjudged the time which meant she'd be at the bus stop an hour later, confidently expecting me to be waiting.

This time it wasn't on! This time I wasn't going to be messed about just because Sandra was older than me. I slumped in my seat, feeling very self-righteous and irritable, and feeling deep down a curious little pain because promises were sacred and friends ought to keep them.

The few street lamps were on in Linton when the bus dropped me off in the main square. The few shops were all shuttered and there were drawn curtains and the glow of lights behind them along the street.

I walked back to my house and took the key from under the mat and let myself into the darkness. Darkness outside never bothered me but for the first time I felt uneasy when the darkness was inside, and a sense of relief when I'd switched on the hall light and the kitchen light.

Mum and Dad weren't back yet. I took the food that Mum had left for me to warm up, looked at it and put it back again. The next and last bus was due at eleven. I'd go back to the square and meet it, I decided, and put on the kettle to make myself a cup of tea. If Mum and Dad turned up in the meantime then I'd have to wait until morning.

I sat in the dining recess, drinking tea with my elbows on the table and one eye on the kitchen clock, and felt rather like a mother whose delinquent daughter has stayed out late.

At twenty past ten I pictured Sandra turning up at the bus stop in Bradford, fully expecting to find me obediently waiting, cross but ready to be pacified and envious of the compliments Mr French had paid her. At twenty to eleven I heard a car go past outside our house and wondered if it was Mum and Dad, but then it wouldn't have gone past. At ten to eleven I put on my jacket and went out, leaving the door open with some muddled idea of giving my neglectful parents a fright when they arrived home and found the house ready for burglars and their younger daughter missing.

Nobody got off the bus. It stopped momentarily but nobody got off and nobody got on. I stood back in the shadows beyond the shelter and watched it start up again and go round the square for the last time.

Sandra could've had a lift home if she'd missed the nine thirty bus. We weren't supposed to accept lifts but she did sometimes hitch rides from local lorry drivers – or said that she did. At this moment she might be safely in her own house, using her mum's cold cream to take off her make-up.

I walked the few yards to Sandra's house and went up the path past the scentless plastic flowers and rang the bell. Nothing stirred behind the curtained windows and the little red lamp that Mrs Pirie switched on in her room when she was entertaining a gentleman friend cast no ray through the swagged lace.

I went home again, finding the house more welcoming since I'd left the lights on but seeming emptier than before. Then I saw Dad's spectacle case on the hall table and a moment later he and Mum came through the back door together.

'Cordy, where on earth have you been?' Mum was flushed and agitated.

'I went for a little walk up the road to see if you were coming,' I said.

Such a good child. Such a little liar!

'Surely you saw the car outside?' Dad said.

'I never noticed.'

That at least was true.

'We must've passed you,' Dad said. 'Your mother had quite a scare, finding the front door ajar and the lights on and no sign of you.'

'I thought you might've gone into the back garden,' Mum said. 'The moon's coming out and the leaves are all silvery, just the way you like to see them.'

'Even you wouldn't be so silly as to sit around in the back garden looking at the moon!' Dad sounded exasperated.

'Never mind, she's back now,' Mum placated. 'Did you enjoy the film?'

'It was super!'

'You didn't come back on the late bus, did you?' Dad looked at me. 'You know the kinds of riff-raff travel on that bus.'

I could've retorted that I didn't because I'd never been allowed to travel on it. However, since annoyance still clouded the air, I said meekly. 'I made myself a cup of tea when I got in. The teapot's still warm.'

'You see, John?' Mum nodded at me. 'I told you there was no need to fret. Did Sandra go straight home?'

'I think so.'

'Not that her mother would notice if – never mind. You'd better go to bed.'

She didn't offer me another cup of tea or ask if I'd eaten. Somewhere at the back of her eyes was the knowledge that I hadn't been truthful.

I said goodnight and went upstairs and closed my bedroom door softly.

When I pulled back the curtains I saw the moon shining silver and I thought of Sandra, hair blowing in the breeze as she straddled the back of some motor bike on which she'd begged a ride or giving the driver of some car her swift, upward glance that promised what neither of us had tasted.

Late nights for me were rare and it was past ten when I woke up. Dad had gone to work and Mum was drinking coffee at the table. She looked tired as if the daylight had drained her.

'There's tea in the pot,' she said. 'Would you like some bacon?'

'Just toast, please. Mum, I'm sorry I gave you a fright last night. I really didn't mean to.'

'I was a bit upset after seeing Susan off,' she admitted.

'She wasn't going to the other side of the world, was she?' I said.

'Now don't take that tone with me, young lady!' Mum had risen and was putting slices of bread in the toaster. 'London might as well be a world away as far as we're concerned.'

'Full of shops and Chinese restaurants.'

'The firm that engaged her are putting her up at an hotel for a couple of weeks. It may lead to her being offered a permanent post when she's finished her course.'

'So why were you upset?'

'You won't understand until you've children of your own and see them growing their hair in styles you don't much like and talking in what Susan calls a flip kind of way and –'

'We can't stay little for ever.'

'Sometimes I wish that you could,' she said wistfully. 'Cordy, about last night –'

'Mum, if you make a solemn promise to someone you have to keep it, don't you?'

Mum gave me an unexpectedly sharp look.

'Every promise ought to be kept,' she said gravely. 'I hope your dad and I brought you up to understand that. If you give your word then you must keep it at all costs. That's important.'

'Yes,' I said.

The bread popped up out of the toaster with a little tinkling sound.

'So!' Mum started buttering the toast. 'What are you going to do today?'

'Just mooch around,' I said.

'Well, don't mooch in the direction of the old Tyler house, will you?' She lifted a jar of marmalade out of the cupboard. 'Those poor people will need time in which to grieve. Losing a child – that must be the most awful thing in the world.'

'Holly Jane was very special to them,' I agreed.

'Every child is special to its parents. If anything happened to you or Susan – but they have a baby, you said?'

'Edward. He's eight months old.'

'Too little to be a playmate for you, but there's still Melanie Deacon. She's a nice girl.'

'So is Sandra,' I defended.

'I never said she wasn't. Her background isn't exactly – you know your dad's always wanted you and Susan to mix with girls from good backgrounds. Those things might not seem important to you now but later on, when you start going out to dances or parties – well, they matter more than you'd think. More toast?'

'No, thanks. I think I'll go out for a bit and – before you say anything I've finished my holiday homework.'

'Honestly? Your dad will be pleased! You know he's always felt that you might be university material one day. That's why he's so keen for you to get high marks in school.'

University material was code for 'not pretty'. I knew that.

'I think I'll give the bathroom a good going over.' Mum absent-mindedly nibbled on a piece of spare toast. 'The tiles are starting to look a bit dingy. I'm trying to talk your dad into buying some of that new thick linoleum for the floor.'

She finished the toast and began happily rooting in the cupboard for cleaning materials.

I went out into the still damp morning, where the last of the little puddles lingered between the cobbles.

Sandra would be home by now and probably still lazing in bed. A remembered dart of annoyance pierced me. Sandra, I thought crossly, didn't know the meaning of keeping one's word.

I walked along to Sandra's house and pushed open the gate. The plastic flowers were still wet and shiny, a few leaning sideways at a perilous angle.

I rang the bell and listened to the musical chimes.

From inside I heard a shuffling noise and then the door opened a crack.

'Yes. What is it?'

'It's only me, Mrs Pirie.'

'Oh, Cordy!' The door opened wider. 'You'd better come in for a minute. If you want Sandra she went out early. I was late home last night so the place is still a bit of a mess.'

The place was actually quite tidy but Mrs Pirie had evidently just got out of bed, feather-trimmed mules on her feet and a dressing-gown – at that time I didn't recognise it as a negligee – wrapped round her, the ends of its peach sash trailing. Her hair was slightly mussed and her face was shiny with cold cream.

'I'm afraid I slept late,' she said, as if it was something unusual. 'I just made some coffee. Would you like some?'

I didn't really want any but coffee had a pleasing, adult sound, so I nodded and followed her through to the kitchen.

'Black or white?' She looked at me.

That was one of the nice things about Mrs Pirie. She asked as if you were quite used to drinking black coffee when most mothers, my own leading the way, doused it with milk without asking.

'Black, please,' I said.

'Help yourself to sugar. I think I'll have a hair of the dog.'

She tipped something out of a bottle into her cup, stirred it round, and drank it straight off.

As the sunlight hit her face I glimpsed faint bruising under one eye where the cold cream had rubbed off. She saw me looking and gave a light little laugh.

'Never trust a man who sells cameras,' she said.

'Cameras?'

'That's his line of business. Selling cameras. Not so good when it comes to dodging a left hook, eh? Ah well, it's a hard life!'

She poured out more coffee and picked up the bottle, grimaced slightly at it, firmly recorked it and pushed it away.

'No good running down that road,' she said with another little laugh. 'You wanted to see Sandra?'

'You said she went out,' I said.

'I figured she'd gone to see you. She wasn't in her room when I looked. Did you have a nice time at the pictures?'

'Yes. It was a lovely film,' I said.

'Good wholesome family entertainment. Isn't that what they say? More coffee?'

'No, thank you, Mrs Pirie.'

The coffee tasted horrible. I wished there was a handy plant pot where I could tip it. Instead I took a big gulp and smiled at her, my teeth on edge.

'She'll turn up pretty soon, I daresay,' Mrs Pirie said. 'She's very fond of you is Sandra. Very fond. Look, dear, if you'll excuse me – I've a bit of a migraine coming on – my own fault but I don't often indulge and I had a bit of a dust-up with my gentleman friend last night.'

'The camera man.' I risked another gulp of coffee.

'Let's not dwell on past mistakes!' she said, fumbling in the pocket of her dressing-gown. 'I don't suppose you smoke yet, do you?'

'I'm never going to smoke,' I said virtuously. 'I promised my dad.'

'And promises must never be broken!' She fished out a cigarette and struck a match. 'That's important, Cordy.'

'Yes, I know.'

I watched her inhale deeply, blow out a thin stream of blue-grey smoke and pick a shred of tobacco from her tongue.

'I'd better be going,' I said, pushing away the dregs of sticky black liquid thankfully.

'When you catch up with Sandra tell her to come in quietly,' Mrs Pirie said. 'I really don't feel too chirpy this morning.'

'Yes, I will,' I said politely, and left her, the bruise under her eye already purpling and her lips clamped tightly around her cigarette.

I went out and walked on into the square. I'm not sure even now exactly what I intended to do but the Bradford bus was just pulling in at the bus stop and I still had money in my pocket so it seemed quite natural to get on the bus.

I was sure that Sandra hadn't gone out early. If she had she'd've come to my house to tell me all about the modelling session and the smashing young man who'd given her a lift home at one o'clock in the morning. Sandra hadn't come home at all. I knew it in my bones.

I couldn't split on her. I just couldn't because promises were sacred. I had to go to French's Photographic Studio in Saddle Street and find out what had happened.

With any luck I'd be back in time for dinner and Mum was so immersed in cleaning once she got started that she certainly wouldn't be worrying about me. I was also lucky because a little crowd of people got on the same time as me so I was quite inconspicuous. I sat down near the back and hoped my luck would hold. The one thing I didn't need was Dad coming out of his office and barging into me!

The Asians were only just starting to move into Bradford back then. The sight of a dark face or a sari-clad woman with a red dot between her eyes was still a novelty. They had begun to open little shops that sold all manner of things and at any other time I'd've lingered to catch the spicy scents drifting from some of them.

This morning I had other things on my mind. I went to the noticeboard next to the bus timetable and looked at the map of Bradford with the red arrow saying, 'You are here!' It took a few moments to orientate myself and work out the way to Saddle Street. Happily it was a good long way from the insurance offices and nowhere near the college. I set off with what anyone passing might have regarded as a confident air, and ten minutes later after backtracking on a couple of wrong turns found myself at the entrance to a narrow, winding side street, with its name boldly posted high on the wall.

There were several small shops that looked dusty and forlorn as if they were never visited, with bulging glass in their windows and odd and ends behind the glass looking as if they'd been there for years and years.

I'd come nearly to the end of the street when I saw 'French's Photographic Studio' on a small sign just inside a shallow archway. It was so small that I nearly missed it.

Inside the arch was a flight of stairs with a half-glass door at the top. I climbed up them, tapped on the door, and then risked turning the handle. The door opened and I stepped into a big room with skylights but no windows and several doors opening off it.

'Mr French!'

My tentative greeting bounced back at me across the space in a series of diminishing echoes. I jumped slightly and looked round in some bewilderment. It didn't look as if anyone ever came here. The floor had been swept but bits of dust were already settling on the wooden planks again and the walls were that peculiar greyish yellow that walls go when paint and paper have faded beyond recognition.

I went across to one of the doors and pushed at it but it remained shut. The second door yielded and I almost tumbled down two steps into the small windowless room beyond with a sink and a steel draining board against the further wall. The tap was dripping but it made only the faintest of little plopping sounds.

The third door was unlocked too and behind it stretched a long narrow room with a skylight in the sloping ceiling and a low platform, like a dais, which raised up the level of the floor at one end. On the dais was a long sofa piled with purple cushions with fringes on them and a camera mounted on a high tripod with a stool behind it.

This must be where the photographs were taken then. I stepped up on the stool and looked through the viewfinder of the camera but I could see nothing because of the black cloth over it. I remember thinking that it was old-fashioned even then.

I stepped down again and stood uncertainly. The whole place had a musty smell about it. There were no photographs anywhere.

I was suddenly conscious of my own footsteps echoing on the floorboards and my own breathing sounding in the silence. I tried to picture Sandra coming here but I couldn't. I couldn't picture Sandra being anywhere at all and in abrupt, irrational panic I went through into the outer room and past the half-glass door and down the stairs into the street again.

Mr French – or his son – hadn't been at work. Maybe he only worked in the evenings. Maybe . . .

I reached the end of the street and realised that I'd run the wrong way, continuing on instead of turning back the way I'd come. I was in a cul-de-sac, with iron railings and a bench and a bit of an excuse for a grass plot littered with old beer cans. There was an old man on the bench, wrapped in an old army greatcoat, nodding his head as if he were dozing.

My arrival must've disturbed him because he opened rheumy eyes and stared at me. He smelled musty like the empty studio and his scrawny hands were filthy, knotted with veins.

I turned and fled the other way, past the archway with the little sign, and the small shops with their pathetic bits of window dressing. I ran blindly as if some horror was chasing me and would catch me if I looked over my shoulder.

A screech of brakes jolted me. I was off the kerb and a car had pulled up inches away.

111

'Are you all right?' The driver, looking shaken, was leaning out, asking me in a loud, worried tone.

'Yes, I – I'm going to catch a bus,' I stammered.

'Better to be half an hour late in this world than half an hour early in the next,' he said.

All adults said that. I'd probably find myself saying it one day.

'I'm sorry,' I said gaspingly, and walked on along the wider bit of the pavement, aware that a patrolling policeman had stopped on the other side and was looking towards the car.

It revved up and went off and my heart started to beat more slowly though the palms of my hands felt damp and there was a sick taste in my mouth.

I still couldn't picture Sandra but I could picture Josie, running out of that same side street with the scarf tied at the back of her neck and all the freckles standing out on her nose and her eyes pale with terror. Had she run out of that same street under the wheels of a lorry? And had Sandra ever reached the studio?

I had threaded my way back to the bus stop and there was the bus waiting and Sandra already sitting in it. I climbed on and went along the aisle with my mouth full of questions and a strange girl tossed back her long blonde pageboy bob and gave me a blank stare.

I sat down in another seat and fished out the return bit of my ticket, and hated the strange girl for not being Sandra or Josie or Holly Jane though Holly Jane hadn't really lived at all but that made no difference because all three had been killed anyway.

I sat with my hands tightly clasped in my lap and watched the world beyond the windows, houses giving place to cottages with the moors brooding behind like some vast, maternal force that kept children from harm.

7

When I got off the bus Mrs Simmons called across to me from the doorway of her shop.

'Cordy! Is Sandra Pirie with you?'

'No, Mrs Simmons.' I went over to her, trying to think of some excuse for being on the bus but her mind was occupied with other things.

'That mother of hers just came in and asked if I'd seen her. She seemed quite agitated.'

'I think Sandra went off somewhere earlier on,' I said.

'Well, it's something that her mother's starting to take an interest, I suppose,' Mrs Simmons said. 'She said you went to the cinema.'

'Doris Day. Excuse me, Mrs Simmons, but I have to go.'

I went off briskly, trying to look as if I was bound on an errand for my mother.

She was laying the table as I went in.

'If you'd wanted Sandra to have a bite with us I'd not have minded,' she said. 'I don't suppose she gets good nourishing food at home.'

'She's bigger than I am anyway.' I slid into my place. 'Mum, when can I have a bra?'

'You're too young.'

'Bras aren't to do with young –' I began.

'And they're not subjects for the dinner table either. Eat your fish.'

'The Japanese eat their fish raw,' I said, scraping the black skin off my piece of cod.

'Don't be silly, Cordy. Would you like some white sauce?'

'No, thanks. Can I have tomato sauce?'

'May I have tomato sauce? Yes, if you must – and don't bang the bottom of the bottle. It comes out with a whoosh.'

The whoosh, I thought, was the best part of it.

'It looks like rain again.' Mum was looking through the window.

'Mum, why can't we have a television?' I asked.

'Your dad doesn't think it would add to our quality of life, dear.'

'What if our Susan got on the television? Would we get one then?'

'Susan's going to be a highly qualified personal representative. She won't be on television.'

'Or I might be.'

'Teachers don't appear on television either.'

'I might not be a teacher,' I said. 'I might be an actress or a famous writer or a model or –'

'Cordy, eat your dinner and stop chattering,' Mum said wearily. I got on with my dinner.

By the time we got to the fruit pie – 'Now don't turn up your nose at it. It's been wrapped up in the fridge, so it'll taste quite fresh!' – the rain had begun again in earnest, splashing down in great gobbets, running down the window panes.

'Well, that puts paid to going out,' Mum said. 'Turn on the wireless, that's a good girl. There might be a weather report.'

'Even if it is raining in London I don't suppose our Susan will be wet, and people call it a radio these days.'

'Wireless sounds more natural somehow. And I wasn't thinking about the weather in London. There are so many buildings and underground pedestrian ways there that nobody ever need get wet.'

'Have you ever been to London?'

'Your dad and I had a weekend there before Susan was born. Mind you, I daresay it was quieter in those – now who's here?' She ended on a faint note of exasperation as the doorbell sounded.

'I'll go!'

This would be Sandra, come to explain. I flew to the front door.

Mrs Pirie peered from under a waterproof headscarf tied under her chin. She had powdered over the bruise but her mascara had run a bit and her eyelashes were spiky like spiders' feet.

'I'm sorry to trouble you, dear, but you haven't seen my Sandra yet, have you?' she asked.

'Who is it, Cordy? Oh, Mrs Pirie.'

Mum came into the hall behind me, her face automatically assuming a slightly forced smile.

'I'm looking for Sandra, Mrs Sullivan. I don't suppose – she isn't here, is she?'

'No, she hasn't been here,' Mum said. 'Did you see her this morning, Cordy? When you went out –?'

'Cordy came round to call for her but Sandra had gone out early.'

'You didn't see her?' Mum looked at me.

'No,' I said, glad that I could be truthful. 'I haven't seen her since yesterday.'

'She probably went into town but she always leaves word. I don't usually worry but – well, you never can tell these days, can you? And Sandra is very independent for her age.'

'I haven't seen her since yesterday,' I repeated.

'Well, I'd better go home in case she's turned up in the meantime.' Mrs Pirie managed a smile herself.

'Would you like a cup of tea?' Mum asked, suddenly becoming the hostess.

'I'd better not. Thanks all the same.' Mrs Pirie stepped back, sending a little shower of raindrops from the edge of her scarf. 'If she does come would you tell her to come straight home, Mrs Sullivan? I don't know how it is but I have the funniest feeling – anyway, I'll see you later . . .?'

She went away on a questioning note. Despite the rain she was wearing high heels that sank into a patch of mud just outside our gate.

'Close the door, Cordy. You're letting in the rain!' Mum said, going back into the kitchen.

'I've nothing to do.' I mooched after her, guilt mingling with anxiety.

'Well, don't get under my feet,' Mum said, scraping plates. 'Why not do a bit of knitting?'

'Knitting! Mum, I hate knitting!'

'Then read a book or do a jigsaw or something, but don't mope around as if you're a friendless waif.'

'What's a waif?'

'A – an orphan I suppose. Neglected.'

'Like in Dickens?'

'Yes, I suppose so. Cordy, stop tipping that chair! You're getting on my nerves, you really are!'

'I'll go and read,' I said in an injured tone, trailing upstairs.

I can't remember now which book I read but I do remember it was a long afternoon. I sat with the book open and read words and phrases and my mind kept on boarding the bus and getting off it and finding my way to Saddle Street and climbing the staircase under the archway to the empty rooms with the skylights and the camera with the black cloth hung over it.

By teatime the rain had stopped again and the sky was labouring to turn blue.

Dad arrived, looking tired and cross. Rain generally made adults cross, I thought, going downstairs to greet him.

'Good day at work, darling?'

Mum kissed him and took his damp coat with a worried air.

'Fairly lucrative, but I got soaked in the car park. So what have you been doing with yourself all day, Cordy?'

'Nothing,' I said.

'How is it that whenever I enquire what one of my daughters is doing I always get the same answer?' He sat down in his armchair and looked at me with a slightly irritable air. 'What have you been doing in school today? "Nothing, Dad." What did you do when you were out playing? "Nothing, Dad." You can't spend your entire life doing nothing surely?'

'Don't be like that, John. Our Susan always had plenty to say,' Mum said.

'Well, sometimes,' he admitted. 'If you hadn't got it into your head to let her go off and live in that flat we might still have a bit of decent conversation round here!'

'I'll get your tea,' Mum said, vanishing into the kitchen with her lips primmed together.

'I've been reading,' I said.

He glanced up at me with a slightly sheepish grin.

'Your old dad's had a hard day earning the pennies,' he said.

'Would you miss me if I left home?' I wanted to know.

'Leave home? Why on earth would you want to do that?'

'I meant later on, when I was older – when I get married or something.'

116

'Plenty of time before you need bother your head about that!'

'About what?' Mum asked, coming in.

'Getting married,' Dad said.

'Don't go putting ideas in heads that aren't ready for them! Cordy, go and wash your hands ready for tea.'

Being married, I thought gloomily as I trailed upstairs, probably wasn't much different from not being married. The only difference seemed to be that you had to cook the meals and clean the house and laugh at your husband's jokes and share the same bed with him. Despite the bruise on her face Mrs Pirie struck me as having a more exciting time than Mum did. When I grew up, I decided, making a kissing mouth at myself in the mirror, I would have gentlemen friends like her.

Perhaps that was what Sandra had done. Mr French had fallen in love with her at sight and whisked her off to the – the South of France perhaps? By now she'd probably phoned her mother to tell her not to worry. In any case there wasn't anything I could say without giving away her secret.

'Cordy, will you get a move on?' Mum called up the stairs.

I put on my ordinary face again and went down to tea.

'Any news in the paper?' Mum enquired as we moved on to the fruit jelly and sponge cake.

'Nothing,' Dad said.

I squished jelly between my teeth and wondered how it could be all right for Dad to say 'Nothing' and not all right for me. The paper was full of news most of which I wasn't allowed to know about. If it hadn't been, I reckoned, he wouldn't have bothered to buy it.

'If it could be afforded?' Mum was saying.

'Possibly.' Dad washed down the last crumbs of cake with tea and put on his considering the practicalities face. 'Cordy might like it.'

'A television set?'

'A piano. You ought to pay attention, Cordy.'

'When I pay attention you tell me you're not talking to me and when I don't butt in –'

'Don't be cheeky,' Dad said without heat.

'It would enlarge her social skills,' Mum said. 'I could teach her. I used to strum quite a lot when I was a girl.'

'There wouldn't be room,' I said. 'You always say there isn't room for a television set so there can't be room for a piano.'

'There's always room for what will enrich our lives, Cordy,' Dad said.

'I wouldn't have time to practise,' I said.

'I thought you spent your days doing nothing,' Dad said, with a wink at Mum.

'It would be nice for the long winter evenings,' Mum said.

She was seeing me as the daughter at home, playing for a couple of ageing parents. University suddenly seemed attractive.

'We'll have to see how the budget stretches,' Dad said weightily.

That meant that we'd be more likely to get a television set before we got a piano. I perked up and had a second helping of jelly.

'Can I go out?' I asked when we were clearing the dishes.

'May I?' Mum said automatically. 'And no, you may not. You were out most of the morning and lolling about in your room most of the afternoon, so this evening we'll have a nice family time. We can play cards if you – You enjoy a nice game of Pelmanism, don't you, John?'

Sandra must've come back by now else Mrs Pirie would've been on the doorstep, asking more questions.

So we played Pelmanism and I won twice and went up to bed feeling that parents weren't so bad after all!

When I look back now I marvel that I could have been so unfeeling, so uncaring. Sandra was supposed to be my friend and I ought to have been worried about her. On the other hand Sandra always gave the impression that she was capable of coping with just about anything. If she said she'd be all right then she would be. So I told myself as I pulled on my shortie pyjamas and bounced twice on the bed – once for luck and once for lots of money – which had been my nightly ritual for as long as I could remember.

Downstairs I could hear the occasional murmur of voices against the background of the wireless. In the morning Sandra would come and tell me . . . The last bit of speculation was drowned in dream.

I woke up not recalling the dream but hearing voices below. Then Mum called up the stairs.

'Cordy, get dressed quickly and come down here, will you?'

I scrambled up and pulled on my shorts and T-shirt and ran down the stairs.

My hair hadn't been combed and I hadn't brushed my teeth but that didn't seem to matter to Mum who turned as I came into the kitchen. Mrs Pirie was seated in the dining recess, holding a cup of tea in both hands and looking as if she needed something out of a bottle to add to it.

'Cordy, Mrs Pirie says that Sandra hasn't come home yet,' Mum said.

'Two nights.' Mrs Pirie looked up at me. 'Two whole nights, Cordy!'

I stood mute, pushing back the remnants of sleep.

'You did go to the Doris Day film with Sandra?' Mum said.

'We got the bus in together.'

'Did you see her go into my house?' Mrs Pirie asked.

'Not exactly,' I said carefully.

Keeping promises sacred was one thing but it wasn't right to tell a whole bundle of lies.

'Meaning?' Mum said sharply.

'It was getting late so I just got off the bus and ran on home.'

'We'd been seeing our Susan off,' Mum explained. 'She has a temporary job as a PR which we're hoping will lead to great things. We got back after Cordy came home.'

'Sandra didn't say anything? About going over to stay with anyone else?' Mrs Pirie had put down her cup, slopping some tea into the saucer.

'No,' I said honestly. 'No, she didn't.'

'Have you rung round her other friends?' Mum said briskly.

'I'm not sure that I know all of them.' Mrs Pirie spoke with a kind of pathetic pride. 'When a girl's pretty and popular –'

Sandra hadn't got any real friends except me, I thought. The boys gave her wolf whistles but the girls at school held apart from her, and because I went around with her at break they didn't include me in many things either. Once I'd seen 'Sandra Pirie, who's your daddy?' chalked on the school wall.

'A lot of people are still on holiday,' I said. 'Anyway Sandra would've told me if she was going off anywhere else. And she didn't.'

'Have you checked her wardrobe?' Mum asked.

Mrs Pirie looked vague. It was obvious that she never bothered much about Sandra's clothes being hung up neatly or even knew for sure just what she possessed.

'She might've run off for a couple of nights just for devilment,' Mum said. 'Did she have any bags with her when you went to the cinema, Cordy?'

'No, nothing,' I said.

'If I were you I'd check round all the same,' Mum said. 'Teenagers can get some funny ideas in their heads at the best of times.'

'If you think so.' Mrs Pirie was fumbling for her cigarettes. 'Yes, I'll do that first. I'm sorry to bother you, Mrs Sullivan.'

'I'm sure she'll turn up very soon,' Mum said, skilfully steering her to the front door before Mrs Pirie had located her matches. 'They always come tripping home when they're hungry, don't they?'

'Josie White didn't,' Mrs Pirie said and I saw her face, rouge standing out on her cheeks and her eyes frightened between the spider-leg lashes.

'Your breakfast's ready.' Mum closed the door and squared her shoulders. 'Dad had his early and went off. He's the week's accounting to do today. Now don't start arguing with me! Sit down and get something inside you!'

I sat down and meekly ate scrambled eggs on toast without noticing that I didn't much like them.

'Is it all right if I go out for a walk or something? It's stopped raining.'

'Oh, go on then.' Mum gave me another sharp glance. 'You're absolutely sure that you don't know where Sandra is? I know you girls with your secret pacts and all the rest of it.'

'Honestly, Mum, I've no idea at all,' I said.

'Better take your mackintosh in case it starts raining again and put on your heavy shoes.'

She poured herself another cup of tea and sat down at the table again.

I put on my heavier shoes and rolled my mackintosh obediently under my arm. When I came downstairs Mum was still sitting over her cup of tea, not drinking it but staring down at it. She was worried about Sandra, I guessed, but she didn't want to upset me by showing it too much.

I turned in the direction of the moor and skirted the drying puddles between the cobblestones. If I could jump the bigger puddle at the foot of the hill I'd take that as a sign that Fay and Fred had returned from Scarborough and would be glad to see me again.

Despite the sun and the wind the puddle was still wide, gleaming dully with a fine layer of dust and dead insects on it. It was too wide to jump without splashing in the middle of it, so it wasn't worth trying and losing the wager with myself before I'd started. I would take it as a sign if a bird started singing before I'd counted to a hundred.

I started counting very slowly because I wanted to give the birds every chance and at forty-nine I heard a chirruping from one of the bushes. That was the sign I needed and I cheered up immensely as I skirted the puddle and ploughed up through the long grass until the track was negotiable again.

I reached the long driveway and went up it and round to the back. Coming to visit the Maitlands was exciting because, unlike other people, they changed subtly from time to time. All the other grown-ups I knew were a bit boring because they fitted so neatly into the little boxes they'd made for themselves. Mrs Simmons would always be gossipy and kind and Mr White, if I ever saw him again, would still be hiding bottles in a shed somewhere, and Mum would always drag Susan and her perfections into the conversation, but with Fred and Fay you could never be sure. They might have changed their minds and made Holly Jane alive again though, on the whole, I rather hoped that they hadn't.

The back door was open and I could hear Fay's voice from inside.

'You'll love it, sweetie. You really will! It's ever so –'

She broke off as I went in and turned to look at me with the lovely wide smile breaking out on her face.

'Hello,' I said.

Edward was propped up in a high chair and she had a small bowl of cereal in her hand and a spoon.

121

'Cordelia, come in! Look, Edward, look who's come to see us!'

She was wearing a long-sleeved blouse with a ruched neckline that just rested on the tips of her shoulders and a full flowered skirt that fell nearly to her ankles, and a white ribbon, to match her blouse, strayed through her curly fair hair.

'Am I too early?' I asked.

'Neither too early nor too late. You always arrive at exactly the right moment!' she said, rising. 'I am being very domesticated today. Fred is sleeping in. All the driving exhausted him.'

'Did it –? Was everything all right?'

'It was beautiful,' she said softly. 'Fred always does it so well. When he takes photographs they have to be perfect. Now me – I cut off feet and heads! Your mother's flowers looked lovely. Roses and lavender are such feminine plants, don't you think? Edward! Honestly, for a baby he's getting terribly self-willed. It must be the male in him coming to the fore. Fred thinks it's marvellous and encourages him. I've been trying to get him to eat this but he's terribly messy. See if you can get him to finish it while I get us some lemonade.'

She handed me the bowl of cereal and wafted towards the pantry.

I looked doubtfully at Edward who stared back at me out of shiny brown glass eyes. Since his mouth was a stitched line there seemed little chance of getting any food down him. I picked up the spoon and finished it myself.

Fay came in again with two glasses of lemonade. Nice carbonated stuff out of a bottle, I noticed, and not the pip-thick liquid that Mrs Simmons dished up.

'That's a good boy!' She put the glasses on the table and wiped the black stitched mouth with a scrap of tissue paper. 'I knew you'd be a good influence on him, Cordelia. You know cereal is terribly dull when you come to think about it.'

'He's a bit little for steak and chips,' I said.

'Oh, I don't know.' She put her head on one side, considering. 'Chopped up small. Here's your lemonade.'

'Thank you.' Taking the glass and admiring the bubbles surging up in it, I said, 'Edward's a very nice baby.'

'He's not bad, are you, wretch?' She bent to ruffle his fur, her fingers tender.

122

'And the lemonade's very good,' I added, drinking it.

'You're such a satisfying person to have around,' Fay said warmly. 'You won't neglect us when school starts again, will you?'

'No.' Conscience pricked me to add, 'Mum likes to see me too.'

'Yes, of course. She must love your company,' Fay said, tipping up her own glass and swallowing in a series of little gulps.

'I couldn't exactly say,' I told her.

Most of the time I irritated her, I thought, with a little twinge of sadness. She liked me best when I was immersed in my homework or agreeing with her that Susan was special. I finished the lemonade, stood up and began to rock my chair.

Tap tap tap. Tap tap tap. Fay had seated herself on the bench alongside the table. She looked up at me, startled for an instant, and then began to tap the bottom of her glass on the table top as if she was beating a drum in time to the chair legs. Her face was full of laughter.

I stopped rocking the chair and felt something sad twisting inside me.

'Sometimes I get under her feet a lot,' I said.

'All mothers say that sometimes!' Fay tapped the glass a couple more times, then spun it round, sending lemonade cascading up the inside. 'I used to say it to – It was lovely yesterday. You would've thought it lovely too, Cordelia. Fred always reads the service so affectingly and then we laid the flowers on the earth – it began to rain but that too seemed fitting and Edward –'

'Was he there?' I asked.

'No, Edward wasn't there.' Fay looked up at me, a sad bewilderment in her face. 'So where could Edward have been?'

'You left him in the back of the car?' I hazarded.

'Yes! Of course that's what we did. Of course!' She smiled and nodded. 'These occasions aren't for children. You know everything that happens to a child before the age of seven is impressed on its subconscious mind. I wouldn't want Edward to link flowers with grief. What games do you play?'

'Games?' Her swift changes of mood were sometimes hard to follow. 'Oh, we play hockey in school and rounders.'

'I mean real games when you're by yourself or in your room,

or lying in bed and playing games in your head,' she explained.

'Pretend games mostly,' I said, considering.

'And you played them here when the house was empty?'

'Sometimes.' Her words had brought Josie and Sandra into my mind and I felt uncomfortable. 'Pirates and characters out of history – that kind of thing. Sometimes I came up here by myself. The house is nicer now there are people in it.'

'Houses always are,' Fay said. 'Without people a house is a shell without a soul. It makes its soul from the people living in it.'

'What happens when people leave?' I asked.

'I think if they are people with strong personalities they leave something of themselves behind,' Fay said. 'If the house stays empty for a long time the images fade and the house becomes a shell again. Fred and I mean to stay here for ages, don't we, Edward?'

'Oh, I hope that you do,' I said earnestly.

'Until we're very old and Edward has taken a wife. D'ye think they will call this the Maitland house one day?'

'I don't think it has a name of its own.'

I was trying to imagine Edward with a wife.

'Perhaps they called it The Laurels or something dreary and unsuitable like that. I want something romantic – from King Arthur!'

'Camelot?'

'Or Joyous Garde?' She had risen and was making little dancing steps without moving from her place. 'That was the castle where Lancelot took Guinevere and when the magic fled he renamed it Dolorous Garde. Castle of Sorrow. Such deep, bitter sorrow!'

The little dancing steps had ceased and she stood motionless, her hands held out in front of her as if she were blind. Her eyes were blank as if she watched pictures in her head that she dare not bring into the open.

I said loudly, 'I think Edward's wet himself!'

There had been terror in the room, wound out of something held inside herself, but my voice roused her. Her eyes came back into the world and she reached for Edward, turning him around, operating a little key in his back. A thin, fretful crying mingled with her voice.

'My fault! I always pot him after meals but we got chatting and I forgot! Excuse me but I must – Edward hates sitting in wet! But then what self-respecting baby doesn't? All right, poppet! Now stop making such a fuss!'

Her fingers moved against the furry back and the crying stopped.

She had forgotten me momentarily and was holding Edward against her, making little soothing noises.

'Where exactly did you have the funeral?' I asked.

To this day I don't know what made me ask it.

Fay went on patting Edward's back but over his head her face had a closed and shuttered look.

'I'm not supposed to tell,' she said flatly.

'But not in Scarborough?'

'We drove round of course – for hours and hours. I'm not allowed to tell the exact spot. Fred never permits that.'

'Did you make a vow?' I asked.

'Oh, nothing like that!' Her expression had relaxed a little. 'As it's you he won't mind my giving you a little hint. If you go home through the garden to where the swing is – where we had our picnic. We put your flowers there. We don't lay flowers from us. Fred makes a contribution to a charity, children's usually. Edward, don't jiggle so!'

She was reaching for a napkin, balancing Edward across her knees, her attitude madonna sweet. I turned and went out quietly, knowing she would remember only later that I had been there.

I went through the yard, past the sheds and into the garden, where the wet weeds speared the sunny air and the path was covered with dead leaves.

Ask almost any adult what best evokes the emotions of childhood and they will name, among other things, the crunching of fallen leaves underfoot, that delicious scrunching sound and the scent of approaching autumn in the reds and yellows and browns. For me childhood contains wet leaves, soaked by yesterday's rain, their colours blurred and run together and the snapping of their edges muted into a dismal squelching sound.

Today, long after, I walk down the stairs and through the

kitchen and pass into the yard. There are still broken flowerpots seen dimly through the cracked and spiderwebbed glass of the conservatory. I walk across the yard and past the sheds and down the winding path that leads to the wall and the gnarled fruit trees where the swing still hangs, its chains rusted, its wooden seat swollen and pitted with woodworm.

The gap in the wall is filled up with long trails of convolvulus that has twined round the high grass, choking it, and draped its white trumpets that smell of death amid the fading green. I could find my way blindfold.

I push through the strangled grass and come out on to the moor where the thorn tree stands, still vigorous, still bending before the wind. Up here the wind blows almost constantly, moaning softly through the crevices in the wall and stirring the dry twigs of the thorn tree to creak softly as if some long-buried dancer arose in her bones and executed a last pavane.

On that day the leaves squelched under my feet and once or twice I almost slipped on them. I came out on to the moor and looked round.

There was no sign of my flowers but further along I saw a flash of pink. It was right, I thought, that Holly Jane should have been given a formal farewell.

The rain had soaked the flowers, browning the lavender, and the wind had demolished the rose petals. I could see that the ground beneath had been dug over and then covered with soil and clumps of grass. It was very sad, I thought, luxuriating in my own feelings. Holly Jane had been so real to them, so beloved. I pictured Fred driving round for hours, postponing the moment, and Fay with the black veil over her fair hair and Edward in the back of the van. I could see wheel marks further down where the track began, grown fainter now, almost indistinguishable from the bent and tangled grasses all around.

It behoved me to enter into the ritual. It made me part of the life that Fay and Fred lived. In later years we could sit cosily by a fire and talk about Holly Jane.

I knelt down on the soaked and tumbled earth and gently lifted the sodden posy and watched a few petals float idly down. And saw as the wind stirred the surface of the soil and a clump of grass broke from its moorings and rolled a few inches. And saw.

126

Impossible now to recapture my feelings in that moment. Impossible to recreate my thoughts. I can remember that I rose stiffly, the posy still in my hand, and walked away down the hill, scuffing the faint marks of tyre tracks as I went, tearing the leaves and the petals off the wet stems and scattering them like confetti. Perhaps I wasn't feeling or thinking anything. Perhaps I was just protecting the world of which I was now a part.

Mum was in the sitting-room, dusting the photograph frames tenderly, her eyes dreaming as she looked at the various studies of Susan and me. In the background the wireless was playing music – I forget what if I ever knew.

'Cordy, shoes!' She looked up as I came through the front door, leaving muddy imprints on the hall linoleum.

I stood and looked at her.

'What is it, dear?' She set down a frame and stared at me. 'Cordy, what's wrong?'

And I heard the stranger that was myself say in a clear, precise tone, 'I found Sandra up on the moor. She's half buried there. Her eyes are full of soil.'

8

That Friday morning should be etched indelibly in my mind, but the mind protects itself. I remember what was done and what was said, and certain images recur easily to my memory. The cereal Fay was giving Edward was cornflakes. Now why should I remember that and not recall exactly how Sandra looked? On her back with soil and clumps of grass covering her and the damp, demolished posy above her face, though whether as a conscience-stricken gesture of grace or an insult is impossible to tell. Perhaps it was no more than the automatic bestowing of respect upon the deceased.

Mum sat me down and went to put on the kettle. At moments of crisis women reach for the kettle. I found myself gulping tea crammed with sugar, while Mum stood, twisting her hands in her apron, saying, 'Try to be calm, lovie. Try to be calm! You're absolutely sure – you are telling me the exact truth, aren't you? You're not playing a – no, no, I can see that you're not. I'd better – your father – no, the police need to be informed. This is dreadful, dreadful.'

She put her hands up to her face and drew them down her cheeks, over the taut muscles, and then untied her apron and smoothed down her skirt as if it was necessary to look respectably tidy when one phoned the police.

'It's 999,' I said.

'What? Yes, of course. I'll ring now.'

I heard her voice, hurried and less fluent than usual. Her words danced and splintered in my head and some drops of tea bounced up inside the cup and left soil-coloured stains on the white china.

'They'll be here in ten minutes,' Mum said, replacing the receiver and looking at me. 'I told them up on the moor behind the old Tyler house. You are sure?'

'Yes,' I said.

'You'd better go and wash your hands,' Mum said, clinging to normality. 'They're all over soil. Hurry now, there's a – and put the hand towel in the laundry basket when you've – I'd better brew more tea. They might fancy a cup. Cordy, move!'

I moved up the stairs as slowly as if lead weights were tied to my feet. I felt cold and numb and beneath the coldness and the numbness a sick fear was shaping itself. Mr French's son must've killed Sandra and buried her up on the moor and seen the flowers and moved them to cover her face more securely than the damp and shifting soil. Fay would be devastated if she ever found out that someone had buried a real girl near the place where she and Fred had laid Holly Jane.

'Hurry up, Cordy!'

Mum's voice echoed thinly up the stairs. I washed my hands and sat on the toilet, trying not to shiver as the numbness wore off.

Downstairs I heard a car stopping and then the doorbell rang. Mum called.

'Pull the chain, Cordy! Hurry up now.'

It was, I suppose, a measure of her anxiety that she neglected to tell me to wash my hands again.

I could hear unfamiliar voices in the sitting-room and I can remember pausing and then coming slowly down the stairs, part of myself splitting off to admire the grave, quiet look on my face, that same other self nodding approval at my demeanour. This is Cordelia who has found a dead body, on her way downstairs to talk to the policeman.

'Hello, Cordy! Your mum tells me you've had a nasty shock.'

My two selves snapped together as the man I'd spoken to in Josie's house stood up, looming large in the sitting-room. Another policeman, in uniform, had taken a seat at the table and was leafing through a notebook.

Forty years back nobody thought of trauma or post-traumatic stress or counselling. But the plain-clothes detective spoke cordially, quietly.

'Do you . . .?' My mother looked from him to me in bewilderment.

'We've met very briefly,' he said. 'Detective Inspector Archer.'

'Yes, I remember,' I said.

129

'Come and sit down and let's have a bit of a chat about it,' he invited.

That was how police grilling began. Sandra had sneaked into gangster films and told me all about it.

I sat down uneasily on the edge of a chair and Mum hovered near me.

'Would you like to have a policewoman in while we chat?' Inspector Archer enquired. 'I have a nice colleague called Joyce.'

I shook my head.

'It could be a mistake,' Mum said shakily. 'Cordy has a vivid imagination and I haven't checked –'

'We're checking right now,' Inspector Archer said. 'You didn't make up the story, did you, Cordy?'

'No,' I said.

'Her mother –' Mum put her hand to her mouth. 'She was here, looking for Sandra. The girl hadn't been home for two nights.'

'Mrs Pirie reported her daughter missing about half an hour ago,' he said. 'We were at her house when your call was relayed from the station.'

'Ought I to –?'

'What I really fancy,' Inspector Archer said, 'is a good strong cup of tea. Sergeant Ackroyd wouldn't turn one down either.'

'Tea? Yes, of course. Yes, I'll make some fresh tea. Just coming up!' Mum said.

Relief shrilled her voice. Tea and the conventions hedged her world against disaster.

She went through into the kitchen and the inspector drew up a chair and sat opposite me.

'This really is just a chat,' he said. 'Sergeant Ackroyd will jot down a few notes as we go along. You won't mind that, will you?'

'No,' I said.

'So let's get a few formalities out of the road first. Your name is Cordelia Sullivan and you're – twelve?'

'Nearly thirteen,' I said.

'Sorry. Correct that, Ackroyd! Now – excuse me.'

Another car had drawn up outside and I could see more policemen getting out. Inspector Archer rose and went out into the front garden to speak to them. When he came back his manner was heavier somehow, the lines in his face more deeply engraved. He was quite old, I thought. At least forty.

'How many cups will we be needing?' Mum fussed out of the kitchen. 'I heard –'

'My colleagues have found – what Cordy reported to you,' he said. 'They'll stay up at the scene and wait for the doctor and the photographer. I'll need to be there myself very shortly.'

'Just two cups then,' Mum said. 'Cordy?'

I shook my head.

'Two cups,' Mum said and went back into the kitchen.

Inspector Archer sat down again.

'Can you tell me what happened this morning in your own words?' he said.

'I went for a walk on the moor and I found Sandra,' I said bleakly.

'How did you happen to find her?'

If I mentioned the flowers that would lead him to the Maitlands. I said carefully, 'I saw where the earth had been dug up. The rain had washed some of it away and I saw a bit of her face.'

'What did you do then?'

'I bent down and scraped away some of the dirt.'

'From her face?'

'Yes,' I said and gulped miserably.

'No need to dwell on that.' He gave me a faint, kind smile. 'So what did you do then?'

'I came home.'

'Did you run?'

'I – I think so. I'm not sure. It was like being in a night-mare.'

'And you came straight home?'

'And told Mum. Yes.'

'It was a terrible shock,' Mum said, coming in with the tea. 'I just could not believe it. I mean – things like that don't happen to people you know.'

'Unfortunately, Mrs Sullivan, sometimes they do,' he said quietly. 'Ah, thank you. Tea will buck us up I fancy. Was Sandra a particular friend of yours, Cordy?'

'She was last year,' I said.

131

'She doesn't mean that like it sounds,' Mum said quickly. 'It's only that as children grow older they begin to have other interests and – Cordy and Sandra never had a quarrel, did you, Cordy?'

'A biscuit would go very nicely with this tea,' Sergeant Ackroyd said, entering the conversation for the first time.

'I have some chocolate digestive.' Headed off, Mum went back into the kitchen.

'I like – liked Sandra,' I said defensively.

'Her mother was telling us that you and Sandra went to the pictures in Bradford together night before last,' Inspector Archer said.

'To see Doris Day,' I nodded.

'We weren't too keen on her going off in the evening,' Mum said, coming back with the biscuits. 'In term time it wouldn't've been thought of, but this being the long summer break –'

'Designed to give teachers a rest and parents a nervous breakdown, eh? You went in by bus –'

'Her dad would've taken them both in,' Mum said, 'but we were seeing our elder girl off. Susan has rather a good temporary job down in London. A PR job.'

'Susan doesn't live at home?'

'She shares a flat with another student near the polytechnic. She's doing a secretarial course there.'

'My own lad wants to be an astronaut,' Sergeant Ackroyd said gloomily. 'Not much chance of that round here.'

'You went into Bradford before or after Cordy?'

'Before Cordy. I helped Susan pack and I took in a skirt I'd altered for her. Cordy had strict instructions to be home on the nine thirty bus.'

'And were you?' He glanced at me.

'Yes,' I said truthfully.

'And Sandra came with you?'

'Together,' I said.

If Mum would only go away for a few minutes I'd tell him that I'd come home alone, but I couldn't do that with her standing there, prompting.

'When you came home did you actually see Sandra go into her own house?' he was asking now.

132

'Not actually. I came straight home in case Mum and Dad were back.'

'We got back about an hour later. We saw Susan off on the late train. First time she's ever been to London. If we'd got back earlier –'

'I doubt it would've made any difference, Mrs Sullivan,' he said. 'So! That wasn't too bad, was it, Cordy? We will probably want another chat with you later on but it wasn't too hard, was it?'

He sounded insistent as if he hoped I might say I'd enjoyed it. I said, 'I can't think of anything else to tell you.'

'She's had a bad shock, you know,' Mum said reproachfully.

'Yes. Not a pleasant thing to happen when you're – nearly thirteen.' He flashed me a grin and nodded to Sergeant Ackroyd who snapped shut his notebook and hastily chewed the last bit of his chocolate digestive. 'Thank you for your hospitality, Mrs Sullivan. We may be back later if there are any new developments.'

The two policemen went out, got into the car and drove back along the village street.

'I ought to ring your father,' Mum said, collecting cups. 'Cordy, come away from the window! It's ill bred to spy on people from behind the nets.'

'They'll be going up to the moor,' I said.

I wondered if they would drive up along the high track that bisected the spongy ground.

'Try not to think about it,' Mum said. Her face was drawn and the cups rattled slightly in her hands.

'Will they tell Mrs Pirie?' I asked.

'They'll ask her to make a formal identification I daresay. Poor woman! What a terrible thing to have to do! If our Susan –'

'Or me,' I said, quick and jealous.

'Either of you. I can't get it out of my mind. What was I going to do?'

'Ring Dad,' I said.

'I can't break it to him over the telephone. Hopefully he'll not have a late meeting tonight. Put the lid on the biscuit tin, there's a good girl.'

For once in my life I looked without craving at the chocolate biscuits before screwing on the lid.

'Do you want any help?' I enquired.

'No. No, there's not much to do. I think I'll make a salad and open a tin of salmon for supper.'

'We haven't had our dinner yet!'

'What?' She put the cups on the draining board and brushed her hand over her face as if she were removing cobwebs. 'Heavens! I'm all muddled up. What do you want?'

'I'm not hungry,' I said.

'You must have something. How about beans on toast?'

'Yes, all right.'

'We have to carry on as normally as possible,' Mum said.

I wondered why but it wasn't the time to ask. Instead I got out plates and Mum opened the tin and put bread in the toaster.

I wasn't hungry but the beans were salty sweet and the toast thickly buttered. Despite myself I finished my share while Mum was still trailing a fork through the tomato sauce and drinking yet another cup of tea.

'Can – may I go out?' I asked.

'No, not yet. There'll be gossiping neighbours and police asking – no, you stay here.'

She sounded cross and sad at the same time. I got down from the table silently and helped her wash up. After a few minutes she said, 'I'm sorry, Cordy. I don't mean to be irritable but I'm so worried – first Josie White runs off and gets knocked down and now Sandra – it's like a – I don't know.'

'A curse,' I volunteered.

'That's silly, Cordy. There are no such things as curses. What was that?'

She had started violently.

'The doorbell. I'll go.'

I darted into the hall and opened the door. Inspector Archer smiled at me and Sergeant Ackroyd nodded at his shoulder.

'Mind if we have another chat?' the inspector asked.

'Who is it, Cordy?' Mum came into the hall with a dishcloth over her arm. 'Oh, Inspector Archer. I didn't expect –'

'We won't keep you more than five minutes, Mrs Sullivan. One or two points to clear up, that's all.'

It was amazing how neatly two tall men could insert themselves through the front door into our hall without anyone actually inviting them.

134

'I'm sure that Cordy's told you everything she can,' Mum said.

'A few details require expanding, Mrs Sullivan,' he soothed. 'Nothing to fret about.'

'I do think – you'd better come into the sitting-room,' she said reluctantly. 'I do think that Cordy's been upset enough, really I do.'

'This is an upsetting business all round,' Sergeant Ackroyd said.

'It's about your visit to the cinema on Wednesday evening,' the inspector said, taking a chair and motioning me into another.

'I'm sure she told you everything,' Mum said.

'The point is . . .' He paused for a moment as if he was marshalling his thoughts. 'You and Sandra went into Bradford together to see the Doris Day film. Right? On the bus?'

'Yes. We did!'

'And watched the film together?'

'Yes.'

'Sat together or did you have a bit of a spat and sit separately?'

'We didn't quarrel.'

'You didn't go into the cinema together either, did you?' he said.

'If Cordy says they did –' Mum began.

'We've had a couple of results already from our enquiries,' he said.

'Meaning?' Mum sounded quite fierce.

'A girl answering Cordy's description bought a ticket and went in alone. The usherette noticed she was by herself and kept an eye on her.'

'I wasn't doing anything!' I said indignantly.

'The cinema staff look out for children watching a film by themselves in case they get bothered by unpleasant people,' he said.

'Nobody bothered me.'

I felt slightly annoyed to think that as I had sat in grown-up and solitary splendour watching Doris Day someone had been supervising me, as if I was a silly kid who couldn't look after herself.

'The point is,' Inspector Archer said, 'that you weren't with Sandra, were you?'

'Cordy?' Mum was looking at me.

'We did go into Bradford together,' I said. 'On the bus.'

'But not into the cinema together. Where did Sandra go?'

The question caught me on the hop. I stared at him dumbly.

'Maybe she didn't say where she was going?' Mum said.

'I promised,' I said.

'Promised you wouldn't tell anybody where she was going?' He had dark eyes and they bored into mine.

'I made a solemn promise,' I repeated obstinately.

In my head thoughts were racing round like greyhounds on a track. I'd been to an afternoon greyhound meeting once on a bank holiday with Mum and Dad and Susan, and hated every minute of it – hated the thin dogs, and the stupid pretend hare and the people yelling and shouting.

'Cordy, after a person dies promises don't count,' the inspector said.

'Sandra wasn't likely to have confided in our Cordy,' Mum said, looking troubled. 'I know they were friendly, Inspector, and God forbid that I should speak ill of the poor girl but they weren't really suited.'

'Where was Sandra going, Cordy?' the inspector asked.

'She said she was going somewhere special,' I hedged. 'We were going to meet up at the bus stop afterwards. Sandra didn't come. I was scared of being late so I just got on the bus.'

'She didn't say where this special place was?' he persisted.

If I told the whole story, about Mr French and the studio, I'd get into more trouble than I'd ever been in during my entire life. Mum would tell Dad and he'd see me as a naughty, deceitful child conspiring with a girl he hadn't wanted me to have as a friend anyway.

'She said she wasn't coming and she'd tell me all about it later, only she didn't come and I couldn't sneak on her so I said she'd been watching the picture,' I said and because it was the easiest thing to do burst into tears.

'She doesn't know any more than she's already told you!' Mum said. 'You can't go on questioning and questioning her – Sandra probably went off with some boyfriend! You can't blame Cordy for that!'

'I'm sorry, Cordy.' He looked down at me. 'I certainly never meant to upset you but it's really important that people tell us the whole truth.'

'Would it have made any difference to her getting killed – if Cordy had said something to us on Wednesday night after we got home?' Mum asked.

'Almost certainly not,' he said gravely.

'I promised Sandra,' I said.

At that moment I felt small and persecuted. Mum gave me a handkerchief and made a sympathetic noise.

'We'll leave it like that for now.' Inspector Archer nodded towards his sergeant. 'If we need anything more I can bring my colleague, Joyce –'

'I don't want her,' I said.

Fright was turning to sullenness. I didn't want some old lady policeman badgering me.

'Well, we'll be in touch,' Inspector Archer said, ominously genial. They were preparing to leave, two tall men who made our sitting-room look small.

'Maybe it was just an accident,' I said, scrubbing my nose with the handkerchief. 'Maybe the person didn't really want to kill her. Maybe –'

'Cordy, I think you've been quite enough of a nuisance for one day,' Mum broke in. 'I don't know what your father will say. I really don't!'

'But it could've been an accident and then someone got scared and tried to hide her –'

'This looks as if it was carefully planned,' the inspector said. 'Mind you, we've a long way to go yet. Thank you for the tea and biscuits, Mrs Sullivan. Bye, Cordy.'

I thought he was going but at the door he turned suddenly.

'D'ye have a boyfriend, Cordy?' he enquired.

'I don't like boys,' I said.

'Did Sandra?'

'I don't know. Honestly I don't!'

'Sandra went on holiday with her mother,' Mum said. 'She and Cordy haven't spent a great deal of time together since school broke up.'

'So you really don't know where she was going when she pretended to be at the cinema with you?'

'I don't like to say this,' Mum said, screwing herself up to leap into the breach, 'but Sandra was a bit forward for her age. My husband never really approved of her as a friend for our Cordy.'

'Children do grow up fast these days,' Sergeant Ackroyd said.

'And you've nothing else to tell us, Cordy?' The dark eyes probed me.

'Sandra was killed, wasn't she?' I said in a small voice.

'There are some very sick and cruel people in the world,' the inspector said. 'Thanks again, Mrs Sullivan.'

The two of them actually left. The sitting-room became bigger.

'I thought they were never going!' Mum said, coming back into the room.

'I didn't want to break my promise,' I said.

'And Sandra really didn't tell you where she was going?'

'I'm fed up being asked the same questions over and over!' I blurted.

'If you didn't know then there's nothing to worry about. Honestly, Cordy, I don't know how you could've been so deceitful,' Mum said, her voice rising. 'Really I don't! You wouldn't catch our Susan telling fibs like that. You know our views on running round with boys.'

'It wasn't me running round with boys,' I said sulkily.

'No, it was Sandra and look where it –'

The telephone rang and made us both jump.

'Yes?' Mum lifted the receiver. 'Oh, John! Yes, I was just thinking of ring – no, not yet. Something's happened. Listen, I – Cordy, don't just sit there! Go and weed your flowers or something! Sorry, John, it's only that the most awful –'

I slipped from the room, grabbed my jacket and went out into the street. Next door but one a policeman was standing at the open door, talking to Mrs Binns.

They'd be making what they called house-to-house enquiries, asking all the neighbours if they'd seen Sandra or me. That was how the police worked, I knew, having discussed the matter often enough with Sandra and Josie when we played detective pretends. First family and friends, and then the near neighbours and then people living further off until the questions spread like ripples in a pool, and people who hadn't done anything wrong but wanted to be private were dragged in.

I turned and ran towards the steep track that would take me up on to the moor and to the front gates of the Tyler house.

When I reached the highest point before the ground levelled out I climbed on to a large flat rock and looked over to where the wall curved round and the land sloped again. I could see the tip of what looked like a yellow tent and several tiny black figures moving systematically along the tumbled grass and the clods of earth loosened by the rain.

Then I jumped down and ran on. I ran up the drive, not counting the puddles, and round to the back of the house. There was no sign of anyone but the kitchen door was hospitably unlocked and I went in.

Everything was neat, dishes draining at the side of the sink, the electric cooker gleaming at the side of the old black range. The door into the rest of the house was open and I went up the two steps and along the passage and saw Fred putting some books in the shelves at the side of the fireplace.

'Cordelia, nice to see you!'

He turned with a pleased expression on his face.

I'd run the breath out of myself and stood gasping at him. My face must have been blotched from crying because his pleased look changed.

'Whatever's the matter?' He put down the last couple of books without bothering to arrange them properly. 'You look – what is it, Cordy?'

'Something awful has happened,' I got out.

'Gently now!' He was by my side in an instant, arm round my shoulders. 'Fay's taking a nap. Come and sit down and tell me what this is all about.'

We sat on the long couch over which Fay had draped some lovely turquoise material.

'Sandra's dead,' I said, and having said it felt suddenly calmer.

'Who?'

'My friend – Sandra Pirie,' I elaborated. 'She's dead.'

'But you told me before – some child was –'

'That was Josie White and she got run over in Bradford. That was an – an accident.'

139

The death itself, yes, but what had happened in the hours before?

'Someone else has died?' Fred sounded bewildered.

'Sandra Pirie. She was killed and buried on the moor not far from your garden wall. The police put a tent up there – haven't you seen it?'

'I haven't been out of the house today.'

'The police are going round asking questions. House-to-house.'

He took his arm from my shoulders and stood up, looked down at me.

'Surely this isn't true,' he said. 'Cordelia, is this a game? If so then it isn't a very nice one.'

'I found her.' My fingers twisting together, I spoke loudly. 'The flowers, the ones Mum sent for Holly Jane, were on top of her. On top of Sandra. The rain had washed some of the earth away. I thought – I thought it was Holly Jane and now I'm all muddled up.'

He didn't answer me at first. He took a few steps in one direction, then a few steps in the other. A long bar of afternoon sunlight arrowed through the big window and struck dazzle from his glasses.

'You say the police are there now?' He stopped pacing and looked at me again.

'Further down the slope from the thorn tree,' I said. 'They went round by the road. I came up the track. Nobody saw me.'

'Another death?' He didn't seem to be asking the question of anyone in particular.

'You can't go there,' I said quickly. 'Don't you see? They'll find Holly Jane. The earth is all crumbling away there.'

'Holly Jane.'

He pronounced the two names as if they were sugar and he was tasting it.

'Whoever put Sandra in the ground saw the flowers and put them on top of her face. They're asking questions. Don't you see? They'll come here and if they see Edward – everything will be spoilt, don't you see?'

He turned his head and the dazzle of sunlight faded, leaving his eyes visible again.

140

'You came to warn me?' he said.

'Not because of – you didn't know Sandra,' I said. 'It's just that – if Edward could go to his auntie's again then the police won't – they wouldn't understand about Edward. There'd be talk and you'd have to move on.'

'Always moving on.' He sounded weary.

'And even when they find Holly Jane they won't think that you've got anything – not unless they see Edward.'

'This girl was a friend of yours, you say?'

'We used to be best friends but –' I stopped, suddenly uneasily aware that my feelings weren't what they ought to be. I was shocked and scared but I couldn't feel any aching inside me. 'She was growing up faster than me,' I finished lamely.

'You say you found her?'

'I saw the flowers,' I said. 'It's all right! I tore them up into little bits and threw them all round, and scuffed out the wheel marks with my heels. But I didn't think of looking for Holly Jane. If the police find her and – couldn't you say it was just a joke or something? Fred?'

'I'm trying to take in the fact that a child's been murdered near our home,' Fred said slowly.

'I think she was killed somewhere else and then put there,' I said.

'I hope they catch him,' Fred said.

'The police are very clever.' I recalled the probing dark eyes, the quiet, pleasant manner and the sudden unexpected questions that came out of nowhere.

'And very thorough,' Fred said.

'I just don't want anyone to get the wrong idea,' I said. 'I don't want you to have to move on.'

Josie was gone and Sandra was gone. Their spaces had been filled. I had to keep tight hold of the dream.

'Not again,' Fred said. 'No, Fay couldn't endure another move. You know, meeting you has made all the difference. You know what she said to me? "Cordelia is a rare and lovely soul. The next time we take a trip we must invite her along."'

'A rare and lovely soul'. Nobody had ever used such words about me before.

'There's the rest of the house to get ready,' I said. 'And the garden to plant! And you have your book to write.'

141

'An Eden to be defended.' He was pacing the room again, head bent. When he stopped and turned his voice was matter-of-fact. 'Look, you'd better go home now,' he said. 'Don't fret about anything. I'll sort it out.'

'And Edward?' I rose unwillingly.

'Edward will go to his auntie's,' Fred said. 'You go home now, Cordelia.'

'We could take a trip to Scarborough,' I said.

'Scarborough. Why not? Pick up Edward when all this has been cleared up. Why not indeed?'

He smiled at me but the sun was glinting off his glasses again.

I went out into the front hall and opened the door. There was nobody in sight but I guessed it wouldn't be long before the policemen came asking questions. Fred would see to it all. Fred, I knew, always saw to things.

I went home by way of the track, not turning aside to stand on the rock and look to see how far the searchers had come. It was going to be all right because Fred had said so. All I had to do was keep faith with what was left of my promise to Sandra. If I told them about French's Studio then they might arrest me for – what was it called? – withholding vital information. Anyway it wouldn't help Sandra now to say any more. Sandra was dead.

The word banged in my head like a sharp stone rattling inside my brain. Sandra was dead and Josie was dead and I still had the Maitlands. They were my lamp in a confused and darkening world.

When I reached our house I nipped over the side wall and started pulling up weeds out of my patch. They tugged out more easily after the rain and I made a big pile of them and decided that when it was really dry I'd make a nice bonfire. That was the sadness of being a leaf. And then the sadness overwhelmed me and I sat down on the back step and cried real tears of grief because Sandra was gone and she hadn't been a real close friend after all. I guess that I'd known that for a long time.

142

9

Mum had taken one look at me when I arrived home and sent me straight upstairs for what she called 'a nice hot bath', as if hot water and bath salts could wash away guilt and sorrow.

'I'll bring you your supper in bed,' she said, bustling in and giving me a raised eyebrow kind of stare when I grabbed the flannel and put it across my chest. 'You need a good night's sleep, young lady. Anyway your dad and I need to talk. I'll have to tell him about the lies, Cordy, and he's going to be disappointed in you. Very disappointed indeed, I'm afraid! But with you out of the road then I can probably talk him round.'

So I had the tinned salmon and the salad in bed as if I was an invalid and Mum gave me a second cup of tea before closing the door firmly and going downstairs again.

I could hear their voices like a stream of broken mumbling sounds below the more strident voices from the wireless. Mum would be talking Dad round. It wasn't often she had to do that because I was generally obedient. Mum, I thought, drifting into a sleep I hadn't even known I needed, was all right . . .

First I walked up the driveway of the old Tyler house. The sun was hot on my head but there was snow in the hollows and when I reached the front door the steps were slippery with ice. I remember that I tried to mount them but my feet slipped from beneath me and over and over I found myself at the bottom again. What made it worse was that I could see Fred and Fay standing in the bay of the big front window, and Sandra and Josie were with them.

Sandra was holding Fay's hand and looking at Fred from under her lashes in the way she looked at bus conductors, and Josie was sitting on Fred's shoulders, bending her head over the top of his head to look at me. She had on a skimpy vest and a pair of navy blue knickers and they were damp and creased from hanging too long on the clothes line in the rain, but it didn't much matter because she was holding an enormous flannel across her chest and when she breathed I could see tiny swellings like very young apples pushing against the flannel.

I woke up with a rushing sound carrying the dream away but it was only someone, Mum probably, flushing the toilet. I rolled over with my face away from the door and practised long, slow breathing as if I was still asleep but nobody opened the door to peek in on me, and when I slept again it was like falling into a black hole and not coming out the other side.

'Your dad's taking the day off work.'

Mum came in, as ever starting the daily announcements without waiting to find out if I was conscious.

'Oh?' I said.

'He's gone to buy a morning paper, though there isn't likely to be much in it yet. Don't just lie there, Cordy! You know Saturday's a busy day.'

Saturdays were general clear-out days even if there was nothing to clear out. Those were the times when fathers went into work on Saturday mornings while mothers chivvied daughters into making everything spick and span just in case fathers decided to inspect all the drawers and cupboards.

'Why?' I asked.

'Because Saturday always is busy.'

'I mean why hasn't Dad gone to work?'

'In view of what's happened,' Mum said, 'he thinks it shows more respect. You'd better put on a skirt and a nice blouse. It –'

'Shows respect?'

'Don't get smart with me, young lady!' There was a pinched look round her mouth. 'I've quite enough to worry about without you getting clever! Your dad needed a lot of talking round I can tell you! He was quite hurt to think that you and Sandra had cooked up a pack of lies together so that she could deceive her mother. Are you sure she didn't say where she was going?'

Her eyes were as probing as the inspector's. If I told her now . . .!

'She said she was going somewhere special. She was going to tell me all about it.'

'Right then. Get washed and I'll get your breakfast on.'

There was no use in arguing as I usually did that having had

144

a bath the night before there hadn't been time to get grubby again. I pushed back the bedclothes and got up, trailed into the bathroom and wiped my face with the damp flannel and cleaned my teeth.

When I went downstairs breakfast was sizzling in the pan. I was hungry which gave me a pang of guilt because it didn't seem right that I should be tucking into bacon and eggs and fried bread when Sandra had been killed.

Dad let himself in and sat down in the sitting-room to read his newspaper.

'Would you like another cup of tea, John?'

Mum bustled through.

There was an indistinguishable murmur, the rustling of paper, and then Dad's step in the hall.

'Feeling better, Cordy?'

He stood in the kitchen doorway.

'Yes thank you, Dad,' I said meekly.

'No more lies, eh?'

I shook my head.

'Good girl. You help your mother then.'

He went back into the sitting-room.

Having him at home instead of safely out of the way at work slowed Mum up. She didn't say anything but there was frustration in her voice as she told him to stay exactly where he was, 'because I only need to give this room a quick once over today'.

I washed up without being told, hating scraping the used plates and then nearly scalding myself by turning the hot water tap too far round.

'Leave them to drain, love.'

Mum, coming in, sounded warm and forgiving.

'Will the police inspector be asking me any more questions?' I asked.

'I shouldn't think so seeing as you've told him everything,' she considered. 'You might have to give a brief statement for the inquest.'

'Will I have to go to an inquest?'

'It's not likely,' she said again. 'They don't usually expect children to give evidence at inquests. I daresay the Coroner will read your statement out.'

145

'Will I have to go to the police station to make a statement?'

'Cordy, I don't know.' She sounded weary. 'Why don't you go for a nice walk or something? Get some fresh air – but don't hang around Mrs Pirie's house.'

I went out leaving Dad immersed in his newspaper, closing the front door softly in case he called me back and told me to stay put.

There was a policeman outside Mrs Pirie's house and a crowd at the gate just as there had been outside the White house. I went past with my head down in case anyone recognised me as the girl who'd found the body, but in those pre-media hype days news was fed in snippets only to the waiting press and my identity apparently hadn't been revealed.

Anyway the reporters there were too busy interviewing Mrs Pirie. I stopped for a moment as her voice, the vowels ever so slightly distorted into a parody of refinement, rang out.

'My only child, yes! My ewe lamb!'

Surely she hadn't really said 'ewe lamb'? Sandra would've died of shame.

'Divorced these ten years. No, he has never taken the slightest interest in us. Sandra was better off without him if the truth be told. We both were though it might seem harsh to say that.'

Someone asked something I didn't catch but the rest of the listening crowd pressed forward eagerly.

'It seems not, thank God. My little girl was not – interfered with in that way. The police were kind enough to tell me at once as soon as the doctor was certain. Yes, it's some slight comfort to me to know that.'

So Sandra hadn't done 'it' after all. I had always guessed that but there had been at the back of my mind the suspicion that she just might – what a show-off she'd been!

I wondered if they'd told Mrs Pirie that I was the one who'd found her. The policeman was moving people along now, his voice loud and officious.

Mrs Pirie stood at her gate, made up, hair combed, a little veil shading her eyes. She looked as if she needed the people there to stop her thinking about what had happened, I decided in a flash of insight, and then she turned away and picked up a can and began watering the plastic flowers.

I ought to have gone up to her and said how sorry I was and

what a good friend Sandra had been, but somehow I couldn't even though I was truly sorry and Sandra had been more of a friend than Josie. Instead I went on quickly into the square where more people were standing about in twos and threes, mainly women with baskets resting on their hips and toddlers in tow.

'It's like the Grant business all over again,' someone was saying.

'The child there wasn't interfered with either.'

'Are you sure? I heard that she was.'

'Anyway the lad hanged himself.'

'Copycat killings. They have them in America.'

I headed into the store where Mrs Simmons was giving her views to a group of customers.

'As the late Mr Simmons always used to say – the crime rate will rise until we get discipline back into the schools. Well, he's been proved right though it gives me no satisfaction to say so!'

'Always had a good head on his shoulders,' a woman said.

'You never said a truer word, Mrs Grace. The late Mr Simmons wouldn't have taken any pleasure in being proved right though. He was very fond of children. Chocolate or plain digestive?'

I moved behind the postcard stand and twisted my neck round to look at the headlines in the local paper.

'Second Death in Linton' the headline ran.

Underneath, a long paragraph informed the readers that following the accidental death of eleven-year-old Josie White after she had been missing from home for twenty-four hours another schoolgirl, Sandra Pirie, after two nights' absence, had been found partially buried high on the moor. Neither girl had been interfered with sexually but there were ligature marks on their wrists. The police were now conducting extensive enquiries.

I wasn't sure what ligature marks were but I was relieved that my name didn't feature anywhere.

The bell tinkled as the women went out. Mrs Simmons said, 'Did you want something, Cordy?'

'I'm just mooching around,' I said, ducking out from behind the stand.

'Maybe I've got a bar of chocolate somewhere. You must be

feeling very sad. You and Sandra were really close, weren't you?'

I nodded.

'And you went to the pictures with her on Wednesday, didn't you? Did she run off after the film or what?'

'She didn't come and see the picture.'

'But you said – you went in together on the bus surely?'

'Yes, but Sandra was going somewhere else. She never said where,' I added.

'Going to see a boyfriend perhaps?'

'She never said.'

'So you came home by yourself then?'

'Yes.'

Being questioned by the police was bad enough but I didn't feel like being questioned by Mrs Simmons as well.

'Well, we shall find out all about it in due course I daresay,' she said, handing me the chocolate bar with a disappointed air.

I thanked her and meandered home again. At least she hadn't heard that I was the one who'd found Sandra's body. I peeled off the wrapping paper and ate the chocolate too quickly, feeling slightly sick when it was finished but remembering to put the paper in the dustbin before I went inside.

'There's absolutely no point in it!' Dad's voice was raised impatiently.

'She might see it in a newspaper,' Mum was saying.

'If she does then she'll probably ring us – Cordy, where have you been?'

'Mooching,' I said.

'It's hard on her not having her friends,' Mum defended.

'Surely my daughter has more than two friends! The Deacon girl – what's her name? And who's this now?'

The doorbell had rung. Mum, going to the front door, returned with the inspector behind her.

'John, this is Detective Inspector Archer. I told you –' Mum began.

'You're the one who reduced my daughter to tears,' Dad said. 'My wife's been telling me all about it. I've been thinking of lodging a formal complaint about the incident.'

'That is your right, Mr Sullivan.' Inspector Archer spoke with what might be termed restrained politeness. 'I did offer Cordy the services of a woman police officer but she refused and your wife was present during the interview.'

'I wasn't crying because the inspector was asking questions,' I said. 'I was crying because I felt sad.'

'And because you weren't telling the whole truth.' Dad abruptly changed sides. 'We brought our girls up to tell the truth, Inspector Archer.'

'Well, it's sorted now.' The inspector took the proffered chair and brought out a typed sheet of paper. 'I'm not here to ask any more questions anyway. This is a short statement based on Cordy's eventual account of events. I decided to come along and deal with it here, rather than attract attention by inviting you all along to the station.'

'What's in it?' I asked.

'I'll read it out and you can stop me if anything's wrong. Then you can read it yourself and sign it if you agree. It's for the Coroner.'

'All right,' I said.

He began to read aloud in a measured, expressionless voice. '"My name is Cordelia Sullivan and I am nearly thirteen years old. I live with my parents at number fifteen, Victoria Terrace, Linton. My friend Sandra Pirie and I . . ."'

The initial lies I'd told about Sandra and me watching the film together had been left out. The statement, cobbled together from my other answers, was simple and uncomplicated by any hint of emotion. I wondered if all police statements sounded like that.

'You read it over and if you agree with everything then sign your name at the bottom,' the inspector said.

'I haven't offered you a cup of tea,' I heard Mum say.

'Not for me, thanks all the same.' He lifted a restraining hand. 'I'm only here because I've been consolidating various statements that were taken yesterday.'

'Are you making progress? Or is that a tactless thing to ask?' Dad enquired, sounding less irritable than before.

'Sooner or later we always make progress,' the inspector said. 'It takes a lot of legwork and a lot of talking but we get there in the end. Is that accurate, Cordy?'

I raised my head and looked at him wide-eyed, innocent. If I told him now that what I'd said still wasn't absolutely true then he'd arrest me for withholding evidence. He might even think that I'd done something to Sandra myself – not that that seemed likely but one never knew.

'Yes,' I said. 'Shall I sign it?'

'You can use my pen.' He unscrewed it and passed it to me.

'Try and make it neat,' Mum said.

I wrote 'Cordelia Sullivan' in my neatest, roundest hand and gave him pen and paper.

'So what happens now?' Dad asked.

'The inquest is set for the beginning of next week.' Inspector Archer stood up, folding my statement carefully and slipping it into the sort of envelope that Dad got his tax demand in. 'In Bradford. The Coroner will read this and I'm pretty certain he won't need to call Cordy. It's all quite straightforward. I'll keep you informed anyway.'

'Do they know how –?' Dad bit his lip, frowning.

'Blow to the temple. No sign yet of the weapon.'

Mr French's son had lost his temper with her then. Perhaps Sandra had been cheeky and he'd clenched his fist and hit her too hard, or her skull had been too thin.

'Cordy, Inspector Archer's just leaving,' Mum said in the tone which meant 'Say goodbye nicely.'

'Goodbye,' I said, my mind still filled with a raised fist, a surprised-looking Sandra as she fell sideways, crumpling at the knees.

'Bye, Cordy.'

I went on sitting at the little table, telling myself that soon they'd find out where Sandra had gone when she'd walked away from me at the bus stop. Sooner or later the police always caught the criminal.

'I still think we could phone,' Mum said, coming back into the room.

'We can't go interrupting her work,' Dad said.

They were talking about Susan of course. They were nearly always either talking to Susan or about her when she wasn't here.

'If we haven't heard by this afternoon then I'm phoning any-way,' Mum said firmly.

'Do what you like.' Dad sounded tired.

'I'll wait a couple of hours.' Mum glanced at me. 'Cordy,

haven't you anything useful to do instead of hanging round here?'

'Why don't you go and do a bit in the garden?' Dad suggested. 'I may have an hour there myself later on.'

I wanted to go and see Fred and Fay but it didn't seem like a good idea to mention the Maitlands again.

'I'll go and tidy my bedroom,' I said virtuously.

'Put any washing you need doing in the basket,' Mum said as I went upstairs.

Mum had already made my bed and folded my shortie pyjamas into the fluffy teddy bear nightdress case which had been a pretty babyish present for an eight-year-old even back then, I thought, forgetting that at the time I'd liked it.

Downstairs I could hear the clattering of cups. Then water gushing out of the tap. Then Dad clumping into the back garden. Apart from his not going into work this was turning out to be a Saturday like any other. If I'd been the one who'd answered the advertisement then where would I be now? I wasn't sure I believed in heaven or hell in spite of Scripture at school. It seemed to me that nobody was quite good enough to go to heaven or quite bad enough to go to the other place.

I lay down flat on the bed, closed my eyes and crossed my arms over my chest. My name was Josie White and I was dead; my name was Sandra Pirie and I was dead. My name was Cordy Sullivan and I could feel my leg twitching.

I sat up, went over to the wardrobe and opened the doors. There was a long mirror on the inside of one of the doors and I stood looking at myself as I'd watched Susan looking at herself. Turning this way and that, trying a haughty expression or a smile. When I tried it I merely looked silly. But I would need a bra soon! When I played hockey at school I fancied that my chest jiggled a bit when I ran down the field.

'Cordy, what on earth are you playing at?'

I'd been so intent on my own reflection that I'd not heard her coming up the stairs.

'I will need a bra soon, when school starts again,' I said, meeting her eyes in the glass. 'I'm not a kid any more, really I'm not.'

'Cordy, I really don't understand you any longer,' Mum said. 'Two of your friends have died and all you can do is stand in front of the mirror and admire yourself! It shows a real lack of feeling! Really it does! I'm not saying that Sandra was the ideal friend for you to have but she deserves some respect surely? You'll get a bra when you're fourteen. That's the correct age whatever these silly fashion articles say. Now comb your hair and come down and help me get dinner. And don't go talking about underwear in front of your father. He's disappointed enough in your behaviour already!'

She went downstairs again with the quick, pattering steps that betrayed her annoyance. I combed my hair, decided that if I'd sat down and wailed she'd've ordered me not to be such a crybaby, gave the teddy bear nightdress case a punch, and followed her into the kitchen.

The meal was a silent one. Our meals never were very lively anyway, I reflected. Dad liked to enjoy his food without children chattering, and Mum always preferred hearing how his day had gone rather than listening to what I'd been doing.

'It's no good, John!' Mum cleared the last of the dishes and gave Dad a determined look. 'Our Susan's bound to have heard something by now. I can't make out why she hasn't rung.'

'You were the one said she was old enough to live in a flat and be an independent young woman. You can't expect her to be ringing home every day, especially now she's got this PR job for a couple of weeks,' Dad said.

'I'll try the hotel.'

'You said you wouldn't call unless it was an emergency.'

It was a waste of time, I thought. Mum nearly always went along with what Dad said but when she dug in her heels there was no shifting her. I could hear her talking in the sitting-room in the rather posh voice she used on the telephone.

'So what d'ye plan to do this afternoon?' Dad asked me. 'Feel like going somewhere with your old – what?'

Mum had come in from the sitting-room. She had a queer, blank look on her face.

'She's not there,' Mum said.

'Maybe she's working this afternoon or she's gone out to do a bit of sightsee –'

'She's never been there,' Mum said. 'I spoke to the manager. He said she's not registered there.'

'He made a mistake then. Did you give the correct name?'

'Of course I gave the correct name!' Mum said on a little flare of temper. 'I'm not likely to give the wrong name, am I? He'd never heard of a Susan Sullivan!'

'Then you rang the wrong hotel,' Dad said calmly. 'It's easily done.'

'I rang the hotel where our Susan's staying,' Mum insisted.

'Did she give you the number?'

'I got it earlier on from Directory Enquiries. I thought that if we didn't hear from her I might –'

'Then you took the number down incorrectly.'

'John, I'm not a complete idiot!' Mum said, flushing angrily.

'I'll try the college.'

Dad rose and went into the sitting-room with Mum at his heels. I heard his voice and the banging down of the receiver.

'Nobody there. Evidently the college is closed on Saturday afternoons.'

'Of course it is, dear. Susan told us that.'

'Then why let me ring the place? What about her flat? Her room mate will know where she's staying.'

'Melanie – I'll ring her,' Mum said in a tone of relief.

I hung about in the kitchen, tipping the chair up and down, hearing Mum's voice becoming quick and excited.

'Well?' Dad sounded impatient.

'Melanie's gone home for the weekend,' Mum said. 'That was the landlady. She has the flat underneath, remember when we went to see –'

'Then you got the wrong hotel,' he repeated.

'You were there when we saw her off on the train, John! I heard the name quite clearly – suppose something's happened?'

'Let's suppose nothing of the kind,' Dad said briskly. 'If there'd been a train crash –'

'John, don't!'

'If there had been we'd've heard. I think you're worrying unnecessarily, honestly I do!'

'I'm trying to remember the name of the company she's got the holiday job with. Can you recall it?'

'The Wells Something or other. She was chattering so much that I didn't catch half she – Hand me the directory. I'll look through it.'

As usual they were making a fuss about nothing, I decided, letting the chair legs hit the floor with a little bang. They pretended that Susan had left home and was independent but the truth was that they fretted about her more than they'd ever done when she was living here.

'Cordy, will you stop tipping that chair!' Mum appeared in the doorway.

'Sorry,' I said.

'Did Susan mention the name of the company to you?'

'I haven't talked to Susan for ages.'

Mum pushed back a straying lock of her hair and gave me a what on earth are we going to do with you? look.

'There doesn't seem to be a company of that name in the directory,' Dad said, coming to the kitchen door.

'It wouldn't be in the local directory,' Mum said. 'It's a London outfit.'

'It must have a branch up north otherwise why recruit temporary help from Bradford?'

'I think we ought to go over to Susan's flat!' Mum said. 'We can talk to the landlady; she's bound to have a key to the place. John, I just can't settle until we know something. Cordy?'

'Do I have to come?' I said. 'I hate being shut up in a car on a Saturday afternoon. And you know I get car sick.'

'She'll come to no harm for a couple of hours,' Dad said.

'Well . . .' Mum hesitated.

'I could go and play with Melanie Deacon,' I said.

'Yes. Yes, that's a good idea. You can bring her back here to play for a bit if you like and then we'll phone just before we start back.'

'And don't get into any mischief,' Dad added.

They talked to me sometimes as if I was about seven years old, I thought, as I promised solemnly not to get into mischief.

I think they'd've made more of a fuss about leaving me behind but they were too worried about Susan to be worried about me too. I watched them drive away and waved cheerfully.

Seeing that I'd said I'd play with Melanie Deacon then I'd better traipse over and invite her back, I supposed. Melanie was a neat, clean girl who had no imagination at all though she did awfully well at gym. However with Josie and Sandra gone I'd better make up my mind to turn her into a friend.

I went upstairs to put on a clean skirt – Mrs Deacon being the kind of woman who noticed things like that. There'd be a service for Sandra the next morning, I thought, though she hadn't often gone to church. Would the vicar give out the same sermon? He wasn't likely to have a stock of them specially for girls who got themselves killed.

I sat down on the end of the bed and stared gloomily at the patterned rug on the floor. The truth was that I didn't want to make any new friends. It was too soon and it made me feel disloyal to Josie and Sandra. I hadn't had time to start missing them yet but in any case I had the Maitlands now.

Sooner or later I'd have to let Mum meet them. I'd need to prepare the ground very carefully because if Mum heard about Holly Jane in reality or saw Edward she'd never let me go up to the old Tyler house again. And if I couldn't do that I'd die. I knew perfectly well that my life would be ruined. I might put on a white dress like that American lady who had written poetry and never never leave the house again. Never leave my room again.

I could picture the people coming into the village and getting out of their cars to take photographs of the house and the window behind which I would lurk invisible, clad in white.

'She hasn't left her room in twenty years,' they would say.

In twenty years I would be thirty-two going on thirty-three. I couldn't picture myself as that old. All I could think was that by that time I'd've probably grown out of the white dress. That made me giggle and the more I tried to stop the more I giggled, until I suddenly heard myself sobbing and I didn't really know why.

I was washing my face in the bathroom when the telephone rang. I grabbed the towel and ran downstairs.

'Cordy, it's Mum. Look, we've decided to go down to London on the train and find out what's happening. We'll leave the car at the station. Is Melanie with you?'

'She's in the garden,' I said.

'Are you all right? You sound funny.'

'I just ran to answer the phone.'

'Ask Melanie if you can stay over at her house. Unless you'd like us to drive back and pick you up to come with us, but you'll be very tired.'

'And car sick,' I reminded her.

'Well, you can't stay there all alone. Ask Melanie if her mum'll mind having you overnight. We'll be back in the morning.'

I called loudly across the empty room.

'Melanie, is it all right if I stay at your house tonight? Mum and Dad are going to London. Yes. OK. I'll tell them! Mum? Melanie says yes. Her mum was going to ask me to stay over anyway. I hope you find Susan. Bye.'

I hung up before she got it into her head to have a word with Melanie. Normally she would've insisted on ringing Mrs Deacon but it was a measure of her anxiety that she hadn't thought of that.

I hadn't actually promised to go and stay with Melanie. I hadn't actually promised to play with her come to that. I was sorry they were worried about our Susan but it had given me a whole evening and a night and what remained of the afternoon in which I could please myself.

I went back upstairs and put on my nice summer dress which had a pattern of little yellow daisies and a yellow cardigan in case it got chilly and I put on clean white socks and strap sandals and because I was being more disobedient than even my parents could imagine I left my room very very tidy and closed the windows and bolted the back door and left the key under the mat and even carefully shut the gate before I took the moorland track.

The world was drying up in the late afternoon sunshine. The grass was rising, freed of the raindrops, and there was a mist of gold-glinted purple where the heather tumbled to mate with the greeny yellow gorse. When I grew up, if I never married, and I couldn't see myself wanting to marry anyone or anyone wanting to marry me, then I could live up on the moor. Perhaps Fay and Fred would let me have a wing of the Tyler house for my own. I would come down of course into the village to check on my parents every day.

I envisaged Mum and Dad as old and frail, but in my mind Fred and Fay would still look exactly the same.

When I reached the high flat rock I scrambled on to it and looked over to where I had seen the searchers combing the ground and the tip of the police tent, but they were no longer there. Only the old cow grazed peacefully in a hollow of mellow sunlight.

I jumped down and went on towards the house. As I went up the drive I found myself wondering if Fay knew now about Sandra. Probably not since she didn't seem to venture very far without Fred and he would've taken good care that she hadn't seen the police activity on the moor.

'Cordelia! this is a lovely surprise!'

Fay came tripping down the front steps, a light caftan patterned with green leaves fluttering around her. She was all vitality today, the fair curls springing about her face as if each one had a life of its own. She held out both hands in a way that might have looked artificial in another person but with her was translated into warmth and welcome.

'I'm not interrupting, am I?' I asked.

'You always say that and the answer is always no! Come in! We have almost finished your room.'

I went with her into the front hall. All the panelling had been polished and the scratches removed from the surface of the wood and the licking tongue of red carpet had been cleaned and matched by tall red flowers in a copper jug at the foot of the staircase.

'They're not real,' Fay chatted, catching my admiring glance at them.

'Plastic?' I thought uncomfortably of Mrs Pirie senselessly watering her garden.

'Silk! Fred bought them for me ages ago to cheer up the winter – not that it's winter yet but our own flowers won't be ready until next year. You see! We are making plans for next year already. It's not often we can manage to do that!'

'They look lovely,' I assured her.

'Have you come for tea? Do say that you have! We have masses of food. Fred buys in bulk from Bradford to save having to go down into the village. You've probably noticed we are very private people?'

'I like private people,' I said.

'Because you're a private person too! Come into the drawing-room and have a glass of lemonade. Fred! Fred, guess who's here?'

'Our friend Cordelia,' Fred said from the head of the stairs.

'How's Edward?' I asked.

'Having a nap. He's cutting his back teeth so he's been a bit fretful. Fred, shall we have some sticky buns with our lemonade? You'd like that, wouldn't you, Cordelia?'

'Sticky buns coming up!' Fred came down the stairs and went down the passage.

In the drawing-room swathes of cool blue material had been hung at the windows and more scarves added to those already pinned against the walls.

It looked like Aladdin's Cave, I thought, and sank down in luxury on the long sofa. Fred came in with the tray, a white chef's hat on his head.

'For Madame and Mademoiselle?' He put the tray on a side table.

'Who are you being?' Fay demanded.

'Monsieur Gaston at your service, mesdames!'

'*Enchantée!*' Fay cried. 'Shall we invite Monsieur Gaston to sit down and have some sticky buns and lemonade with us?'

'He'd like that. I don't suppose he gets paid very much,' I said.

'I labour for love alone!' Fred removed his hat which threatened to slide over his glasses and began pouring the fizzy yellow liquid.

'How long can you stay?' Fay asked, nibbling round the edge of an iced bun.

'As a matter of fact . . .' I hesitated, then went on. 'My parents have gone down to London overnight to see my sister – she has a holiday job down there. They were rather hoping . . .'

I left the sentence unfinished.

'They've given you permission to stay overnight!' Fay put down the bun and clapped her hands together. 'That's marvellous! Isn't that marvellous, Fred?'

'Your parents didn't object?' Fred looked at me.

'They didn't object at all,' I said, truthful in the letter if not the spirit.

'We are having sausages and mash and tinned peas for dinner,' Fay informed me. 'And lots of brown sauce. Or do you like tomato? Have we got any?'

'I love brown sauce,' I said.

'And a kind of whipped thing with bits of lemon in it. You must be psychic, Fred, because you made far too much for just two of us!'

Memory is a strange thing. Some days – whole days sometimes – stay in my mind with absolute piercing clarity. Others become blurred and confused when I try to recapture the exact sequence of events. So it was on that Saturday evening. I remember when the sound of Edward's crying – was there a time switch in his back? – sent Fay upstairs to change his nappy and I remember how she carried him downstairs and let me hold him while she and Fred went off to put sheets and pillowcases on my bed. I remember how we laughed as we squidged the brown sauce into the peas and mash and nobody said a word when I put both elbows on the table. I remember that we spent a long time looking through Fay's seed packets, arranging them in the pattern she planned for next year's garden, and I remember her taking Edward up to his cot, expressing the hope that he would give us all a peaceful night's sleep. I can't recall exactly what we talked about or why the jokes seemed so hilarious.

'Does Fay know about . . .?'

I do remember saying that when she had taken Edward up to bed.

He shook his head, pushing his glasses up on his nose.

'There was no need to upset her,' he said. 'Fortunately she never listens to the radio and we don't buy any newspapers so it's easy to shield her. I take it they haven't arrested anyone yet?'

'Not yet. I think there's going to be a special church service tomorrow morning like there was for Josie. Will you –'

'I think not.'

He spoke with a kind of dignified finality.

I think Fay returned then and nothing more was said.

I do remember that the evening wrapped itself around the house like a soft lavender shawl that stole the colour from the vivid scarves and muted the last arrows of the dying sun.

'Bedtime I think, ladies?' Fred came in with mugs of hot chocolate.

'It has been a long day,' Fay admitted.

'And the night may be interrupted if Edward's teeth begin to hurt. Will you do the honours?'

'Yes, of course. Are you going to work?'

'I may do a little.'

'On your book?' I asked.

'Routine translation work I'm afraid.' He grimaced slightly. 'I don't get much time for my own book.'

'Poor Fred doesn't get much time for anything because so many other things demand his attention,' Fay said. 'He used to take the most wonderful photographs, Cordelia! Not just use the camera but develop them himself! They were greatly admired. Weren't they, Fred?'

'I haven't used a camera in a long time,' Fred said. 'Drink up, ladies!'

We drank up and then Fay took my hand and went with me up the wide, shadowy staircase to the upper floor where the gloom was dispelled by occasional lamps set into the walls or perched on half-moon tables in the corners.

My room had been painted and a green rug lay on the polished floorboards beside the bed. There were green curtains patterned with daffodils at the window and a vase crammed with dried green grasses on the chest of drawers.

'Would you do me the most enormous favour?' Fay asked.

Her voice sounded tentative.

'Yes, of course,' I said promptly.

'Would you wear Holly Jane's nightdress?'

She was holding it across her arm and now she bent and spread it over the yellow and green patterned cover on the bed. The pattern showed through the fine white cotton with its bands of lace threadwork.

I remember looking at it and suddenly feeling chilly.

'I miss her so much,' Fay said softly. 'Would you . . .?'

She hadn't seemed to notice that I'd arrived to stay overnight without so much as a toothbrush.

'Yes,' I said. 'Yes, I'd like that.'

'I won't look.' She made a prim mouth and turned her back.

I undressed quickly in case she turned round suddenly and pulled the white lacy garment over my head. It was slightly too large for me, its sleeves falling over my wrists and its scalloped hem covering my toes. Under my bare feet the rug felt soft and prickly at the same time.

'Ready?'

'Ready,' I said.

Fay turned and looked at me. I thought for a moment she was going to cry and stiffened in embarrassment but she only said. 'Her hair, I think, was darker than yours. Goodnight, Cordelia. God bless.'

She went out and closed the door softly behind her and I stood looking at my reflection in the mirror on the back of the door. Cordelia Sullivan wearing white as I had imagined but somehow being Holly Jane.

I waited until I'd heard a door elsewhere close and then I took off the lacy shroud and pulled on my vest and knickers and the rest of my clothes and became myself again, the nightdress neatly folded and placed next to the vase of dried grasses on the chest of drawers.

There was a hot water bottle in the bed and somehow that reassured me more than anything else could have done though I wasn't really conscious of being in need of any reassurance. I flicked off the switch on the side of the wall lamp and curled up under the covers.

This was the first time I had slept in a house that didn't contain either my parents or someone else's parents. I wasn't prepared for the silence which was underlined rather than mitigated by the sighing of the wind as it rushed through the heather and gorse and twisted the limbs of the thorn tree a little more.

I heard once the sound of Edward crying and then feet tapping along the gallery and then silence again save for the wind.

When I woke next the room was full of greyness and the hot water bottle was lukewarm and rubbery to the toes. It wasn't quite dawn and the sky beyond the open curtains was still spiced with dark clouds but I could see the outlines of things quite clearly, and the wind beyond the window had a different sound.

There was another sound. I could hear someone walking on the gravel under the window. Crunch! Crunch! Crunch!

I pushed back the covers and tiptoed to the window and looked down, pressing my nose flat against the glass. Fred was marching up and down on the gravel strip. Up and down. Up and down.

I was about to open the window and call down, 'Hi, Fred!' Then he made a smart about-turn and stood staring straight ahead, and I moved back to the bed and huddled there, because even with his glasses and thick pullover and gardening trousers and heavy boots that went crunch, crunch, he hadn't looked like Fred at all.

161

10

I must have gone back to sleep because the next thing I knew was Fay tapping at the door.

'The water's hot and I put towels out for you! Take your time. We're going to have a proper Continental breakfast in your honour today.'

Her footsteps tapped away across the landing. The crunch, crunch of Fred's marching feet assumed the semblance of a dream not fully remembered.

The bathroom wasn't a place where we'd played very often, being a chilly cave painted a kind of vomity green with a dingy bath and a marble washstand with rusty taps. Someone – Fred I guessed – had cleaned everything and polished the taps and put a striped rag bathmat on the floor but the walls were still a vomity green and the place had a dank, musty feeling about it.

I had my bath, though it was rather a quick one because while I was soaping myself I suddenly recalled that one game we had played here was Brides in the Bath, Sandra having nicked a paperback about the case. We'd made Josie be the victim and Sandra had been the evil husband and I'd been the maid who discovered the body, the husband's girlfriend and the detective, but half-way through the game we'd got scared because the cistern had suddenly gurgled and a thin stream of brownish water, which Sandra swore was blood, had oozed from the taps.

I got out rather hastily, dried myself on the big towel that hung over the rail, and scrambled back into my clothes. I ought to have pulled out the plug and wiped round the bath in the way that Mum insisted but the room seemed a long way from the other rooms in the house and I went downstairs.

Fred was singing in the kitchen, rather loudly and without much tune but his voice sounded reassuring and when I stepped down into the kitchen I saw that he was cutting bread, letting the pieces fall neatly to left and right, never ceasing the quick, slicing motion as he looked up and smiled at me.

'Did you sleep well, Cordelia?' he enquired. 'Some people find it hard to sleep in a strange bed.'

'I slept like a log,' I said, feeling cheerful again because everything was normal. 'I'm afraid I forgot to empty the bath.'

'Don't worry about it. I'll see to it later. Fay is just seeing to Edward.'

'Fay has seen to Edward,' she announced, coming in. 'He's having a nice little nap. Shall I get out the chocolate?'

'For breakfast?' I said in surprise.

'It's very good for the digestion,' Fred said. 'Gives you energy.'

'It also tastes wicked,' Fay said. 'I love wicked-tasting food.'

'Ice-cream with caramel sauce,' Fred said, starting to butter the bread.

'Smoked salmon and peanut butter!' Fay cried.

'Together?' Fred asked.

'Probably separate,' she agreed.

'Chicken cooked in brandy with baked potatoes bursting with butter!' Fred said.

'Lobster patties!' I supplied, having had one once at a party.

'Yuk!' Fay said, making a silly face. 'Chocolate mousse!'

'The eggs are ready,' Fred said, bringing us down to earth.

We sat at the kitchen table as we had sat on that first evening as if we were completing a circle and ate hard-boiled eggs and bread and butter with a thick layer of plum jam on each slice and slabs of dark chocolate broken into irregular pieces, and drank coffee with cream lying thickly on the top.

'What are we going to do today?' Fay asked.

'I have to go home,' I said regretfully. 'Mum and Dad will be home.'

'Perhaps they've gone off somewhere for a second honeymoon – to Paris or the South Sea Islands?' Fay suggested.

I considered the notion but decided that my parents were highly unlikely to be so obliging.

'Anyway, I might get on with my book for an hour or two today,' Fred said.

'Have you finished the translating work?' Fay enquired.

'Sending it off in a couple of days. You must have something nice when the money arrives.'

'Edward needs a little coat for autumn and – Cordelia ought to have something too! What would you like, Cordelia?'

'I don't want anything,' I said, embarrassed.

'How about a nice dressing-gown for when you come and stay over?' she said.

'That'd be lovely but –'

'A dressing-gown it is then,' Fred said, suddenly brisk as he rose from the table. 'Green? Yes, green would be nice. Now we'd better get on.'

'Fred is in a working mood – a writing working mood,' Fay said to me. 'He has so little time in which to write and then the book itself takes a great deal out of him. Some days he can only manage a couple of sentences, can't you, Fred?'

'And sometimes more.' Fred was brushing crumbs into the palm of his hand.

'I'd better go,' I said, and got up from my seat.

'So Fred will be writing and Cordelia will be going home and Edward is having his nap,' Fay said. 'What shall I do, Cordelia?'

She asked the question as if I was the grown-up and she was waiting for instructions.

'Maybe Edward would like someone to read to him while he's napping,' I said.

'That's a splendid idea! Poor Edward mustn't be allowed to feel left out,' she exclaimed. 'Thank you, Cordelia!'

She whisked out of the kitchen, her airy caftan floating behind her.

'Thank you for having me,' I said politely.

'You know you're more welcome than anyone else I can think of,' Fred said.

'See you soon!' I said and went through the half-open back door into the yard.

Not until I was at the end of the drive by the front gates did I think of looking at my watch. A silver one that Mum and Dad had given me for my twelfth birthday – gold was for twenty-one and even Susan hadn't got one of those yet. It was past ten o'clock. It couldn't be, I thought, tapping the watch face and holding my wrist close to my ear to check on the ticking.

It was like old legends, I decided, where time stopped or ceased to count when you were in a particular, enchanted place. I wouldn't have been too surprised if I'd reached the village and found only ruins of some long-past civilisation.

Nothing of the sort happened, of course. Instead I saw Dad's car parked outside the house with a police car behind it.

'Cordy! I was just going to ring Mrs Deacon.' Mum had opened the front door. 'Inspector Archer wants a word with you. Hurry up!'

There was nothing for it but to walk up the path and join my mother in the hall. She delayed a moment to brush imaginary grime off my skirt with her hand before giving me a little push in the direction of the sitting-room. She hadn't been back very long, I thought, because she still had her high-heeled shoes on and her eyes looked tired as if she'd been awake all night.

Dad looked tired too, shielding his face with his hand, a cup of tea at his elbow. The inspector was seated at the table and Sergeant Ackroyd was perched rather uncomfortably on the window ledge.

'Where's Susan?' I asked, and thought guiltily that I hadn't spared her a thought while I'd been up at the Tyler house.

'She wasn't at the hotel,' Mum said. 'We were just going to ring the police when they arrived. You have to find her, Inspector. It's driving me crazy not knowing –'

'We have to keep calm, Mary.' Dad shifted his hand and spoke heavily.

'It's no good telling me to keep calm!' Mum said, her own voice so tight that it seemed about to splinter. 'I'm worried to death and so are you if you'd only admit it! We went everywhere, Inspector! Knocking up hotels in the middle of the night –'

'Useless exercise,' Dad put in.

'I was so sure she'd be there, maybe in an hotel which had a similar name. In the end we caught an early train back and decided to report her missing – we could have done that before and saved ourselves a journey, but I was so sure –'

'Susan would be terribly cross if you sent the police looking for her,' I said.

'Do you know where your sister is, Cordy?' the inspector asked.

I shook my head.

'Sit down and keep quiet then,' Mum said. Her face was very cross.

I sat down meekly on the nearest chair, wishing I hadn't come home.

Inspector Archer leaned forward slightly, his manner quietly friendly.

'At the moment we've no reason to believe that anything's happened to your daughter, Mrs Sullivan,' he said. 'She's entitled to go where she likes without supervision. On the other hand you tell me that she hasn't travelled far alone.'

'Only to Bradford and when we agreed to let her move into a flat we helped take her things over. I wasn't in favour of her leaving home but my wife felt a bit of independence wouldn't hurt her.'

'You can't blame me for this!' Mum said sharply. 'We both agreed that she accept the holiday job. You can't turn round now and –'

'You said it was a PR job with a company called Wells?' the inspector put in.

'Wells and Cholmodely. I couldn't remember that second name. We can't find a phone number in any of the directories. It's just a holiday job but she was hoping – we were both hoping that it would lead to something more permanent when she finishes her course. She was chosen to represent the college on a pamphlet, you know.'

'I didn't approve of that either,' Dad said. 'It gives young girls the wrong idea – you can't be too careful these days.'

'We'll check on this firm,' Inspector Archer said. 'There won't be anyone there today.'

'Her room mate went home for the weekend and when we phoned her she said she didn't know any more than we did.'

'You saw her off on the London train?'

'On Wednesday evening. It was her first visit to London and we wanted to give her a bit of a send-off. We expected her to ring when she arrived but we haven't heard a word since.'

'You expected her to ring, John. I told you the train would get in very late and she'd be busy from then.'

'May we have a recent photograph of her?' Inspector Archer asked.

'She had one taken ready for the pamphlet. It's to advertise the various courses the college offers. She gave me a copy on Wednesday. You won't – I don't want to lose it.'

'I'll make sure you get it back, Mrs Sullivan.' He took it from her, looked at it for a moment, then put it carefully away. 'Pretty girl! Does she have any special boyfriend?'

'She hasn't any boyfriends yet,' Dad said. 'Well, not in the sense you're meaning the term. Eighteen is the age we regard as suitable for romantic goings on. Anyway Susan's a sensible girl. She wants to get her City and Guilds before she starts courting.'

'She could've gone to friends for a few days.'

'Then she'd've told us!' Mum said in an irritable little burst. 'She said she had a holiday job. She wouldn't tell us that if she was spending a few days with a friend. Our Susan doesn't tell lies, Inspector!'

'And I don't see the point of these endless questions,' Dad said. 'Surely you ought to be out there making enquiries!'

'We've been looking into the Grant case,' the inspector said.

'But surely . . .?' Dad looked at him.

'That was eleven years ago,' Mum said. 'Cordy was just a baby and Susan a tiny girl. I don't see what that has to do with our Susan!'

'Nothing at all probably. Cathy Benson was only nine. She was a pretty child judging from the photographs I've seen.'

'I didn't know her,' Mum said. 'Not personally that is. There were more children in the village then but several people moved into town – more convenient for work and shopping I suppose. Wasn't she found . . .?'

'Where Sandra Pirie was found. Yes.'

'Everybody knew that Larry Grant had done it,' Dad said soberly. 'It really isn't wise to let people like that wander at large in the community. Oh, we never thought there was any harm in him –'

'I did!' Mum said. 'The moment I saw him trailing after the children when they went off to the sweetshop – he had a funny look in his eyes. I never allowed Susan to play out of the garden. I blame the parents myself. Fancy leaving a child of nine to play with someone like that and not keeping a close eye on her.'

'Larry Grant confessed anyway, didn't he?' Dad looked at the inspector.

'Yes. Yes, he made some kind of a confession but it didn't really stand up to close examination. His father got a top lawyer in and we were obliged to let him go. We being the police. It was before my transfer here.'

'But he hanged himself.' Mum sounded puzzled.

'Oh, it was suicide all right. He had wit enough to realise that he was only out on police bail and enquiries were still being made. It seems to have been a nasty affair.'

'But that's past,' Dad said. 'Inspector, my daughter is missing now. And there was Sandra and –'

'Cordy, why did you go to French's Photographic Studio?' Sergeant Ackroyd asked.

I think we had all forgotten he was there so that his dark brown voice sounding in the midst of us made us jump. I shot up my head and stared at him, wondering confusedly if all the blood was really draining from my heart.

'What on earth are you talking about?' Mum said. 'What studio? Where?'

'Cordy is going to tell us,' Inspector Archer said.

'I don't know what you mean.' I could hear my voice gasping and I stopped.

'You know exactly what I mean,' the inspector said. 'You went to Bradford on Thursday morning, didn't you?'

'Of course she didn't –' Mum started to say. 'Mrs Pirie came round to ask if we knew where Sandra was and then Cordy went out to play.'

'She got on the bus and went into Bradford,' Sergeant Ackroyd said.

'No, I didn't!' I said.

'Cordy, you've been identified –'

'Mrs Simmons never saw –' I stopped, stared at the penetrating dark eyes boring into mine and heard myself whimpering.

'Don't let's have a crying jag,' the inspector said wearily. 'It doesn't get us anywhere. You weren't seen getting on the bus, Cordy, but a motorist has come forward to report narrowly missing a child who came hurtling out of Saddle Street on Thursday. He was puzzled because Josie White had run out of

168

the same street. Anyway he thought it worth reporting. Now, please let's have the whole truth this time.'

'I think a policewoman ought to –' Sergeant Ackroyd began.

'I don't want any old policewoman,' I said sullenly.

'Cordy!!' Dad looked imploringly at Inspector Archer. 'I must apologise. My daughter has been better –'

'No offence, Mr Sullivan,' the inspector said easily. 'When people are scared they often say things they wouldn't normally say. If you don't want a policewoman, Cordy, you'll have to put up with me. You did go to French's Studio, didn't you?'

I sat mute, listening to the thudding of my heart.

'Cordy?' He spoke my name gently.

'Yes,' I said.

'Did Sandra tell you that she was going there?'

'You're just putting words in her mouth –' Mum began indignantly.

'Yes,' I said, and then more loudly, 'Yes!'

'She told you she was going there?'

'I promised not to tell.'

'So you promised first to make out that you and Sandra had gone to the cinema together and come home together. And then you admitted that Sandra had gone off by herself. Why didn't you tell us the whole truth?'

'I got muddled up,' I said desperately. 'I broke my promise a bit but then – I didn't want to be arrested for holding back evidence. Anyway that's why I went to French's Studio.'

'Cordy, I cannot believe you could be so disobedient,' Mum said. 'You know perfectly well that you're absolutely forbidden to go anywhere out of the village by yourself. Inspector, I hope this didn't make a difference to that poor girl?'

'Sandra Pirie was killed sometime on Wednesday evening, Mrs Sullivan. Cordy was watching Doris Day at that time.'

'In French's Studio?' I asked in a small voice.

'We reckon so. Cordy, what exactly did Sandra tell you?' He leaned forward with his eyes fixed firmly on me. 'I know you promised her but promises can't count when someone's been killed. What did Sandra tell you?'

'She answered an advertisement in the newspaper,' I yielded. 'It wanted models for a teenage magazine. She – wanted to make some money so she could buy her mum a surprise present.'

169

'Oh, dear Lord!' Mum said and began to cry softly.

'Was this the advertisement?' The inspector had taken a cutting from his pocket.

'Yes. She said that she'd rung up for an appointment or written. I can't remember which. She gave a false name – Tara something.'

'Why on earth didn't you tell us this before?' Dad was staring at me as if he didn't recognise me any longer. 'Why tell a pack of lies?'

'The studio has been rented out over the last few years to a Mr French,' Sergeant Ackroyd put in, 'but the son of the original owner has been in Australia these last ten years since shortly after the old man died.'

'Coming to Josie . . .' Inspector Archer paused and looked at me.

I thought of the note left in the cleft of the wall that I'd flushed down the toilet. They could take me to the police station and torture me, but I'd never tell about that!

'Did she . . .?' Mum was wiping her eyes.

'It looks as if she went there too,' he nodded. 'She slipped away while her mother was shopping in Harvey's, got on the first Bradford bus and went – we believe to the studio. She was probably kept locked up there overnight, but either the man calling himself French decided to release her or she managed to struggle free. She was in a blind panic and ran under the wheels of the lorry. There's still a lot to find out.'

I was finding out things myself. Josie had had a lot more pluck and gumption than Sandra or I had ever imagined. I was sorry that we'd always made her be the unimportant person in our pretend games.

'And now our Susan's missing,' Mum said.

'I hardly think –' Inspector Archer began.

'She told us she was going to London on a holiday job. We saw her off on the train! Since then we've not heard one word and she wasn't at the hotel or any other with a similar name and we can't get in touch with the firm if it exists! And instead of looking for her we're wasting our time talking about other girls,' Dad said.

'If you'd rung us last night instead of rushing down to London yourselves then we do have the resources to make enquiries more speedily,' he said.

'I panicked,' Mum said. 'It was my fault, Inspector.'

'The point's academic,' Inspector Archer said.

'Cordy, did Susan say anything to you?' Mum asked abruptly.

'About her holiday job. Did she tell you anything at all? If she made you promise not to say anything –'

'Susan never tells me anything,' I said.

'You're sure?' The inspector looked at me.

'Yes, I'm sure!' I said loudly. 'Our Susan never said anything to me about anything at all, and I never gave her any promises! And if you go on asking millions of questions then I want – I want a solicitor!'

'Cordy, don't be so cheeky,' Dad said.

'She doesn't mean to be,' Mum leapt in with. 'She's had a lot on her mind recently what with losing two of her best friends and then the new girl getting run over.'

'New girl?' Sergeant Ackroyd had raised his head.

'The Maitlands who just took the old Tyler house. I haven't actually had the chance to meet them yet, but Cordy got quite friendly with their little girl – Holly Jane, wasn't it, Cordy?'

'You should've checked them out before letting Cordy play with her,' Dad said. 'I told you so at the time.'

'John, I was going to but there was the business about Josie and then Susan getting the holiday job and the memorial service and then Josie's funeral – and then we heard the Maitland child had been killed too. I can't be expected to see to everything, John!'

'These Maitlands lost a daughter too?' The inspector's eyes were very bright. I lowered my own, desperately trying not to shake.

'In – Scarborough, wasn't it, Cordy? She was staying with an auntie or something, you said. I ought to have gone up with condolences or an offer of help or something, but I was run off my feet with everything else. I did send up some flowers.'

'The Maitlands haven't been into the village since they arrived,' Dad said. 'A mite stand-offish if you ask me.'

'I don't suppose that they felt much like socialising after what happened and so soon after they moved in too.'

171

'A terrible thing to happen,' Inspector Archer said slowly.

'One can only be thankful they've still got the baby,' Mum said.

'Is something bothering you, Cordy?' Sergeant Ackroyd asked.

'Will she get into trouble for not telling you everything about Sandra in the first place?' Mum enquired anxiously.

'Withholding evidence is an offence, Mrs Sullivan,' Inspector Archer said. 'However, in view of the circumstances, I can promise you no further action will be taken. Cordy, this Holly Jane –?'

I heard myself give a small, stifled shriek.

'What's the –' Dad looked at me.

'There's a wasp on the light shade,' I said.

Mum, who was allergic to wasp stings, echoed my shriek on a louder note and backed towards the door.

'I can't see any wasp,' Dad said.

'It's crawling round the fringe. Up there!'

Sergeant Ackroyd rose ponderously, exchanged glances with his superior and suddenly clapped his hands high in the air.

'Got it!' he said and sat down again, raising an eyebrow at me in a way I would have called sardonic had I then known the word.

'About the Maitlands –' Inspector Archer resumed.

'Do you think our Susan went to French's Studio to pose for a magazine?' I asked.

'She went to London,' Dad said. 'We took her to the station.'

'She might've got out at the next station and come back,' I argued.

'About the Maitlands,' Inspector Archer said.

'Yes?' I eyed him warily.

'This child they've just lost. Holly Jane you said?'

'Holly Jane Maitland.'

'You've been going up to the house to play with her?'

'Actually more with the baby, didn't you, Cordy?' Mum said.

'Holly Jane went to Scarborough?'

'To stay with her auntie,' I said.

'Is something wrong?' Dad said. He sounded uneasy and bewildered.

172

'It's only that when house-to-house enquiries in connection with Sandra Pirie were being carried out,' Sergeant Ackroyd said in his ponderous way, 'Mr Maitland said there were only himself and his wife in the family. His wife was asleep at the time so the constable didn't speak to her.'

'Holly Jane had been run over by then,' I said.

'He didn't mention that to the constable,' Sergeant Ackroyd said.

'He didn't want to make the policeman uncomfortable!'

'He didn't mention a baby either.'

'A baby isn't a real child,' I said. 'Not really!'

'Mr Maitland said that he and his wife had no children.'

'But Cordy's been playing with the baby, haven't you?' Mum said.

'His name is Edward.'

'Has anyone seen this baby or the girl who was run over?'

'Edward was staying with his auntie too,' I said. 'He was! Then Holly Jane got run over and they fetched Edward home.'

'But if Holly Jane was away – Cordy, you told me that you were going to play with her when you went up there,' Mum said.

'I'm welcome there any time,' I said. 'They consider me to be a most tremendously interesting person.'

'One is tempted to agree,' Inspector Archer said.

I knew the word for that tone all right. It was sarcastic.

'And they have – had two children?' Mum said.

'Holly Jane was run over when she was staying with her auntie,' I said doggedly. 'By a motor bike. She was!'

'Surely you can check this out?' Dad said, looking at the two policemen in a rather helpless way.

'Oh, we'll certainly check,' Inspector Archer said.

'You can't!' I said.

'Why not?' He fixed me with a long steady look.

'It would upset them terribly. Fay – Mrs Maitland is delicate.' I put my hands together, weaving my fingers tightly. 'She has nerves, awfully bad nerves. She doesn't go out very often – like nuns, you know. Because of the other children, you see. Eloise and – and Linnet. She lost them and she can't bear to be reminded. They neither of them can!'

'You're saying the Maitlands have lost more than one child?' the inspector said.

'Why on earth didn't you tell us about it?' Mum said.

'Because it's just another silly made-up story,' Dad said. 'Cordy, you have to stop this!'

'I'm not making it up!' I insisted. 'Fred – that's Mr Maitland – he told me about them. They were burnt up in a fire a long time ago. I didn't make it up, honestly!'

As if in answer to my voice the telephone rang shrilly. For a moment we all stared at it. Then Mum moved slowly and lifted the receiver as if she was in some kind of dream.

'Hello? Yes. Oh, how are you? I wanted to thank you for – I don't understand. She – what? But surely she – I see. Yes, there must have been some mistake. No, of course not! Very sad. Yes. Goodbye.'

She put the receiver back into its cradle very slowly and turned to look at me.

'Mary?' Dad said.

'Where did you stay last night, Cordy?' Mum asked.

'With – Melanie,' I said.

'That was Mrs Deacon, Melanie's mother,' Mum said. Somehow I knew what was coming next. 'She wanted to know if you'd like to go over for tea. She says she hasn't seen you for the last couple of weeks.'

The room was silent. Had there really been a wasp there, the fluttering of its wings would've sounded like a hurricane.

'Where did you sleep last night?' Mum asked, her voice suddenly rising. 'Don't dare try to get out of this one, young lady! Where did you sleep?'

'We never leave her alone in the house overnight,' Dad said. 'In fact we very seldom go out, do we, Mary?'

There was a picture in our school library which some old pupil had donated probably because they didn't want it any longer. It showed a little boy in a velvet suit standing in front of a row of men in dark clothes with two girls in long, frilled dresses peeping round the door. Underneath the picture was written, 'When did you last see your father?'

I knew exactly how that little boy felt now as they all stared at me.

'I went up to the Tyler house,' I said.

'And stayed over with people we don't even know? I can hardly believe it,' Dad said.

'I didn't want to go and stay with Melanie,' I said. 'She isn't really a friend of mine.'

'She didn't come over to play here yesterday then?'

It felt as if Mum had suddenly become the police.

'I – no,' I said flatly.

'And you went over to spend the night with people we hadn't even met? Why on – why didn't you say something? How dare they assume that –?'

'They thought that you knew,' I said loudly. 'Fred – Mr Maitland said they'd love to have me stay but I had to ask my parents first. It wasn't their fault.'

'But with strangers – anything might have happened,' Dad said.

'Well, it didn't!' I said. 'Nothing happened at all. I had a room to myself and I had a Continental breakfast. They haven't anything to do with what happened to Josie or Sandra. They wouldn't have given me a Continental breakfast if they were bad people.'

'But you should've said something.' Mum sat down on the arm of Dad's chair.

'You wouldn't have listened,' I blurted. 'You were too busy worrying about our Susan. You never listen to me! You only notice me when I'm tipping chairs! You don't see me! You don't see anybody except our Susan!'

'Someone taking my name in vain?' Susan said from the doorway.

Outside a taxi that had arrived unnoticed even by the sergeant drove away.

'Oh, thank God!' Mum said faintly. 'Thank the dear Lord!'

'It said in the newspaper that Sandra Pirie had been found dead,' Susan said, putting down her suitcases. 'I decided to come home. The front door is open, Mum. Did you know?'

'I've been worried to death,' Mum said, hugging Susan hard.

If I'd gone missing and then turned up she'd've reminded me to wipe my shoes on the mat.

'About me? I'm fine, Mum, honestly. I was just alarmed when

I read about Sandra. What happened?' Susan said, disengaging herself.

'It's a long story, love. Are you sure you're all right? What about the job?'

'It didn't work out,' Susan said lightly.

'I don't understand. And the hotel – you must've got the name wrong. Cordy, let your sister sit down! She's been on a tiring journey,' Mum said.

I slipped thankfully from my seat.

'There wasn't any PR job, was there?' Dad had risen suddenly, standing between me and the others. I couldn't see his face but I could see his fists clenched at his sides. 'You weren't staying at the hotel either. You've been off with some man, haven't you? Haven't you?'

'She's home!' Mum said. 'That's what matters. Who cares about any old PR holiday job? We've been that fretted, love, not knowing – working you all those hours and no job in the end.'

'There never was any job, was there, Susan?' Dad asked.

'I'd really rather not talk about it just now,' Susan said in a careful polite little voice.

'Looks as if we shall have to call off the bloodhounds,' Inspector Archer said cheerfully. 'I'm delighted to see you're safe and well, Miss Sullivan.'

He was back on the other track, ready to continue his investigations, to nail any lies still floating about.

I slid along the wall into the hall and through the front door, ducked lower than the garden wall in case Sergeant Ackroyd was looking through the window and reached the bottom of the moorland track and then I ran faster than I knew I could run up towards the gates of the old Tyler house.

11

Imagination can distort memories. When I look back now, trying to see myself as I was then, I look down a long passage and see a figure gilded by time into a slender child with an idealistic nature. I look at my past self with sympathy. And sometimes, now, walking along the street I catch sight of some other girl, hurrying through her own life, eager to be grown up, and fancy that I know how she feels. It's only an illusion. I never can fully recapture Cordy as she was then. I can never catch up with that figure at the end of the passage in my mind as she scrambles up the steep track, varied emotions churning inside her.

The picture I conjure up is slightly blurred around the edges. I can see the old house, scarcely changed in outward aspect today so many years later, and I can smell the wind as it scythes through the heather and the yellow buds of gorse, but I find myself not looking at the Cordy I was but inside her again, racked by emotions too complicated for a child to understand.

I was breathless by the time I reached the gates and there was a stabbing stitch in my side before I slowed down momentarily and then gathered speed again, dashing round to the back of the house and arriving, scarlet-faced, in the conservatory where Fred was potting some plants and Fay sat at her ease in a wicker chair, humming a tune and weaving an invisible web with her fingers.

They both looked up as I skidded to a halt just inside the french windows.

'Oh, how lovely!' Fay spoke eagerly, her restless fingers stilling. 'I was just thinking that we required a third person to liven us up and you come on your cue! Isn't that marvellous, Fred?'

'Have you run all the way, Cordelia?' Fred enquired, looking at me.

'We have fizzy lemonade,' Fay said. 'Shall we have some?'

'There isn't time,' I got out, feeling the piercing of the stitch grow less.

'There's always time for lemonade,' Fred said amiably, then

paused, set down the pot he was holding and said, 'You haven't been running for fun, have you? What's wrong?'

'The inspector –' I said, feeling my breaths slowing down. 'He knows about Holly Jane and Edward – well, not everything. He knows that Holly Jane was run over and that Edward went to stay with his auntie – Mum let it out. I didn't tell, honestly!'

'You told the police about our children?' Fred said slowly.

'No, I – Mum said she'd sent flowers and that I'd been playing with Edward. They were at our house asking questions about Sandra and – I didn't tell! I don't break promises, I really don't. But Inspector Archer will come here. I know he will! He wants to clear everything up neatly. The police are like that.'

'They're coming here?' Fred was staring at me.

'I'm positive they will,' I said. 'Inspector Archer keeps on coming back until he's got answers. You can tell him that it's just pretend, can't you? It's not against the law or anything. He wouldn't say anything to anybody else. I'm sure he wouldn't!'

'But we couldn't possibly tell anyone,' Fay said.

She was looking up at me with a blank, terrified look in her eyes.

'But he'll find out,' I said. 'He's the kind of person who goes on and on until he finds out everything. When he finds Holly Jane – after you buried her the man took the flowers and put them on Sandra.'

'But we never buried Holly Jane,' Fay said, clutching at one bit of what I was saying.

'But you said – on the moor near the thorn tree –' I stammered.

'We had a funeral,' she said. 'It was beautiful. Fred spoke the words and we laid the flowers but we don't go round digging up the countryside.'

'Then where is she?' I said in bewilderment.

'Holly Jane is in the once was,' Fay said. 'Isn't she, Fred?'

'But you have to show them!' I argued. 'They won't mind about Holly Jane. They just want to find out what happened to Sandra.'

'Who is Sandra? Is she anybody we know?' Fay enquired.

'She's dead,' I said bluntly.

'Like Holly Jane. Did she have a funeral too?'

'Fred, the police will come here again – to check up!'

I turned to him appealingly but he was looking at Fay. Behind the glasses his eyes did rapid calculations.

'Fay, dear one, go upstairs for a while,' he said.

She rose in a flurry of caftan from the wicker chair and looked at us both, her fingers pleating the thin material of her skirt.

'Fred, what's going on?' she asked uncertainly. 'Why are the police going to come here? I don't like this game, Fred.'

'Everything is going to be fine,' he said. 'You go upstairs now, dear.'

'For how long?' She looked confused and unhappy, like a child left out of a party.

'Not for very long. Go on now.'

'Will there be lemonade afterwards? Cordelia needs some.'

'Yes, of course. Sticky buns too,' he said patiently.

'Don't be too long then.' She patted his arm and drifted out.

'Fay is – not very well today,' he said, looking after her. 'I think you ought to go home again, Cordelia.'

'If you tell the police that it was a pretend game, just to make Fay feel better about the children who were burned up,' I urged, 'then the police will go away again. You won't have to move on!'

I don't know what he would have replied because at that moment we heard brisk footsteps down the side of the house and Inspector Archer came round the corner.

Even though he was, as usual, in a grey suit with a dark tie you could never mistake him for anything other than a policeman, I thought.

He walked through the open french windows as if someone had invited him to tea, and gave me a little nod of amused recognition.

'Hello again, Cordy. You can run like the wind when you've a mind, can't you?' he said pleasantly.

'You are . . .?' Fred looked at him.

'Detective Inspector Archer. You'll be Mr Maitland?'

'Fred,' I said.

'We haven't met before,' the inspector said, ignoring me. 'However, you had a visit from one of my officers, I believe?'

'In connection with the poor child who was found near here. Yes indeed.' Fred gestured to the inner door beyond which the

179

drawing-room lay, its vast expanse reaching the front of the big house.

'After you, Cordy,' Inspector Archer said.

If he fancied that I was going to run away then he had another think coming. I walked with some dignity into the drawing-room and sat down on an upright chair near the door.

'Do sit down, Inspector.' Fred motioned to the sofa but the other stayed on his feet.

'I don't expect to trouble you for long, sir,' he said.

'What can I do for you, Inspector?' Fred took the arm of the couch. 'As I told your officer when he called, my wife was not feeling well and was taking a nap, but in any case there was nothing useful I could tell him. We neither of us knew the girl.'

'This is merely a technical point to set the record straight.' Inspector Archer was completely at his ease. 'In our business we do a lot of rather tedious double checking. You and your wife only just moved into the district, I understand?'

'We've rented the house, yes.'

'May I enquire your line of work, sir?'

'Translations for various academic bodies.'

'You're by way of being a linguist then? I envy you. Schoolboy French is my only other language. What tongues do you speak?'

'French, Polish, Czech, some Latin,' Fred said.

'German?'

'That too. I don't see –'

'I just wondered,' the inspector said. 'I understand there are only your wife and yourself living here?'

'Only the two of us,' Fred said.

'So if I were to tell you that we've received information about the presence of two children here you'd say we were misinformed?'

'I would say your officer made a mistake, sir,' Fred said.

'Always possible, but the officer noted that you had distinctly told him that your family comprised only your wife and yourself. He didn't actually speak to your wife.'

'I believe she was taking a nap at the time,' Fred said. 'Fay isn't very strong. Another reason for our choosing a rural existence.'

'Yet we have received further information to the effect that you have two children,' Inspector Archer said thoughtfully.

'There must be some mistake,' Fred said.

'Even so.' The inspector's dark eyes were steady and probing.

'Holly Jane and Edward aren't exactly children like you mean children,' I said helpfully.

'Holly Jane and – who?' Fred looked at me.

'You can tell the inspector about them,' I encouraged. 'He won't say anything. He won't!'

I stopped because Fred was simply looking at me, face blank.

'What on earth is the child talking about?' he said.

'Cordy here assures me that your daughter, Holly Jane, was killed recently in a traffic accident in Scarborough and that you have a baby called Edward.'

'I cannot imagine what put that into her head,' Fred said, and rose as feet pattered across the hallway and Fay came in. 'Darling, the inspector here has the most extraordinary – he seems to think we're hiding away two children.'

Fay had paused just within the door. All the quicksilver sparkle had fled from her face and the caftan looked less colourful.

'We only have a visiting child,' she said politely, making a tiny motion of her head towards me. 'You are . . .?'

'Inspector Archer, Mrs Maitland. We're making enquiries into the death of a local girl –'

'We haven't met any children except Cordelia,' Fay said.

'And you have no children of your own?'

The green eyes moved to Fred and then moved indifferently back to the inspector.

'There's only Fred and me,' she said.

'They aren't exactly children!' I said heatedly. 'Edward is – well, he's unusual. If you showed him to the inspector –'

'I'm afraid that Cordelia's been weaving fantasies again,' Fred said. 'She is rather a lonely little soul and she's apt to spin tall stories.'

I remember having the strangest sensation as if the room was turning upside down and we were all four standing on our heads – no, not all of us. I was still the right side up but everything and everybody else was turning around me, assuming unfamiliar angles. I heard myself say, 'But you can show Edward to the inspector! There's nothing wrong about having a baby like Edward. There's no law! You won't have to move on!'

'I've no intention of moving anywhere,' Fred said. 'I wish that you'd stop this nonsense, Cordelia. You're wasting everybody's time!'

'But you have to show Edward to the inspector!' I was on my feet and half crying now. 'I'm not telling lies or making him up. I'm not! He's a teddy bear, Inspector. He's just a teddy bear! We pretend him like we pretended Holly Jane, because of the children who were burned up. Why don't you show him Edward?'

Fay was just standing there looking at Fred. He had taken a step away and was shaking his head. The room was filled with odd, distorted angles.

'You're becoming a nuisance,' he said coldly. 'We've made you welcome and you repay us by telling lies.'

'It's not lies,' I cried. 'Mum sent flowers –'

'You've not been telling these stories to your mother, have you?' Fred said.

'I think that's enough, Cordy,' Inspector Archer said.

He sounded sorry for me.

'There is a teddy bear! There is!' I said passionately. 'His name is Edward and Fay feeds him cereal – not feeds. Pretend feeds – he doesn't really eat it. Holly Jane was a pretend too but I didn't find out right off. She had to die when I started coming here before they knew they could trust me and Fay cried and said there were onions in the stew –'

'I don't think I need to trouble you further, sir,' Inspector Archer said.

He had the look of a man who has almost completely lost patience and is holding in the last remnants of good humour with great difficulty.

'I don't understand,' Fay said. 'Who has been killed?'

In the end there was no loyalty in the grown-up world, not even in the world where Fred and Fay lived. In a moment the inspector would arrest me because by this time, in his opinion, I'd told too many lies not to be arrested.

I turned and ran into the front hall and up the stairs, sobbing as I tore open the doors of room after room. All the places where we had played our games, Sandra and Josie and me; all the rooms that little by little were being changed to fit in the Maitland universe.

There was no sign of Edward anywhere. Some part of me guessed that this kind of thing had happened before – the rumours, the questions, Fay's play-acting in obedience to Fred's instructions. I couldn't understand any of it but I knew I wasn't completely a liar.

I could hear footsteps below and Fred's voice raised angrily.

'Cordelia! Come down at once!! How dare you –?'

Edward was in a cupboard in a small room with the pram in it. He sat in the darkness with a nappy on and a bib round his neck, and I turned the key in his back as I flew along the gallery to the head of the staircase.

I'd picked up something else as well, bundling it and the bear together. It spiralled darkly shining over my arm.

They were in the hall staring up at me. I held Edward aloft by one leg and cried in triumph, 'I found him! She hid him in the cupboard. I found him!'

And Fay drifted to the newel post and clung to it as she called anxiously, 'Do be careful, Cordelia! Fred, tell her! She's hurting Edward!'

It was too late for her to try and mend the secret Eden.

'It's a teddy bear!' I shouted in fury. 'A stupid, stuffed teddy bear! And this is all that's left of Holly Jane, I suppose! What did you do with the rest of her? Did you chop her up and throw bits of her into dustbins? Did you?'

I threw the long dark wig down and Fay caught it, her hands outstretched, her face suddenly glowing though there was at that moment no ray of sunlight in the hall.

'Fred, it's Holly Jane,' she said. 'Oh, Fred, I prayed you'd change your mind!'

'For pity's sake –' Fred took a step towards her but her voice ran on.

'Holly Jane can come alive again. It was all a terrible mistake, Inspector. The doctors thought she was dead but she was on a life support machine and she made a miraculous recovery. Look, Fred! Holly Jane's come home.'

She had pulled on the wig over her own short fair curls,

pulled it on with the ease of long practice and, turning briefly, showed for a second the profile I had glimpsed on that first evening when I'd looked up at the round window and seen –

'See? I'm all better now.' She pirouetted very slowly, the long dark hair whipping across her face. 'Good as new! Is my new bedroom all painted? In pink? I love pink, you know.'

'Take the wig off,' Fred said in a tired, flat voice. 'Holly Jane's dead. We decided it was best.'

'She's not dead,' Fay pouted. 'I won't be dead!'

'Not before strangers, my dear. You know the rules,' Fred said.

'But they're not strangers,' she cried. 'We never ask strangers into our house, do we? So they're friends and I'm not dead.'

She wanted to turn the world right side up again but it was too late. It was all smashed and spoiled.

'You're not Holly Jane!' I shouted. 'I thought she was a big doll you could bury but she's only a wig. And this isn't a baby. It's a stuffed bear!'

And I flung him down the stairs and stood tremblingly as he turned over and over and landed with an obscene squashy sound in the hall.

Fay gave a long cry, like a howl heard in nightmare, and sank to her knees beside the stiff little shape. His crying sound that had woven like a threnody through the brief interchange of words stopped abruptly.

'Edward? Edward!' Fay's howl shaped itself into words. '*Mein Gott!*'

'Fay! Remember the rules,' Fred said, but she picked up the bear, cuddling him close, and turned her face up to him.

'He's dead,' she said quaveringly. 'His little neck is broken, Fred.'

And Fred stopped and raised her, holding her as she cradled the bear.

'Poor little chap,' he said.

'It was very sudden. You know how he loves crawling on the stairs. Was it my fault, Fred?' she asked.

'It never was,' Fred said.

'My other children burning. I can still smell the burning,' Fay said. 'Their bones were all mixed up with the others. I couldn't even lay a flower or ask someone to say Kaddish.'

'We shall have a funeral,' Fred said.

'Shall we, Fred? Like the other funerals, with beautiful words and much weeping?'

Her voice was eerily eager.

'Like all the others, *liebchen*,' Fred said, and they went slowly towards the kitchen together, her head leaning against his shoulder, the long dark hair floating over his supporting arm.

'You'd better come downstairs,' Inspector Archer said quietly.

My hand clung to the banister as I shakily descended.

'I wasn't telling lies,' I said.

'I know.' He sounded weary.

'I never meant to spoil it all. I never meant to hurt Edward.'

'I know that too, Cordy. Come along home now.'

Unexpectedly he put his arm round my shoulder as he led me from the house.

I don't think we said anything at all as we walked down the drive and along the track. There didn't seem to be anything left to say.

'Tell your parents that I'll be along later today,' he said when we got into the street. 'There's a lot of legwork for us to do.'

I nodded, wondering if the questions were finally done, and he climbed into the police car where Sergeant Ackroyd was already sitting and went off in a burst of exhaust smoke.

Our front door was still open. I went in reluctantly, bracing myself for a scolding, but I needn't have worried. Dad was in his armchair and lifted his eyes from his newspaper only to say, 'No more running about all over the countryside, young lady. Understood?'

'Understood,' I said gratefully, and went out of the room and up the stairs again.

Susan and Mum were in the big bedroom. The door was ajar but though I couldn't hear any words they were clearly having a very long conversation.

I closed the bedroom door and sat on the edge of the bed. It wasn't over yet I knew. Fred and Fay would be questioned and their lives turned inside out, and Inspector Archer would be back later. At least he knew that not everything I'd told him was a lie now, but I didn't care about his good opinion. I craved the

185

enchantment that Fred and Fay had offered, until they turned traitor and in betraying me toppled their own world.

'Dinner's ready,' Mum said, rapping sharply on the door.

I'd lived a whole life since breakfast time.

'I'm not hungry,' I said.

'Now don't be silly, Cordy! We all have to eat,' Mum said, opening the door and putting her head in. 'This has been a very worrying time for us all, and the best thing we can do as a family is pull ourselves together and act normally. So we won't say one word about you running out of the house like you did or about Susan's job coming to nothing. We'll go down and have our dinner and –'

'Lunch,' I said.

'Dinner. Lunch. Whatever you call it it's lamb chops and minted potatoes. You're lucky to get that because I'm worn out with all the rushing about on trains and there wasn't time to do the beef so I can't think what your father will say! Wash your hands and face and don't forget to pull the chain. Susan! If you know what's what you'll put on that longer skirt. You know your dad's views on the subject!'

Susan, emerging from the other bedroom, shot a knowing look at the back of Mum's head. Then she looked at me.

'We'd better go down and act normally,' she said.

I thought that nothing would ever be quite normal again. In the course of a few days everything had changed. Susan was wearing more make-up than I'd ever seen her wearing before and her face looked – harder somehow, her eyes more deeply set. There was something about her that reminded me of Mrs Pirie suddenly.

'I've a taxi coming at four o'clock,' she said.

'You're going back to – London?' I questioned.

'No, back to the flat. It'd drive me crazy staying here.'

'Dad'd run you back,' I said.

'He's wasted enough time running round on my business,' Susan said with a little laugh. 'Time I grabbed some independence! Come on!'

Was she really going to the flat or was she going somewhere else to meet some man or other? I knew that I'd never ask and she'd never tell me.

'Come along, girls!' Mum had on her cheerful, let's pretend that nothing bad ever really happens face.

Dad had folded his newspaper and was already in his seat.

'Pity about the beef!' he said.

'Darling, there simply wasn't time!' Mum said, apologising as she dished up the chops. 'I can cook it for tomorrow if you like.'

'Sunday is beef day.' He frowned at his plate.

We ate in silence except for Mum who kept up a series of trivial remarks to which nobody paid any attention. Only once did Susan speak and then she sent me a sympathetic look and said, 'Bad luck for you about Sandra.'

'No point in mulling over sad events,' Mum said. 'Inspector Archer said he'd be back later on to let us know what's happening.'

'I thought we were going to have a nice family meal and set other things aside,' Dad commented.

'There's no dessert,' Mum said.

'Surely there's a bit of cake left?' Dad looked as if he had just heard famine was imminent.

Mum cut what was left of a lemon cake and handed it round, big thick slice for Dad, medium for Susan, thin for me, the merest sliver for herself.

Susan got up without being asked and made some coffee. We always had coffee on Sundays.

'I'll wash up,' I said, feeling as if I was acting in a play that had been going on for years in which everybody spoke their lines without even thinking about them.

'Try not to smash up too many,' Dad said, making his usual joke.

Nobody had mentioned the Maitlands or asked whether or not I'd lied about their having children. It felt as if someone in the family had cancer and it had been agreed that nobody should say anything about it.

'That's my taxi,' Susan said. 'I'll get my case.'

'It's the police car again,' Mum said.

'Don't they know it's Sunday?' Dad said irritably.

Mum went to open the front door. Inspector Archer was by himself, looking as if he'd just stepped in from some other play.

'I'm sorry to interrupt your afternoon again,' he said.

'Would you like some coffee, Inspector?' Mum asked too brightly.

'Nothing for me, thanks, Mrs Sullivan.' He did take a chair though, his eyes moving round from one face to the next.

'Did you go up to the Tyler house?' Dad asked.

'Cordy, you'd better –' Mum looked at me.

'I'd like her to stay,' the inspector said.

'Well, do the Maitlands have children or not?' Dad wanted to know.

'Two. At least it seems Mrs Maitland had two children,' he said. 'She was married before. A couple of toddlers.'

'And they died?'

'At Dachau. In the furnaces there.'

'My God!' Mum put her hand up to her mouth. 'Oh, my Lord! John, did you hear that?'

'What was – what you said?' I asked.

'Dachau. A concentration camp. You won't have heard –'

'We did a bit about it at school,' Susan volunteered. 'It was a very long time ago though, wasn't it?'

'Nearly twenty years. Mrs Maitland – that wasn't her name then – was in her early twenties. She lost her entire family there. Somehow she came out alive. She'd met Fred Maitland there and they got together after liberation. There were never any more children.'

'But the girl – Holly Jane?' Mum looked puzzled.

'Invented, just like the baby, Edward.' Inspector Archer glanced at me. 'Their way of staying sane, you understand. When their odd behaviour began to attract comment anywhere they simply moved on. Cordy didn't know at first what was going on. Then she promised not to say anything. That's a promise she felt obliged to keep.'

'They got her to tell lies, you mean,' Dad said.

'They admitted her into their secret. She was trapped. Anyway, I've had a long talk with Mr Maitland.'

'But what about Josie White and Sandra?' Susan demanded. 'Could they have had something to do with –?'

'Enquiries are still progressing,' the inspector said. 'Their alibis for the requisite periods appear to be non-existent. We shall certainly be seeing them again. Police investigations are necessarily slow but we get there in the long run.'

'Fay and Fred wouldn't hurt children,' I said on a breathless note.

'One hopes not, but the abused can become the abuser.'

'But they weren't abused surely. According to the newspaper –' Dad leaned over to pick it up.

'No, Josie and Sandra weren't abused. An odd feature,' the inspector mused. 'Anyway that's it for now. I wanted to set your minds at rest about Cordy. She was desperately trying to keep her promises.'

'You'll be seeing Mr French's son now?' Mum asked. 'I know he's supposed to be abroad but travel's so much quicker these days.'

'We'll certainly be bearing him in mind,' he agreed. 'I'll see myself out. Apologies again for intruding on your Sunday. Cordy, it might be wise if you made fewer promises in future, especially when they involve telling lies.'

Mum went with him to the front door.

'Dachau!' she said softly on returning. 'Those poor people! How terrible their memories must be.'

'Not in front of –!' Dad glanced in my direction.

'I've heard about those camps!' I said indignantly.

'But there's no need to dwell on the horrors of the past,' Mum said. 'Your dad's quite right, Cordy. Least said –'

Outside a car drew up.

'Looks like my taxi.' Susan was on her feet, picking up her suitcases. 'Do I get a fond farewell or what?'

'I take it that if your mother rings up this evening you will be in the place where you say you're going?' Dad said.

Susan turned a hard little face towards him.

'If I wasn't watched and spied on and cross-examined all the time,' she said, 'then maybe I wouldn't need to –'

'Now we agreed to say no more about that!' Mum said in a fluster. 'It was a misunderstanding, just a – it's only that we worry about you, Susan. You know that we do!'

'I'll be fine, Mum. See you, Cordy!'

Susan mouthed a kiss at me and went out.

'It comes to something,' Dad said heavily to nobody in particular, 'when a father can't show some natural concern about his daughter.'

'Wave from the window, John!' Mum said, coming back in. 'You know we always wave.'

The two of them stood and waved. They went on waving until the taxi had disappeared down the street.

'She waved back,' Mum said with satisfaction, turning round. 'It's not in our Susan to bear grudges.'

It seemed to me that they were the ones who ought to have a grudge since they'd been scared out of their wits because Susan hadn't told them the truth.

'She's not eighteen until February.' Dad sat down again. 'I'd always imagined her bringing home a nice local boy at the right time.'

'They grow up fast these days,' Mum said.

'Wanting to be adults before they've finished with childhood.' He looked sadly at me. 'I daresay that you'll be the next one. Wanting to wear nylon stockings and lipstick before we know it.'

'Wanting isn't getting,' Mum said grimly.

'Childhood's such a precious time,' Dad said. 'You grow up quickly enough as it is.'

'It seems to me,' I said loftily, 'that nobody in this family will let me grow up!'

'We'll treat you like an adult when you start behaving like one,' Mum said.

'Sneaking off to stay with people we don't know,' Dad said.

'Crazy people.' Mum thinned her lips.

'They weren't crazy!' I said indignantly. 'At least – Fred knew the children weren't exactly real. It was just like – suppose I died then you might get a doll or Mum might put on a wig and pretend – well, I bet you'd do something like that if our Susan got burned up in a fire!'

'That's a very wicked thing to say!' Mum said, trembling. 'Don't you dare try to upset me like that!'

'Sorry,' I muttered.

Nobody seemed to care that I'd been upset, that two girls I'd played with were dead and that Fred and Fay – I didn't want to think about Fred and Fay yet.

'I'll make some tea,' Mum said.

190

'Not for me, love.' Dad stifled a yawn. 'I feel like catching up on some sleep. We didn't get more than a catnap in the train last night.'

'Can – may I go out?' I ventured, without much hope.

'You may not,' Mum said flatly. 'After what's happened I don't know when I'll be able to trust you out of my sight again! All those lies! And me telling you to take up those flowers. They must've thought me a gullible fool.'

'They didn't! Honestly, Mum, they didn't. Holly Jane was a real pretend to them, don't you see?'

'Your own common sense should've warned you,' Dad said. 'They were only using you in their sick little games.'

'No they weren't!' I forgot the Maitlands' betrayal of me when Inspector Archer had arrived and spoke fiercely. 'They liked me. They liked me for myself. They did!'

'Don't contradict your father,' Mum said.

'I'm nearly thirteen. I've the right to an opinion of my own!'

'It seems to me,' Dad said, raising his voice slightly as his face got redder, 'that you haven't got many sensible opinions of your own! You're too easily led, Cordy! Letting that Pirie girl coax you into lying in order to cover up for her while she went swanning round in that skimpy red bikini like a blasted tart!'

That was when the world stopped for me. I saw everything in our bright, shiny sitting-room frozen, the family photographs seeming to leap from their silver frames, my father sitting down again too slowly for the movement to be measured.

'Dad, how did you know that Sandra was wearing a red bikini?' I asked.

Mum stood by the table, both hands over her mouth. Above them her eyes were bright and fixed, like Edward's eyes.

Why didn't Dad say he'd read about it in some newspaper or other? Why didn't either of them invent some casual, consoling lie?

Dad was getting up again and his face was old. Older than I'd ever seen it.

Mum took her hands away from her mouth and said, 'John.'

The way she spoke the name held more agony than I had ever imagined.

191

He didn't answer. He went past her to the door and pulled it wide open, and trod through the hall and opened the front door and went down the path and turned right towards the steep track that led up to the moor and the old Tyler house.

I must have moved though I can't remember doing so because I found myself at the front door, heard my voice thinly pursuing him.

'Dad? Daddy!'

Mum came to my side and put her hands on my shoulders and spoke into the air above my head.

'It's better so,' she said.

12

At the time I believed that was the end of childhood. It wasn't, of course, because you carry bits and pieces of childhood wherever you go. But as I stood at our front door and heard Mum's voice something inside me gave a little shiver and died.

I have wondered since if she guessed what was going to happen. In the moment I knew only that my impulsive question had killed something as surely as if I'd picked up a hammer and swung it at my existence.

Mum put me aside and closed the door. Incredibly her face and voice were completely calm as she said, 'We never get much time together these days, love. Let's have a game of Monopoly and a nice quiet evening.'

She had effectively closed the door on any further questions or revelations. I went and got out the Monopoly set and put out the board and put the cards and the flimsy pretend money in neat piles and found the dice, and we sat down to play with as much concentration as we would have shown had we really been bidding for Park Lane. With only two of us the game went on for ever. Twilight rushed down from the high ground and threw a blanket over the village and still we counted our pretend money and rented out little green houses and sighed with relief when we didn't have to go to jail. Darkness ate up the twilight and Mum said that I'd won and made us hot chocolate and told me that I'd better get to bed as there was a new week ahead.

It's a terrible thing to remember but I'd enjoyed our time together. I felt privileged because I'd had her undivided attention and Susan hadn't been mentioned once.

After I'd gone to bed I lay awake for a while, expecting to hear Dad's key in the lock or the ringing of the telephone. All I could hear faintly from downstairs was the sound of the kettle boiling as Mum brewed endless cups of tea.

Nearly forty years later I stand outside the wall of the old Tyler house. Through the cleft in the stones through which I have just squeezed myself I can see the rusted chains of the swing with the seat hanging sideways and nettles growing up towards the lichen that softens the outlines of the two fruit trees that never bore a second generation. Not far off is the twisted thorn tree, and I think not of my father but of Larry Grant whom I never knew, of his body swinging there and his parents moving away. I don't know who found him but I know who drove him to the knotted rope and the sharp thorns.

Villages can be cruel places. There is gossip and there are sidelong looks and significant nods and sighs and half-completed phrases. The Grant boy must've suffered greatly before he took that last walk.

I am thinking about the Grant boy because I don't want to think about Dad. I don't want to picture him walking up the steep track, leaving his life behind him, making his solitary way to the thorn tree and there taking off his belt and looping it.

The police came in the morning to inform us. They'd kept the Maitlands for questioning most of the night, taking everything slowly and gently, trying to separate fantasy from fact, eliminating them from the enquiries, and had the decency to give them breakfast and a lift back home when the questioning was done.

Somehow what happened the day after we played Monopoly is vaguer in my mind than anything else. I was sent upstairs while Mum was told and sometime later Susan arrived, red-eyed and subdued, and she and Mum hugged and left no room for me. There were newspaper headlines which nobody forbade me to read.

'Insurance Agent Child Killer' was the least lurid of them, and yet when I think of the tabloids these days I realise the publicity was relatively low key.

'We won't be driven out until we're ready to go,' Mum said proudly. 'We have done nothing to be ashamed of!'

She was a proud woman was my mum. She was questioned too of course, for many hours, admitting that on the evening she and Dad had seen Susan off on the London train he'd gone back to the office to clear up some paperwork, and then when they'd driven home he'd dropped her at the house and then driven off again saying he had business to attend to.

'I was worried because my daughter wasn't in the house though the lights were on and the door ajar, so I went into the back garden in case she'd gone out there for some reason. John – my husband – joined me there – he must've driven down the steep track. He said he'd been to see a client and I – I tried to believe him though it had crossed my mind that he might be having an affair. I was angry and puzzled and I was going to ask him what was going on, but then Cordy – my younger daughter – came in. She'd walked to the village to see if we were on the way. I told her that we'd both just got home. I couldn't start letting her know that I was worried about – well, there possibly being another woman, could I?'

She had given evidence at the inquest, her voice flat and clear, her face very pale under a small black hat. Funny to think of it now but people still wore black in those days.

I went to the inquest. Mum thought I ought to stay away but for once I insisted. I wanted to know, you see.

Susan came with me, seeing herself as the protective elder sister with her arm round me, her make-up subdued.

There were reporters there and photographers and everybody in Linton who could find a seat.

The Whites didn't come. I have never known what happened to them. Did Josie's dad simply find another shed in another back garden where he could stack away the bottles? By now he has probably drunk himself to death or so my cynical side tells me.

Mrs Pirie did come, wearing a black coat with a real fur collar. I can't recall her face clearly but I do remember the fur collar, and the high heels on which she swayed into court flanked by two strange gentlemen – friends, I supposed.

Susan was nice that day – especially nice because she was seldom nasty to me. She put her arm round me and hurried me away at the end after the Coroner, who wore his glasses near the end of his nose, like Fred, had given his verdict.

'While the balance of the mind was disturbed' is a compassionate phrase. It suggested that Dad didn't know precisely what he intended to do when he left our house and turned in the direction of the moorland track, but even then I knew that he was thinking very clearly.

I've come here to put a full stop to the affair, to make some sense out of what happened all those years ago. No, it hasn't haunted me down the decades. Life adapts itself to us. The child

Cordy is grown up now. I tell myself that fiercely but the truth is that ever since I drew up in the altered village I call Linton I have felt that child hidden in me now growing stronger, struggling to find a voice.

I look for a long time at the thorn tree and then I go back through the cleft in the wall and congratulate myself on my continued slenderness.

I stand for a moment looking at the swing with its clinging nettles and see in my mind's eye Holly Jane swinging on it with her long dark hair flying out in the breeze, and the sandpit that was never dug shapes itself with Edward making sand castles in the middle of it. Fay said they had gone into the once was but the truth was starker.

Holly Jane and Edward existed in the never had been, though I see them more clearly than I see Josie or Sandra. In this place I see them more clearly than I see my own children or the grandson I recently acquired.

I walk back towards the house, and the echoes of the past are all around me. Fay still throws crusts for the birds and sways to the music in her head and somewhere in the empty house the ghost of an old gramophone churns out the bell chorus of *Hansel and Gretel*. And Cordy watches and listens and is drawn into Eden.

The back door is ajar and the cracked and broken french windows offer no barrier to the casual visitor. One might expect to find graffiti on the walls and used needles and condoms in the weeds but the house has escaped that kind of ugliness. It broods quietly, seeming to stir within its bricks and stone as my remembered tread sounds on the unpolished floor.

For a moment I don't recognise him. He has retained his thick hair but it's silver now and there's a stout walking stick at his side. Then he looks up from the moth-eaten old sofa that still graces the drawing-room and his eyes are the same behind dark-rimmed spectacles.

'Don't get up,' I say quickly and cross the vast expanse of dusty floor to shake hands.

'Nice to see you again, Cordy – you don't mind if I use the old name?'

'No, of course not. It was good of you to come.'

196

'I'm not quite decrepit yet,' he says. 'In fact I have a shrewd suspicion that you regarded me as pretty ancient back then!'

'And I was very young,' I say.

'Nearly thirteen!' He smiles at me, displaying still good teeth. 'How scrupulous you were in small matters!'

'And such a liar in anything that mattered!'

'Don't be too hard on yourself!' He motions with his stick towards a chair, low and armless. 'You were in a difficult position. Wanting to be loyal and at the same time –'

'Terrified that I was going to be arrested for something or other.'

I sit down on the low chair and find myself meeting the intense dark gaze again.

'Nowadays it would be more scientific,' he says. 'DNA testing, improved forensic knowledge and techniques, psychological role playing – I'm glad I'm retired!'

'Are you enjoying your retirement?'

'I've been enjoying it for twenty years. I still do a bit of gardening and chair the Neighbourhood Watch Committee – not that anyone does much more than humour me!'

'You tracked me down,' I remind him.

'Did you know that your mother wrote to me about ten years ago?'

'Mum did?' I stare at him. 'She never said!'

'I read in your local paper about her death.'

'Three months ago. It was a heart attack. She'd had a couple of mild attacks before but the final one was very sudden and final.'

'I'm sorry,' he says.

'Better that than a long-drawn-out dying,' I say.

'She had, I think, a long-drawn-out living after . . .' He leaves the sentence delicately unfinished.

'She stuck it out in the village for nearly six months before she decided to sell the house and move south. This is the first time I've been back here since it all happened.'

'A great deal has changed. You're happily married?'

'Yes. Yes, I am. Two sons and a daughter – Mary Susan. She just had a baby.'

I can hear my smug, adult tone, catch his eye, and smile.

'Boy or girl?' he asks.

'A boy. Joshua. You?'

'My wife died a couple of years ago. Two sons, four grand-children, all plotting a surprise party for my eightieth birthday and wondering if they will manage to keep it a secret from me, for the next couple of years.'

We both laugh and I think fleetingly how strange it is that we should be seated here in this same room so many years later.

'You said in your letter . . .?' I prompt.

'That I would like to see you informally up at the old Tyler house. Yes.'

'You knew it was still unoccupied then?'

'From time to time there's talk of turning it into a youth hostel or a residential home,' he tells me, 'but the plans never come to anything. Now and then someone rents it for a short period but nobody stays. There are odd stories about it, of course –'

'There always were!'

'And I understand the occasional pack of ghost hunters camps out here for the weekend but nothing much happens except in their own overheated imaginations.'

'You didn't ask me to come all the way up here again just to talk about ghost hunters,' I say.

'No. No, I didn't.' He frowns slightly, looking at me over his spectacles before he says, 'You know, I never knew your father well. In fact I only met him on two or three occasions. He struck me as a decent man.'

'Yes. Yes, I know.'

'He didn't fit the profile of – the kind of man who abducted young girls and killed them. He was a family man not a loner; he had a steady job, a house, a car, a loving wife – did you never wonder why?'

'Sometimes,' I admit.

'After I retired it went on nagging at me.' He speaks thought-fully now. 'I did a little digging on my account long after the case was closed. You know he was the only son of elderly parents who died before he met your mother?'

'Yes. That much I know. He was ten years older than Mum,' I say. 'She was brought up by an aunt and they met just after the aunt died.'

'Did he ever tell you there'd been a younger sister?' he enquires.

'No. He never talked about his childhood. How did you –?'

'Just digging around during my retirement. I had time in which to indulge my curiosity. Yes, there was a sister – Sarah.'

'He never mentioned her. Did my mother know?'

'Probably not. The sister was delicate, couldn't play games, had to have a special diet. Died when your father was about ten.'

'I don't see what that has to do with anything,' I protest.

'Cordy, your father didn't molest Josie or Sandra. He only took pictures of them. Oh, he may have adjusted a shoulder strap here or pushed back a ringlet there but he didn't hurt them. He didn't touch them in any criminal way.'

'You talk as if there were other girls.'

'Over the years when he was renting French's Studio, taking photographs there when he was supposed to be working late at the office, there must've been many girls. The advertisement was only one way – towards the end – of getting subjects to pose for him. We found photographs in the old studio, you know. Literally dozens of them. Nothing very shocking. Young teenage girls, in coquettish poses. In most cases the face was out of focus.'

'Did you talk to any of the girls?' I ask. My mouth feels dry.

'There was no point. No charges would ever be brought and the girls themselves never made any complaints. They were in the cupboard under the sink in French's Studio, by the by – you didn't find them?'

I shake my head.

'I was scared,' I say. 'Sandra was missing and I was going to get into trouble for lying. I don't understand why he did it! I don't understand why he had to take photographs, maybe touch –'

'A shoulder, a suspicion of a breast – the subjects were young. I think he was never allowed to touch his sister. Oh, I can't prove it, but I can imagine it. Can't you picture it, Cordy? A noisy little boy who isn't ever permitted to run and jump with his sister or climb trees with her or do any of the things that boys like doing? Sarah was an invalid, not to be touched or teased. Wouldn't you agree that part of his childhood went missing and somewhere

199

deep inside he wanted that innocent contact after he'd outgrown the age when it would be appropriate?'

'Amateur psychology,' I say. 'What difference does it make now?'

'None I suppose. Merely the curiosity of a retired police officer has been half-way satisfied. He never set out to hurt them. That's the point.'

'And Josie wasn't really knocked down by a lorry and Sandra was never hit over the head and – the little child the Grant boy is said to have killed – was she –?'

'That we'll never know. Your mother never said.'

'My mother?'

I rise abruptly from the low chair and take a turn or two about the room. On one wall the rusted, tattered remnant of a silver lace shawl hangs limp against the discoloured wall.

'She wrote to me ten years ago. She gave me no instructions but I think she wanted you to know the truth one day.'

'What truth?' I demand irritably.

'I think you'd better read the letter for yourself.'

He takes an envelope out of his jacket pocket and hands it to me.

'I'll be in the garden,' he says.

He levers himself somewhat stiffly out of his seat on the sagging sofa and moves towards the door. He looks his age when he moves, his stick tapping. I hear it tapping down the passage towards the kitchen again.

I sit down again and take the letter out of the envelope. Mum's neat small handwriting leaps up at me with a date of ten years before on the right-hand side.

Ten years ago Robert and I were going through a sticky patch in our marriage, coming to terms with middle age and the astonishing speed with which our children grew up and became people instead of children. Susan had just divorced her husband and was off somewhere or other with her lover. We kept in touch spasmodically but her job took her abroad a lot and she had never had children. When she did come she brought exotic gifts and a fund of anecdotes and looked smarter and more well groomed than I can ever hope to be, but whatever closeness had existed between us had dwindled away down the years. Mum had just recovered from her first mild heart attack and had gone to the seaside to recuperate. Had the illness inspired her to write to Inspector Archer?

I read the letter slowly, hearing my mother in each matter-of-fact phrase.

Dear Inspector Archer,

By now you are, of course, retired and may not recall me since you obviously dealt with many other cases after the one in which my family and I were involved. Although the case was closed when my husband died I have always sensed that you were never completely satisfied with the conclusions reached at that time. I myself am not in good health at present and because I have prided myself on being a truthful and law-abiding woman I feel that I must write to you with the full story, though it will not help those who are gone.

I hope you will believe me when I tell you that my late husband was a good man. He loved his family and he worked hard to support us. Nobody can ever deny that fact. That he had another side to him I found out not long after we married. Physical intimacy, if you know what I mean, meant very little to him. He was what might be termed inhibited, the consequence of his upbringing perhaps though I never enquired. I myself have never found that part of human experience to be important save for the begetting of children. But we did love each other and our girls.

John had always taken a great interest in photography you know. When Susan and Cordy were small he was forever taking snaps of them, very good ones too. He might, I think, have become a successful photographer but his father had wished him to go into the insurance business and John would not have stood up against his father's expressed wishes.

I cannot say exactly when his love of children and his photographic hobby began to become an obsession, nor exactly when he rented French's Studio, giving as his excuse the overtime he was required to put in at work. I am convinced there was no harm in it. Nobody ever complained. No irate parent ever arrived on our doorstep. But some of the pictures he took were inappropriate without being obscene.

Sometimes I think he was born out of his time. He would have been happy in the Victorian age when shy, repressed men like Lewis Carroll found their greatest pleasure lay in being with young girls, in worshipping their grace and their innocence, in capturing it for all time on film. These days we always think the worst of men like that, don't we? Even thirty years ago there were whispers and rumours about men who liked to watch little girls playing, and these days it is unwise to cuddle a child or get into conversation in case someone misunderstands.

I never talked about it with him but we both knew that the girls he made friends with and took photographs of were not from Linton. I don't know how Josie White came to be at the studio. Perhaps she saw an advert and just turned up there with the idea of having an adventure. I do know that John must've been horrified when she did turn up. She knew him, you see. No, that's a lie. It's a lie!

We went to the theatre in Bradford the night that Josie White disappeared. We had dinner with Susan and then we went to the theatre. It was a treat for me because we seldom went out. The play didn't interest me very much and during the interval when Susan was getting drinks at the theatre bar John told me that Josie had turned up at the studio. He didn't know what to do about her. He thought of taking her home but then it might all have come out and at the least there'd've been gossip. I said that I'd see to it for him and I slipped out of the theatre. John told Susan that I'd gone to telephone Cordy to make sure she was all right. It isn't far from the theatre to the studio and I walk very fast.

Josie was there, locked in and becoming scared. Very scared. John had bought her chips and lemonade and told her to wait until he came back. I didn't know what to do. She'd started to cry and say she was going home and that meant she'd tell her mum that John had the studio. So I tied her hands together and put a scarf round her mouth – her own scarf – and I told her that it was a game. She was a stupid child. She let me do it. I meant to lock the door again but I'm a fair-minded woman and she deserved a chance, so I left the door unlocked. I'm a religious kind of woman, Inspector, and it seemed to me that if she managed to get out then that would be a sign that John's hobby had to stop, and if not – but I didn't have time to think about that. I had to dash back to the theatre as it was and even then Susan started asking where on earth I'd been because the play was almost over. I said I didn't feel too well and later on, driving home, I told John that I'd fixed things.

I think I meant to go back myself the next day but the house was in such a mess. It really needed a good cleaning. And by that time Josie had been reported missing. I simply didn't know what was best to do. And then the news came that she'd run out into the street and been knocked down by a lorry. She had taken hours to get her hands untied and pull down the gag.

It was an accident, Inspector, but I think it was a sign. Josie would have told about the studio and about John and me being there. When she finally found the courage to get out then Fate took a hand. She wasn't meant to tell, you see.

I pause here, anger filling my eyes, my fingers clenched on the edges of the letter. How could my mother have done what she did? How could she have made such a bargain with destiny? Josie might've suffocated or fallen down the steep iron stairs or – I shake my head and continue reading, the words sharp spikes now as the past unravels.

John didn't know about Josie still being in the studio. I told him that it was all fixed and he'd better stay away from Saddle Street for a few days. It was a terrible shock to him when his secretary reported having seen the accident. It was a shock for me too. I mean, you don't expect the finger of God to set everything right for you, do you? But I was sorry about Josie. There was no harm in her. I still wish that she'd never turned up at the studio, never taken it into her head to run off like that. We went to the service and both John and I went to the funeral. One must do the correct thing.

Sandra Pirie was a different matter. I never liked her much and it upset me that she and Cordy became so friendly. What happened that Wednesday evening when we saw Susan off to London was quite simple really. John told me a girl called Tara Fallon was coming to be photographed that same evening. We had a bit of an argument about it actually and that made me angry because we never disagreed, but I could see that his hobby was going to cause trouble, that it had to stop. And that wasn't fair because he never hurt them, only looked at them. Only photographed them.

Anyway I told him that I'd deal with it and he dropped me off at the corner and I went on up to the studio while he went on to Susan's flat. That Pirie girl was waiting, not someone called Tara Fallon at all. I knew that she'd not be fooled by talk of games so I just – I must admit that I lost my temper which is something I was reared not to do, and I hit her very hard. She slipped and hit her head on the corner of the dais where John liked to pose his subjects. It was an accident, almost like Josie's, but it shook me up. I went back to Susan's with some flowers I said I'd stopped off to buy – a good luck gift to celebrate her job.

After we saw Susan off at the station I told John what had happened. He was terribly upset about it. Anyway we went to the studio and found her still there. I had been half hoping that she might have got up and walked away, lost her memory or something. But she hadn't. She had on a bright red bikini under her clothes – most unsuitable for a young girl. We tied her hands and put her in the boot of the car and then I cleaned the floor of the studio and wiped the door knob and the stair rail. John said he'd got rid of all the photographs. I don't know whether he did or not. The police never said. We buried Sandra near the old Tyler house. We had to use an old spade we kept in the boot for when the winter comes and there are snowdrifts, and there wasn't time to dig very deeply. It was raining and the earth kept slipping away. John was in a dreadful state. I was quite worried about him. I was sorry about Sandra too even if I wasn't very keen on her. There was a posy I'd given Cordy for the Maitland child nearby. Maybe they'd just tossed it away but I put it on Sandra. Everyone deserves some mark of respect.

John promised he'd stop taking photographs. He never meant anything bad to happen to the girls, you see. He just wanted to capture their beauty and their innocence before the world spoiled it. When we got back the door was unlocked and the lights on but there was no sign of Cordy. We put the spade in the shed and then Cordy walked in. She'd gone out looking for us.

I'm afraid she behaved very badly when she lied to you about going to the cinema with Sandra. I couldn't say anything of course but I was disappointed in her. We brought our girls up better than that.

There isn't any more to say, Inspector. When Cordy heard John mention that Sandra had been wearing a red bikini, we knew then that she'd guessed, and John – he loved us very much, loved the girls too much to deprive them of both parents. And it was my duty to look after Cordy and give our Susan advice and keep the house neat and clean. A man could never have done that.

I wish you every happiness in your retirement. I am truly sorry the whole affair turned out as it did. There was never any intention to hurt anyone, but when duty demands one must act. Don't you agree?

Yours sincerely,
Mary Sullivan

I read the letter over again. I can't help myself. As I read I see it unravel in my mind, the way things happened. I see my dad horrified at finding Josie White on the doorstep of his studio, making some excuse to persuade her to wait there until he can tell my mother what has happened.

Mum, I think, was always the stronger one in that marriage.

I see Mum slipping away from the darkened theatre to hurry to the studio and see her, in fury perhaps?, gagging and binding Josie, telling her it's only a game. And sweet, silly little Josie takes all night to pluck up the courage to release herself and then still waits. I wonder what other threats kept Josie where she was for so long.

And I see myself coming back alone from the cinema, worrying about Sandra, and my parents coming through from the kitchen, looking distraught because, as I thought, they were anxious about me when the real truth was that they had just buried Sandra up on the moor and hidden the spade in our shed as Mr White had hidden empty liquor bottles.

I feel sick and shaken, my fingers trembling as I force the closely written papers back into the discarded envelope. On the envelope I see that the address my mother put has been crossed out and another hand has added a forwarding address. On the

205

top left-hand corner of the envelope the words 'Strictly Private' are blackly printed.

Mum took a risk. Someone else could've opened that envelope, read the contents of the letter, taken it to the police, set the wheel turning again.

It might have ended up in some dead letter office somewhere. I wish that it had, because I don't want to deal with the reality behind my mother's self-justifying words. I went off up to the old Tyler house looking for fantasy and never guessed that the true fantasy was in our own small house where all the conventions were observed, where my gentle, child-worshipping father was deferred to as the master, the disciplinarian, and my mother cleaned and tidied and sorted cupboards in an endless battle against the rage lurking within her.

I don't want to remember these things. I don't want to know these things. I want to catch hold of all my lost innocence and pull it round me like a shawl to shut out the cold. But I will remember them.

I turn and walk slowly out of the big shabby drawing-room and along the passage into the kitchen. There is dust here and mould thickening in the corners of the window panes and the sad musty smell of an abandoned room.

I go through the back door which has swollen with the rains again and hangs loose like a parody of itself on the evening I first met Fred and Fay. There's no need for me to call the inspector. I have guessed where he'll be and I walk without haste across the yard and the garden where the grass is waist high and Fay never planted her seeds.

He has clambered through the space between the stones, further destroying the long creepers that bind the wall. I go towards the thorn tree and silently hand him the letter.

'You didn't give it to the authorities,' I say.

'It was too long afterwards and would have served no purpose.'

'But my mother –'

'Did what she felt she had to do. Nobody can do more. She and your dad must've loved you and Susan very much, don't you think?'

'She wanted you to know the truth,' I say.

'Perhaps.' Inspector Archer hands the envelope back to me.

'Or perhaps she wanted to shoulder the blame, to lift some shadow from your father's name. Who knows? Your father might've been the one who drove round to the studio to gag and bind Josie, slipped out to silence Sandra and got your mother to help him bury her.'

'Susan might remember which one went out during the interval,' I say.

'And will you ask her?' he enquires softly.

'No,' I say. 'No, I never will.'

'And I am too old to trouble myself about a forty-year-old case,' the inspector says.

He is looking at me intently through the horn-rimmed spectacles. I tear the envelope and its contents into myriad pieces and I throw them out into the taking wind as Fay once threw the crusts of bread.

'My car's down in the car park. Can I give you a lift anywhere?' I ask as politely as if we had just enjoyed an unimportant reunion.

'One of my family is waiting down in the café by the supermarket,' he says. 'I'll be going now before they come looking for me! Oh, there is this. It was privately published a couple of years ago but attracted very little attention.'

He takes a slender volume from the pocket of his comfortably worn jacket and gives it to me.

I look at it in silence.

'You've not seen it before?'

I shake my head numbly.

'I daresay they are both gone now,' Inspector Archer says in a matter-of-fact tone. 'They'd be into their late eighties, early nineties by now. The book explains a lot. I picked it up in a second-hand bookshop.'

I look at the dark brown cover with the title in stark white characters: *Memoirs of a Dachau Guard* by Frederick Mannheim.

'Fred? But I thought –' I say at last.

'English educated and Fay herself was half English. She grew up here and was visiting her Polish relatives when the war came. She was a prisoner and Fred was – the title explains it.'

'But he loved her,' I say. 'He was a kind man. How could –? Wasn't anything real?'

'Some of them were idealists, you know, who were hardened

207

by conditions, corrupted by the power they were given. He never was but he had to obey certain orders or be shot himself. And he was hardly more than a boy. After the war he took care of her. It was his way of making reparation. And there was a bond between them. They knew the same things.'

I am back in the bedroom with Holly Jane's nightdress folded on the chest of drawers and the faint greyness before dawn curling through the window, and I hear the crunching footsteps on the gravel below and when I look down I see Fred marching, on some long-abolished guard duty, see him about-turn and catch a glimpse of a face I cannot recognise.

I open the book and look at the dedication inside.

'To our friend Cordelia in memory of Holly Jane.'

'It all happened a very long time ago, Cordy,' the inspector says.

'It happened yesterday,' I say softly.

Then I set off across the moor, away from the crumbling wall and the broken swing and the tiny bits of paper scurrying ahead of the wind, and hear somewhere inside my head the sweet bell sound of the children's song, and Fay swaying as Fred watches her lovingly flashes into my mind. It seems to me as I hurry across the moor that somewhere the music and the dancing continue. In the once was. In the might have been.